THE COURAGEOUS BELIEVER

THE COURAGEOUS BELIEVER

THE UNCONVENTIONAL AGENT BEAUFONT™ BOOK 8

SARAH NOFFKE

MICHAEL ANDERLE

This book is a work of fiction. All of the characters, organizations, and events portrayed in this novel are either products of the author's imagination or are used fictitiously. Sometimes both.

Copyright © 2022 LMBPN Publishing
Cover by Fantasy Book Design
Cover copyright © LMBPN Publishing
A Michael Anderle Production

LMBPN Publishing supports the right to free expression and the value of copyright. The purpose of copyright is to encourage writers and artists to produce the creative works that enrich our culture.

The distribution of this book without permission is a theft of the author's intellectual property. If you would like permission to use material from the book (other than for review purposes), please contact support@lmbpn.com. Thank you for your support of the author's rights.

LMBPN Publishing
PMB 196, 2540 South Maryland Pkwy
Las Vegas, NV 89109

Version 1.00, September 2022
eBook ISBN: 979-8-88541-834-8
Print ISBN: 979-8-88541-835-5

THE COURAGEOUS BELIEVER TEAM

Thanks to the JIT Readers

Veronica Stephan-Miller
Christopher Gilliard
Dave Hicks
Jackey Hankard-Brodie
Dorothy Lloyd
Diane L. Smith
Deb Mader
Jeff Goode
Angel LaVey

If we've missed anyone, please let us know!

Editor
The Skyfyre Editing Team

For Martin, my robotic expert and friend. And my second reader on all books. You're so cool

— Sarah

To Family, Friends and
Those Who Love
to Read.
May We All Enjoy Grace
to Live the Life We Are
Called.

— Michael

CHAPTER ONE

Zelle Corp, Manhattan, New York, United States

"Mirror, mirror on the wall, who's the richest of them all?" Jackson Zelle said, looking into his reflection in the glass door that led to the research and development lab in Zelle Corp.

He grinned at the disfigured reflection that stared back. Zelle was extra giddy that day, knowing that soon he would be one of the richest men in the world. There was no stopping it. The best part was he'd profit from the demise of love—the most despicable thing in the world.

People killed for love. It drained money, happiness, and health from the world. Jackson Zelle had seen it happen over and over again throughout his lifetime. He'd witnessed it firsthand during his time as director of finance at the FGA.

From an early age, people were programmed to care about love over all else, and that money was the root of all evil. It was love, and finally, Jackson Zelle could fix the world by destroying love. Best of all, he'd make more money than God.

Pushing the door to the lab open, Jackson Zelle commanded the attention of every scientist in the large space. They all looked up, straightening at the sight of him. Mostly because his burned face and many scars always jolted people. Also because he was their feared leader, and for a good reason. Jackson Zelle hadn't lost everything to lay down and die or crawl back to the impoverished life he had been born into.

Instead, the man who was totally self-made had figured out exactly how he'd make Zelle Corp the most successful company in the world—using a series of magitech projects that were destined for greatness. It didn't even matter that the FGA had thwarted many of his efforts as his company launched. That had always been a part of the plan.

Jackson Zelle knew Agent Paris Beaufont couldn't resist sticking her nose into everything, making anything connected to love her business. The halfling had tried to stop him, outmaneuvering him at every turn. All of that had been a distraction while Zelle Corp positioned itself for world domination.

A series of projects would position the company at the very top, and then Jackson Zelle would be ready for his ultimate goal —destroying the FGA. It would take a lot of money. It had already taken a lot of planning. The CEO was so close now.

"Continue," Jackson Zelle commanded, looking out over the various workspaces. The company was still growing, and as profits increased, so too would this department space. Soon his main brand would take over its own floor. Until then, it shared the space with the smaller projects meant to fund its development and launch.

Striding by a group of men wearing white lab coats, Jackson Zelle nodded to his head scientist, Dr. Marty Dupree. The man was tall and overweight, covered in tattoos and with small eyes and entirely too big of a nose for his face. Jackson Zelle was ugly now, after the plane crash and fire, but if he so desired, he could have surgery and fix his face. Dr. Dupree had been born ugly, and there was no fixing him. What he lacked in looks, the scientist made up for with brains.

"What's the status of Project X?" Jackson Zelle asked the man, noting the pieces of robotic equipment strewn around the closest workstations. Project X was what they were calling the venture that would take over the world and make an ultimate fortune. Better yet, it would finally end love and all the misery it caused.

"It's right on schedule," Dr. Dupree answered. "Our biggest hurdle is funding, but the development aspect is on point, and I'm hopeful we will have a successful prototype for you soon."

"Good," Jackson Zelle stated sternly, striding on, leaving the scientist and his team to continue their work. He cut his eyes to the many realistic human body parts strewn around on the workstation before turning his focus to the next area, which involved his more immediate project and the one that would fund Project X.

The other main research and development area was full of computers powered by magitech. A long bed sat next to the main workstation where a test subject lay, wires attached to her head, neck, and chest.

"How's it going?" Jackson Zelle asked the scientist in charge of Project Snow White.

"We're ready to launch," Dr. Jessie Raven answered with confidence. He was much shorter than the main scientist but not that much more attractive with his round red nose, receding brown hair, and unkempt beard. He had a forgettable face and a nerdy laugh. "I've just completed testing. As you can see, the subject has responded as intended."

Jackson Zelle glanced at the woman who was asleep. This was part of the intended outcome. "This occurred after the stimuli were administered?"

"After twenty minutes. According to our monitoring of the subject's frequency waves, she's progressively going into a deeper sleep."

"Can she be awoken easily?" Jackson Zelle asked.

"At this stage, yes," the scientist answered. "After several sleep sessions, produced by the initial stimuli, she'll be comatose."

"Good," Jackson Zelle affirmed with mild satisfaction. "You have my permission to take the subject to the final stages to ensure it works."

"What then?" Dr. Raven asked.

"Then, we roll out Project Snow White nationwide," he answered.

The scientist drew in a breath. "I understand you intend for this project to be a funding source for Project X, but you understand that sleeping people don't spend money, right?"

"I understand that completely. We're making money on admission, advertising, and membership," Jackson Zelle explained. "What happens to our brides afterward? Well, I'll already have their money then. They'll be one less headache for me and for the men they've made miserable. Finish testing and roll this out to the media and events pronto."

Jackson Zelle then turned and walked back to his office on the top floor of the skyscraper. It was perfect timing that Paris Beaufont had recently gotten engaged to be married. That had given him the idea for Project Snow White, which would make him a fortune capitalizing on brides obsessed with planning the perfect wedding. He'd ensure the bride-to-be didn't lose sleep over her wedding. She'd get so much sleep, she'd do little else.

CHAPTER TWO

Little Pleasures Farmhouse, Outskirts of Boulder, Colorado, United States

"Stop yawning and wake up, would you?" Faraday snapped in Paris' face.

She lifted her head up, blinking at the little squirrel who had some nerve. Glancing over her shoulder to the bar along the restaurant dining room of the large farmhouse, Paris grinned at her Uncle Clark. "Put squirrel on the menu for tonight?"

"Stew or kabobs?" he asked, cutting up garnishes for the specialty cocktails for dinner service later.

Paris liked he hadn't missed a beat. Her uncle, who was wearing a starched suit under his apron, never missed anything—not even a blond hair out of place. He was the head chef for Little Pleasures, a councilor for the House of Fourteen, and the manager of the Beaufont family.

She hoped that soon he'd have more of a social life, but Paris wasn't sure how he could juggle that and everything else he did so expertly well. He'd started dating a mortal who lived at the House of Fourteen since her aunt was a Mortal Seven.

Apparently, things were going well between the couple,

according to Liv, who said Clark was never home anymore and always distracted during council meetings. Paris reasoned he'd spent all of his life studying and working. He deserved to have his head in the clouds for once, and he did seem to be in a good mood lately.

"If you two are done making threats, I need you to make a decision." Faraday flicked his tail as he stood on the table in front of several open catalogs.

Paris winked at her uncle. "Are we done making threats? I hadn't planned on being done. But I guess…"

"Well, I'll circle back to it in just a bit," Clark replied, heading for the kitchen area. "I need to go and retrieve some more ingredients for prepping."

"You know we have employees for that," Paris called after him.

"They don't do it right," he said over his shoulder, disappearing in the back.

Paris shook her head. "I swear, that man would do everything himself if he could."

Faraday tapped his foot on the table, his paws on his hips. "Stop stalling and make a decision."

Paris yawned again, glancing down at the thick catalog. "Why? Why do you care?"

"Because it's your wedding," he began, continuing to tap his foot. "Because Hemingway put me in charge of getting you to make decisions since he's got to take care of the farm. Oh, and it's your wedding, once again."

Paris sat back in her seat. "It's his wedding too. Why do I have to do this now? This type of thing isn't for me."

"Most brides want to be in charge of making decisions," he argued. "You have to pick the colors because that dictates everything. You can't pick invitations until that's done. If you don't pick those out, you can't invite people. Then no one comes to your wedding."

"Perfect!" Paris threw her hands up in the air. "More cake for me."

"You can't pick a cake unless you know the theme and the colors," Faraday continued, ignoring her.

Paris rolled her eyes at the rodent. "When did you become such a know-it-all about wedding planning?"

"I know about many things," Faraday stated. "This is your only wedding, and I fear if you don't take it seriously, you'll regret it. Also..."

Faraday looked away rather sheepishly.

Paris arched an eyebrow at him. "What?"

"Well, it's nothing."

"What, Squirrel? Out with it."

He averted his gaze. "I never had a wedding. I never had anyone I wanted to marry. Well, I never really dated, actually."

"Which makes it nearly impossible to get hitched," Paris joked.

"I get to live vicariously through you now," he went on. "I mean, it's not that I wanted to have a wedding, but I want you to have one. I want it to be magical, but that involves making some decisions."

Paris pushed the catalog at him. "Then you plan the wedding. Pick your favorite colors. What are they? The color of uranium and cheese?"

He snickered. "That's quite accurate, but I can't do this for you. It's your wedding. Not mine. I will help you."

"Get a wedding planner," Subfar said from a neighboring table. He'd been so quiet, with pages of newspapers and other notes and books piled high around him, Paris had forgotten he was there. She hadn't thought he was listening to their silly conversation about wedding colors when he was studying the stock market and funding sources to help her with FGA budget issues.

"Say what?" Paris asked, directing her attention to the Protector of Wealth. He had stringy black hair like his twin,

Subner, but his wasn't as unkempt. While both men had narrow faces and high cheekbones, Subfar appeared less serious than his brother.

"A wedding planner," Subfar said, stretching his arms overhead and yawning like Paris had been doing earlier. "They are people you employ who take care of many of the arrangements for a wedding. I don't think they normally make personalized decisions for brides, but for a price, I'm sure they will. Like the squirrel said, most brides like to make these decisions."

Paris sighed. "I'm not most brides. I want to be married. Who cares about a wedding?"

"Every woman ever," Subfar stated. "Much wealth is spent on creating a lavish affair. The wedding industry is big business."

Faraday nodded in the elf's direction. "He would know."

"Speaking of business," Paris said, taking a sip of her coffee. She needed to get to work soon. "Have you found a funding source for me yet?"

Paris had pretty much promised the Protector of Wealth her firstborn child in exchange for a huge sum of income that would save the FGA from bankruptcy. The contract she signed with Subfar was over a hundred pages long and stipulated everything he must deliver to her and by when and that it was a sustainable way to maintain money for such a length of time.

Because Mama Jamba had said that Paris had to agree to whatever Subfar asked to get the funding to support the FGA, she hadn't read the terms of the agreement. She didn't have time to read through a huge contract, nor did she understand the legal language when she had perused the first few pages. Paris signed it and asked the Protector of Wealth to get to work.

The FGA didn't have much longer before the board of directors panicked and sold the company off. Worse yet, Saint Valentine was concerned that it would go bankrupt and be dissolved entirely. Time was crucial. Paris would deal with her part of the contract after the fact. She wasn't sure what Subfar would do to her when he found out she couldn't have children, but she decided to worry about that later.

"I think I've found a benefactor to loan us the money for our initial investments," the Protector of Wealth replied. "I still need to decide the right strategy for stock trading based on the current market and your desired goals. If saving the FGA is your intended outcome, there are several ways to get you there, some ways being better than others."

"That's exactly what needs to happen," Paris said with conviction. "I don't care how we get there, though. We're running out of time."

He glanced at her sideways. "Really? You don't care how you get there? What if it's selling dangerous magical items on the black market? Or poaching the protected and nearly extinct forgy from the rainforest?"

"What's a forgy?" Paris asked.

"A magical cat-like creature," Faraday answered.

"Then no. I'm not up for doing anything unethical."

"That's key," Subfar said. "The end doesn't justify the means when it comes to making money. How you do it when determining how much you make, for how long, and whether you keep it. If you want a lot of it, then I can have it for you tonight. If you want a lot that you keep, then you'll have to wait a few more days. If you want a lot that you keep and has sustainable growth over a long period of time, well, then—"

"I get it," Paris interrupted, finishing her coffee, already used to the long rants the Protector of Wealth went on regularly. "These things take time, and you have to find the right one. Let's do it, and if you need any help, Sherlock is available."

From the other side of the dining room, the great detective lowered his ballpoint pen and glanced up from his journal where he'd been writing. "Are you sure about that?"

"Are you available should Subfar need assistance?" Paris asked him, getting to her feet.

"Do you have a case for me to solve?" he asked in his distinguished British accent.

She pointed to the catalog of wedding dresses, venues, decorations, invitations, and everything else related to such things. "Do you want to pick out my wedding colors?"

"Not really," he replied after considering the notion for a moment.

"Well, then no, I don't have anything for you just at the moment," she told him.

"Can't you find a mystery on your own?" Faraday asked. "Turn on your crime radar or whatever it is."

"That's quite accurate," Sherlock Holmes retorted. "I prefer the ones that Paris assigns me. They are more complex than the ones I find on my own."

"Because drama follows me around," she joked, picking up her squirrel and getting ready for work. "I suspect that after foiling his efforts to murder his hometown, Jackson Zelle will be up to something treacherous yet again. It's very likely that once I figure out what that man is up to, I'll have a mystery revolving around him. In the meantime, you can solve the mystery of why I have to wear a dress or feed a bunch of people just to tell the love of my life he's my forever person."

"I'm not sure there's much of a mystery there," Sherlock Holmes replied just as Hemingway Noble strode through the door, tracking in mud from the field.

He stopped as soon as he realized what he'd done and peeled off his work boots.

Paris crossed the space, meeting him by the door. "Thankfully, Uncle Clark is in a good mood and won't be all whiney about that mess today."

"I'm never whiney," Clark said, coming back from the kitchen, carrying a stack of linens that would need to be folded for that night's dinner service.

"No, but especially lately...you're...." Paris observed, tilting her head to the side and trying to come up with the right description for him. "Lately, you're...."

"Happy," Sherlock Holmes supplied.

Hemingway nodded. "Yes, and it looks good on you."

"Why, thank you," Uncle Clark replied. "Nothing makes me happier than a full day's work and going to bed tired and feeling accomplished."

"Sleeping beside another person," Sherlock observed.

Clark gawked at him, his eyes wide. "That's quite the assumption to make."

"It isn't one." The great detective stated, pointing to his hair. "That's not your usual hair gel."

"I've decided to try something different," Clark replied. "I'm allowed."

"You're not wearing your usual aftershave," Sherlock Holmes continued.

"You smell me?"

"I believe we all do," Sherlock said, winking. "Those are the same clothes you wore yesterday, but they've been freshly laundered."

"I like to wash my clothes. Sue me."

"You do laundry on Wednesdays and Sundays," Sherlock Holmes countered.

Clark stuck his hands on his hips. "How could you possibly know that?"

"Easy," the detective replied. "You have three favorite pairs of trousers. The rotation restarts every Monday and Thursday. Furthermore, you have a favorite suit jacket and wear that up to three days in a row, but never four, always laundering it on Wednesday or Sunday. Lastly, I overheard you tell Hemingway that you were excited because it was laundry day and that only happens twice a week. I deduced that since it was on a Wednesday and you were a very practical man, you'd spread out those days, making the other one on Sunday."

Clark lowered his chin, regarding the man through a hooded gaze. "Your point is?"

"That you're staying at your girlfriend's house," Hemingway said. "Who can blame you? When you find someone you want to spend all your time with, that's what you do."

He leaned in and kissed Paris on the cheek.

She smiled, pressing into him. "I'm happy for you, Uncle Clark. Are we still on for later?"

"I'll come by later to take a look at the FGA space you need renovated."

"I'll check out any obstacles the building might have when it comes to magical changes," Faraday said, straightening in Paris' arm and tapping the side of his face, and staring at Hemingway.

"What?" he asked, giving the squirrel a sideways look.

"Where's my goodbye kiss?" Faraday asked.

"On someone else's lips," Hemingway replied with a laugh.

Paris giggled too. "Okay, you merry bunch, have a good day. We're off to work."

Hemingway blew her a kiss. "I love you."

"Have fun." Uncle Clark waved.

"Good luck." Sherlock Holmes waved.

"Mazel tov." Subfar waved.

Paris and Faraday strode out the door for a full day at the FGA, feeling refreshed and ready for the challenges to come—knowing there would be many. There was never a dull moment as an agent for the Fairy Godmother Agency.

CHAPTER THREE

Fairy Grounds Coffee Shop, First Floor, FGA Tower, New York City, New York, United States

"You're so boring," Christine muttered as they stood in line at the coffee shop. "How can you not want to plan every aspect of your wedding?"

"For starters," Paris began, holding up a finger, preparing to tick off reasons. "I have a brand new position as the director for a branch of the FGA that's been shut down for a long time. I'm trying to keep this place from going belly up. Jackson Zelle is most definitely planning to come after me and the FGA. Oh, and then there's that whole 'I don't really care' about weddings thing."

"Are you sure you're a girl?" Christine asked, pushing her orangey-red hair out of her face.

"Not all girls sit and fantasize about their wedding day," Paris argued.

"Yeah, some of us read books."

"Well, not me," Paris remarked. "I was spelled not to like reading or be curious so that I didn't learn anything accidentally about my personal history and therefore learn that my entire life was a lie."

Both of the other women gave her blank looks.

Finally, Christine shook her head. "You're so weird."

"Are you sure about this?" Paris asked her friend who had dragged her into the coffee shop run by the pixies. "You know how this lot loathes me."

"That's because you insult them and refuse to drink their coffee or eat their food," Christine pointed out.

"That's because I don't eat sugar, their coffee sucks, and they have tiny fairy brains."

Because the universe loved to set Paris up, the person in line moved away right then, putting them right in front of Ivy, the manager of Fairy Grounds. Her little cherub-like face blossomed red at the sight of Paris.

"Hey," Paris said, drawing the word out and trying to sound natural.

"I heard that," the small pixie with pink hair and wings said, flying behind the counter, her eyes narrowed.

"About how she's getting married?" Christine asked. "Yeah, it's super exciting."

"No, about how we have tiny fairy brains," Ivy fumed.

"Well, technically, you do," Paris explained. "I mean, look at the size of your head relative to mine. Birds have tiny brains too, but it doesn't mean they are dumb."

"Actually, turkeys have been known to die from standing open-mouthed, drinking rainwater falling from the sky," Christine related.

"Then there's the kakapo," Penny began. "They are so stupid that much like the dodo bird, they've nearly made themselves extinct. Their diets consist of berries that only grow once, and every four years, they freeze when confronted by a predator instead of fleeing, and the male's mating call confuses the female instead of what it's intended to do. There's like less than two hundred left in the world."

Paris turned to the women beside her and offered a disingenuous smile. "Did you all say you were my friends? Because if so, I want my friendship bracelets back."

"You're real smart, Ivy," Christine said, angling around Paris. "Which is why you know the name of the best wedding planner and can refer Paris to them. She needs their help badly."

"Yes, and not only does no one know who this person is that is so amazing at wedding planning, but only you pixies can get Paris on the list to work with them."

"Will you help?" Christine asked.

"No!" Ivy exclaimed. "Next in line."

"Well, we tried, guys," Paris said, grabbing her friends by the arm and turning around. "The pixies loath me because of their own shortcomings. Nothing to be done about that. I'll just have you all plan the whole thing."

"Although we would do an amazing job," Christine began, shaking Paris off. "Planning your wedding is a huge job, and I already happen to have one."

"Me too," Paris said. "So we're eloping."

"You're the director of the Advanced Love branch of the FGA," Penny argued. "You have to have a huge wedding."

"You're also a Beaufont," Christine added. "Mama Jamba and Papa Creola will be there. It's bigger than when the king of the fae got married."

"My mother was his best woman," Paris offered.

"Do you see what we mean?" Christine insisted. "You can't just have a small backyard wedding."

"My mother did," Paris declared. "It was in a giant's backyard."

"Yeah, and she's a Warrior for the House of Fourteen," Penny countered. "You work for an organization that's devoted to protecting and nurturing love. If you don't have a huge and lavish wedding, what hope do you give other women they will find their Prince Charming?"

Paris chewed on her lip. "I guess you're right."

"Of course we're right," Christine insisted. "This is not just about you. This is about sending a message and affecting the love meter. It will also give me a reason to drop ten pounds to fit into my bride's maid dress for the wedding of the century."

Paris didn't like the idea of being the center of attention, but she did love the idea of marrying Hemingway. As a bonus, there was a real possibility the wedding would positively affect the love meter. It would get press coverage since Paris was a Beaufont and also a director for the FGA. The guest list alone would have people talking. Big weddings for queens and princesses often increased love worldwide, making Cinderellas fantasize about their own future unions.

Sighing, Paris resigned herself. "Fine. I'll have a big wedding." She returned her attention to the pixie hovering behind the counter. "Ivy, can I please have a referral to this wedding planner?"

"No!" the angry little jerk said.

Paris refrained from mouthing off yet again and drew in a breath. "Name your price."

The manager of Fairy Grounds squealed in protest. "I can't be bought."

"Of course you can," Christine argued. "Everyone can be."

"It doesn't have to be money," Penny reasoned. "Do you want Paris to introduce you to a dragonrider or ask the king of the fae if you can stay in his weekend mansion or ask a burning question to Mother Nature? She can connect you with just about anyone."

Paris laughed at her friends, who were always impressed by all the people Paris hung around—not realizing they were normal and weird, all at the same time.

Ivy seemed to have softened slightly, as though the idea was starting to appeal to her. "There's something that you can do for me."

"What?" all three women asked in unison.

The pixie looked around at the busy coffee shop, hesitation

on her round face. She flew in closer to Paris and leaned forward. "I need you to go to Sundry Charms and buy me something."

Paris tilted her head to the side, surprised by the tame request when she was expecting something so much bigger. She thought that Ivy would ask her to endorse her bad coffee or, even worse, actually drink it. "You need me to run a shopping errand for you?"

The pixie, who had no personal space issues, flew in even closer, whispering in Paris' ear. "I need you to get something secret for me."

"Okay." Paris drew out the word, glancing at her friends who could still hear Ivy, and wondered if it was something illegal. There was no telling with Sundry Charms. The place sold all sorts of strange oddities. "What is it?"

"Well, I'd get it myself, but Jenny, the shop owner, doesn't like me," Ivy explained.

"No." Paris pretended to be surprised.

The pixie flashed her an annoyed look, her wings flapping vigorously to keep her afloat. "Most people who aren't you and that new age mystic who runs Sundry Charms find pixies to be very positive and happy people."

"It's true," Christine chirped. "You, Paris, are, like, the only person I've known the pixies not to like or vice versa."

"Again, give me back my friendship bracelet," Paris joked, turning her attention back to Ivy. "What can I get for you? Jenny likes me."

"That's the other part of it," she replied, whispering, her voice nearly inaudible over the flapping of her wings. "It's a Smarten Up Shortcake."

"A what?" Paris asked loudly, making Ivy flush red.

"A Smarten Up Shortcake," she replied quietly.

"Why would you need that?" Paris asked, trying to keep the laugh out of her voice.

"Because…" Ivy answered. "You'll have to test it on two other fairies first."

"Because?" Paris replied.

"Because some batches have the opposite effect," Penny answered for the pixie. "It always depends on several different factors. Jenny doesn't guarantee anything with it."

"Well, I can't take the risk of losing my brain right now," Paris said.

"You're half magician anyway," Christine said, holding up her hands. "Don't look at me to volunteer. I like my wits, and I'm keeping them this week."

"Sorry, me either. The effects can last for up to a month. I can't risk that."

Paris frowned. "Yeah, well, then I'll have to find someone who doesn't care."

"Or someone who doesn't know," Christine offered.

"That's deceptive," Paris pointed out.

"It is, but you need a referral," Ivy said. "So get me the Smarten Up Shortcake and proof it worked on at least two fairies. I'm sure you know someone who doesn't rely on their intelligence you can test it on."

Paris thought for a moment as something occurred to her. She grinned victoriously. "Okay, I think I can help you. I'll get you that shortcake, so get ready to get me my referral."

CHAPTER FOUR

Dwyer's Polishes, Second Floor, FGA Tower, New York City, New York, United States

"Fascinating," Faraday gasped, his eyes wide. "So the building has feelings?"

"Don't we all?" Paris joked, sidling up next to Dwyer, the shoe shiner, who was mixing together some sparkling polishes that were no doubt magical.

The squirrel glanced up at her from his place on the shoe shine station. "Well, according to rumors spread by the pixies at Fairy Grounds, you don't."

Paris sighed. "Here I am trying to help those ungrateful jerks."

"Maybe if you stopped calling them jerks," Faraday offered. "Insulting them in general…."

Dwyer grinned easily, slapping a rag over his shoulder. "I think you have feelings."

"Thanks," Paris replied, smiling back at her friend, who was also one of the most knowledgeable people in the FGA. That was why Faraday was meeting with the shoe shiner, to find out how the skyscraper would react to renovation magic.

As a structure that held a lot of fairies and magic, it took on their properties and became alive itself. In this way, it was similar to how Happily Ever After College, the House of Fourteen, and the Gullington reacted to changes. Each of those places was different, just like the diversity of the people inside of them.

"Of course, some say that you eat kittens based on your demon blood," Dwyer stated. "I won't judge you if you do. One year I became anemic and ate steak nonstop."

Paris couldn't help but laugh. "I'm a vegetarian."

"Because you can't bear to eat animals since your best friend is one," Dwyer guessed.

Paris shook her head. "Because I know how filthy that creature is."

The squirrel glared at her. "Ha-ha."

"What have you learned?" Paris asked Faraday.

"That probably due to the gravitational forces caused by the magnetic poles—"

She held up his hand. "Minus the science and insert things I understand."

He thought for a moment. "It's hard to explain because the positive electrons create an electron well—"

"Layman's terms, nerd," Paris interrupted again.

"Magic makes the building emotional," Faraday said at once, crossing his arms and giving her a grumpy look.

She smiled at him. "Wasn't hard, was it?"

"You made me dumb down a fascinating set of principles that are brought about based on the—"

Paris plugged her ears, shaking her head and humming. When she saw Faraday halt his explanation, she removed her hands.

"So what does this emotional, moody building mean for our renovation efforts in the basement?" she asked.

"It means," Dwyer began, "That you need to be respectful of its feelings. Ask permission. Look for signs it doesn't want you to do something. The FGA Tower will tell you."

"What if we do something it doesn't like?" Paris asked. "Like put too many bean bags in the department space."

"One is too many," Faraday stated decisively.

Dwyer laughed. "Your efforts will be futile. The building will delete your efforts."

"So we have to work within its confines," Paris said, looking around.

"The FGA Tower strives for balance," Dwyer added. "It won't allow you to create a shiny, glamourous space if your departments aren't successful or happy. The areas and renovations have to meet the level of the divisions."

"Yeah, which was why the basement was dark and flooded when the Advanced Love branch was shut down."

"It was the biggest problem at the FGA," Paris offered. "Which is why the twenty-sixth floor kept taking us there."

"That's the floor that directs employees to places that have concerns," Faraday stated.

"It should have taken us to the finance department," Paris muttered.

"The finance department was considered a success," Dwyer argued. "It was only once you uncovered that Jackson Zelle was a villain the department failed, bringing the FGA with it."

"We'll recover," Paris encouraged.

"I wonder where the twenty-sixth floor would take us now?" Faraday mused. "I mean, now that Advanced Love branch in the basement is being managed once more. Is it still the biggest problem area?"

"Well, I do have a lot of work to do down there," Paris replied. "Then again, I'm not supposed to do too much at once, so change is slow. Hopefully, my ragtag crew is making progress down there."

"I vote that we should check out the twenty-sixth floor," Faraday said, batting his eyelashes at her, begging.

She shook her head. "I don't feel like landing in a hovel right now. I know where the places are that demand my attention without the twenty-sixth floor directing me or the possessed elevator taking me on a mysterious journey."

"Okay, so we're off to the basement then." Faraday hopped off the shoe shine chair.

Paris pointed at the shop behind them. "Unfortunately, what's demanding my attention right now is a stupid errand for a pixie who thankfully knows how stupid she is. We're off to Sundry Charms."

CHAPTER FIVE

Sundry Charms, Second Floor, FGA Tower, New York City, New York, United States

When Paris and Faraday walked into the shop with assorted foods, convenience products, and magical items, she nearly turned around and went right back out. She just didn't have patience for hippies...ever. After her trip to the Redwood National Forest in Humboldt and nearly becoming a carefree hippie herself, her tolerance levels were much lower.

The dryads and devas had spelled people subject to their forces to let go and want to waste away in the forests. Paris' fairy blood made her susceptible to these cosmic forces. She still hadn't fully come to terms with the fact she shucked off her shoes and had all but committed herself to the idea of living inside of a tree and marrying a man named River during her time in the forest.

Thankfully Hemingway had reminded her of who she was, and Paris had awoken. Since then, though, she'd had a major aversion to hippies. No one was a bigger hippie than Jenny, who owned and operated the Sundry Charms. Sadly, she appeared to have leveled up on the hippie scale.

The woman with flowing brown hair who looked as though she had raided one of Santa Claus' elves' closets was sitting in the middle of her shop in a tailor position. All the shelves with various goods and products had been pushed back to the walls.

Around Jenny, who was wearing green pants, a red and white horizontally striped shirt, and a pointy green hat, was a circle made out of flower petals. She had her hand by her nose and was pressing one nostril closed, taking a breath. She then held and pressed a finger to her forehead before closing the other nostril and exhaling.

"I'll be with you once I've devoted myself to pranayama," Jenny said, her eyes closed and moving her hands to rest on her knees as she sat in the lotus position.

"Oh, good, this will be fast," Paris muttered to Faraday, who snickered at finding the sundry shop looking more like a yoga studio.

"You need Smarten Up Shortcake?" Faraday asked, having been informed of their errand on the walk over. "I can go and check the shelves for them."

Jenny cracked an eye open. "They are in the back room."

"I'll retrieve them," Paris said. "You can put it on my tab."

"You don't have a tab," Jenny argued, opening her eyes all the way.

"I'll start one. I work here, so I think it's safe to say that you can track me down if I don't pay up."

Jenny shook her head. "Your exchange for goods isn't the issue. It's that I'll have to retrieve them. They are in an awkward spot."

"About like me right now," Paris said, mostly to the squirrel who was looking around the strange circle where Jenny sat, odd symbols written in chalk on the floor beside her.

The hippie offered a subtle smile. "I invite you to share the space with me and join in this meditation of mindfulness."

"I'm good," Paris said.

"Have you taken time to connect with your prana—your vital lifeforce—today?" Jenny asked.

Paris nodded in an exaggerated manner. "I've hardly done anything else today."

Faraday copied her movement, nodding adamantly. "We're so connected with our prana that we're like one."

Jenny gave him a calculated look. "Prana permeates all of reality. You are always one with it but must continuously reconnect as the material world tries to separate you."

"Damn material world," Paris mumbled, looking around the shop.

"It's like our Wi-Fi at the farm," Faraday joked. "I'm always having to reconnect with it because the router is faulty."

"In Sanskrit, there are five different types of prana," Jenny continued in her airy voice, obviously in yogi mode.

"Cool, cool, cool," Paris remarked dryly. "Sorry to interrupt your session with the Force, but if you and the Jedis can pause for a moment, I just need to grab a quick batch of Smarten Up Shortcake."

"For you?" Jenny asked. "You seemed stressed but not to the extent that your intelligence is failing you."

"It's for a friend," Paris said in a rush.

Jenny pursed her lips, a doubtful look on her face. "How about instead of using magical food to fix your problems, you come and meditate with me? I think you'll find clarity and mental space after connecting to your prana through the practice of Nadi Shodhana breathing."

"It's not for me," Paris explained.

"Then why doesn't your friend come and buy it?"

"Because they are embarrassed," Paris answered, knowing it was best to avoid telling her it was Ivy, who she apparently didn't like. Although hippies were supposed to love everyone, it appeared they still had grudges when their prana didn't get along with someone—like the pixie.

Jenny didn't seem to be buying this. "Come. I invite you to share this meditative space with me."

"I'm good."

"It's remarkable how taking time to enjoy the silence allows you more time than if you were to rush to your next task."

"Seriously, I'm good."

"Come and meditate with me," Jenny insisted.

"No, thanks."

"Do it or no shortcake!" Jenny yelled, her face suddenly flushing red.

Paris and Faraday both widened their eyes at the sudden outburst.

Jenny softened instantly, embarrassed but quickly covering it up. "I just think that if you allow yourself to let go, then you'll find that meditation is both a restorative and creative boost for you. Come and sit and share the silence with me."

Paris cut her eyes to her squirrel before glancing back at the crazy hippie.

Jenny let out a breath. "Do it, and I'll give you the Smarten Up Shortcake."

Letting out her own breath, but hers much heavier, Paris resigned. Of course, she couldn't just stroll into the shop and purchase the magical food. Nor could she take it to Ivy and get the referral for the wedding planner. Everything had to be a wild goose chase.

Resigning her frustration, Paris trudged into the circle of flowers, waving for Faraday to follow her. "Come on, Squirrel. If I have to connect with my prana, then you're doing it too."

CHAPTER SIX

Casual Romance Department, Third Floor, FGA Tower, New York City, New York, United States

If the FGA Tower responded to the vibrations of a department and the building changed accordingly, then Paris' old and first division was doing surprisingly well. She wanted to be happy to find the Casual Romance department bustling with activity and everyone working so well in the space. However, if she was honest with herself, it made her a little sad to think the department, which had been more than a little defunct when she started there, was performing successfully without her.

"You know the sign of a good manager," Faraday said, jumping up on a chair and then a table so he was higher up, "Is they can create leaders who can take the reins and manage without them."

"Are you saying that I did this?" Paris asked, going unnoticed as fairy godmothers hurried back and forth, discussing cases or reviewing reports in the open department space. The areas designed by Holly and Isha hadn't changed much. The Cozy Corner was spruced up a bit more. The conference table was filled with people, whereas it used to just be the two employees and Paris. One thing that hadn't changed was Doris Frederickson, still asleep in her chair, taking her mid-morning nap. That would be followed by a snack, some work, and then a late morning nap.

"I'm saying that you're a part of this," Faraday explained. "You molded a fairy godmother into the type of manager who could take over in your absence and lead the department, continuing its success."

"Yeah, I guess it's like parenting," Paris related. "If you do a good job, then you raise children who don't need you anymore."

The squirrel lifted an eyebrow at her. "Strange for you to suddenly be spouting parenting advice."

"I can't have children, but I've deceptively signed a contract with Subfar to give him my firstborn child in exchange for a huge and sustainable funding source," she said.

"You do realize he's probably going to murder you when he finds out that you've lied to him."

"Well, maybe he won't find out," Paris said. "I mean, I'm just now getting married. It's not like I planned on popping out a baby right after the wedding."

"Yes, but he's an immortal man who is sticking around for the rest of your life," Faraday countered. "I think he's going to get suspicious when a decade passes by and you haven't made good on the deal."

"I'll deal with it then." She waved a dismissive hand. "For now, I've got to find a couple of fairies to feed this to."

Paris held up a box of a dozen Smarten Up Shortcakes. She and Faraday had finally gotten Jenny to give them what they'd gone there for. It only required they lay around in Shavasana and "Let go." It was known as corpse pose and was apparently the hardest of the yoga exercises. Humans are programmed to "Do," and that move required the opposite.

Paris hadn't found it so hard and was thinking she could have used the nap time if she wasn't so busy. Now she was feeling quite groggy, but she had the shortcakes and was that much closer to getting the referral for the wedding planner that she "had to have." She hoped there would be a benefit to this wild goose chase that helped her work, but that might be an overly optimistic notion.

"What is your current task, and how much progress have you made?" the voice of Alfred, the magitech AI said from behind them.

Paris turned to find the refined man dressed like a butler standing behind them with his usual neutral expression.

"Excuse me?" Paris asked, confused.

"Oh, it's you, Agent Beaufont," the man replied in his posh English accent, making a note on an electronic tablet. "You won't have a productivity score to record."

"What in the world is going on here?" Paris asked, looking at Faraday as the AI moved on to another group.

"What's going on is maximum efficiency," Holly, the new manager for the Casual Romance department said, striding over, having come around the corner with Isha.

The fairy godmothers looked as they normally did, Holly wearing hot pink workout pants and a top that matched her fake nails. Her long fake blonde hair was tied up in a high ponytail, and she was sipping a green shake. Isha wore all-black yoga pants, a hoodie, and a sweat band that pushed her short black hair out of her face.

"We have Alfred record all the fairy godmother's tasks, and then we compute their productivity scores at the end of the day," Isha explained.

Paris blinked at the pair. "Hi, my name is Agent Beaufont. Can you tell me where the two loafs who used to work here are? Are they napping in the back or doing crunches in the Wellness Area?"

Holly shook her head. "Paris, it's us. Don't you recognize us? I'm wearing a different eyeshadow today."

"I did that self-tanner this morning," Isha added. "I told you I went too dark."

Paris laughed. "I think it went to your heads. Here, have a cookie." She held up the box of shortbreads.

"Oh, she does recognize us," Holly said, pursing her lips. "She thinks we're stupid and is trying to smarten us up with that magical shortbread. Well, no thanks, ex-boss. I don't have to do what you say anymore."

Paris laughed. "When did you ever do what I said?"

Holly shrugged. "There was that one time you told me to take my feet off the conference table, and I did."

"Didn't you have to go get a cup of antioxidant tea anyway?" Isha asked.

The other woman nodded. "Yeah, probably."

"Although talking to you health nuts is bringing back fond memories, I'm fairly busy," Paris began, holding up the box of Smarten Up Shortbread. "I need you two to eat one of these and tell me if it makes you smarter or dumber. Or give me two of your fairies who can stand to gain or risk losing brain cells for a month. I need your help."

"Don't you have an entire branch with a dozen employees?" Holly questioned. "Go and make one of your employees do it."

"I have three employees," Paris told her. "I can't afford for anything to happen to them."

Faraday motioned around. "Thanks to Paris' recruitment efforts and management, you have a bustling department with plenty of test subjects."

Holly shook her head, but this gesture was cut off by Isha.

"I'll do it," she stated, holding out her hand.

"You realize that if the shortbread doesn't work, then you'll be dumber for a month," Holly interrupted, stopping her friend. "You never know which way that cookie is going to go, which is why Paris wants you to test the batch."

"You're smarter than you look," Paris teased.

"Thanks," Holly chirped. "Hopefully, I don't look too smart. I want to be hot, not look like some nerd."

"No one would think you're that smart based on how much collagen you have in your lips," Paris joked.

"I want to take the risk and have shortbread," Isha said, redirecting the conversation back on track. "I'm having some challenges finding solutions for a few cases. This might be exactly what I need to fix things."

"Or it might turn your brain into Jell-O for a month, and then you'll be of no use to me," Holly argued.

"It's worth the risk," Isha countered. "You should try it too because when it works, you'll be jealous if I'm smarter than you. Also, I'll need someone who is on my level."

"What if your level is a dumb one?" Holly asked.

"Then we'll be dumb together," Isha answered.

"Fine," Holly said, holding out her hand. "If this does make us dumb, then you, Paris, have to manage the department for the month. I'm taking my brainless hot body to Jamaica."

"Deal," Paris agreed at once, willing to take the risk. She opened the box and handed over two cookies.

"Oh, my angels," Holly said, nearly inhaling the cookie. "I haven't had a real carb in a month."

"I'm breaking my intermittent fasting for this," Isha added.

Paris and Faraday exchanged uncertain looks.

"How do we know if it works?" Paris asked the squirrel.

Before Faraday could answer, Isha slapped her forehead with her palm. "Oh, my angels! I'm so stupid."

Faraday deflated. "That's how we know."

Holly gawked at her friend. "Yeah, right. I'm a total idiot."

Paris sighed. "I guess this batch is no good. Ivy isn't going to help me."

"Well, maybe we try another batch on someone else," Faraday offered as Holly and Isha both stared at the floor like their brains were melting. They appeared deep in thought, but

Paris supposed they were probably thinking about nothing at all.

"Yeah, maybe we give these two ladies another batch and see if we reverse the effects of the first dose," Paris said.

The scientist squirrel nodded. "I wonder if that will just take them up to their normal intelligence or supersede it."

"Ish," Holly said to her friend, looking up from the carpet.

"Yeah, Hols?"

"Are you thinking what I'm thinking?" Holly asked.

"Yeah…"

Paris frowned, feeling bad for her dumb friends. "Are you thinking that thinking is hard?"

Both women shook their heads.

Isha's mouth fell open, but it was Holly who spoke first. "For case number 216, we need to create a diversion that will pair the lovers by giving them something to relate to. Then with case number 818, which has proved quite complex, we're going with a multifaceted approach using events related to the potential lover's interests. Then with case number 799…well, I've suddenly got solutions where I just had problems before."

"Yes, and I was just thinking, there should be some function-ality on the FGA's website. Why aren't we taking messages from Cinderellas and Prince Charmings? We could be hearing directly from them about their problems and solving them instead of relying on the tele-eventor to report issues and opportunities."

"That's genius," Paris said, her mouth falling open as she glanced at Faraday.

He shared her expression. "It worked."

"Of course it worked," Holly stated. "The probability of it not working was four to one, giving us fairly good odds."

"You said that you were so dumb after you ate the cookie," Faraday pointed out.

"That's because in comparison to our intelligence now, we were really dumb," Holly explained.

"Yes, I like this idea for the website," Isha said, off in thought as she headed back for the elevator. "I'm going to talk to someone in IT about implementing it right away."

"Good idea," Holly said over her shoulder, striding in the opposite direction. "I'm going to send fairy godmothers into the field to manage the cases I've just had breakthroughs on."

Paris grinned, looking at the box of Smarten Up Shortbread. "I'm going to get a referral for the best of the best in the wedding business."

CHAPTER SEVEN

Although Paris would have liked to deliver the Smarten Up Shortbreads to Ivy right away and get her referral, it appeared she'd have to wait. When she and Faraday buzzed down to Fairy Grounds, she found the coffee shop closed due to a shortage of ingredients—both for pastries and drinks. It seemed Ivy really did need the cookies to smarten her up since stocking the coffee shop was her job, and she was out of supplies before late morning.

With twenty minutes to spare before the first big meeting, Paris allowed Faraday to convince her to go on a field trip. She could have gone down to the basement to check on her department but didn't want that stress right before the big board meeting.

This was her first one, and there was a lot of pressure. She knew the board of directors was seriously considering selling the FGA or shutting down the company altogether. Saint Valentine had asked her to attend with him and the other directors to hopefully change the tone of the very dark meetings.

"I don't want to wind up drenched and cold to the board meeting," Paris said to Faraday as they stood in front of the door that led to the twenty-sixth floor in the stairwell.

"That's where the twenty-sixth floor took us when Advanced Love branch was the problem area in the FGA," he argued. "You're making those departments and that space better. I'm sure this floor of mystery will take us somewhere else that needs help."

"That's just the thing," Paris argued. "I'm not sure we should be doing this right before the board of directors meeting. I need to show up looking professional and not all disheveled."

"How about showing up looking like a motorcycle cop?" Faraday questioned. "Is that one of the options because that's the look you've gone for."

Paris glanced down at her leather jacket, pants, and boots and smirked. "I look tough and sleek."

"Ready to slide onto a motorcycle," he teased. "Because you have that meeting soon, that's exactly why we need to do this right now. If there's a problem area within the FGA, the twenty-sixth floor will take us there. We need to know what the potential problems are in the building. Knowledge is power, and that's what we need to arm ourselves with before the big meeting."

Paris sighed, resigning a little. The squirrel was probably right. Paris was extra nervous about the board meeting, so this was a good way to kill time beforehand and take her mind off it.

Slipping her fingers onto the metal handle for the twenty-sixth floor, she drew in a breath. "Okay, are you ready to pass out and be transported to a mysterious location?"

He winked. "Like you even have to ask."

Paris laughed, turning the knob and pushing the door open, ready for whatever came next.

CHAPTER EIGHT

Saint Valentine's Office, Matters of the Heart, Fiftieth Floor, FGA Tower, New York City, New York, United States

As Paris had expected, for a moment, she did black out. It was as if she had gone to sleep when she stepped through the door to the twenty-sixth floor. When she awoke, it wasn't on the mysterious floor, and it wasn't cold and wet in the basement like before.

She and Faraday stood on a familiar floor in an office that usually she only found herself in by invitation. Thankfully she wasn't drenched or cold or feeling like the world was caving in on her as she had when she had been transported by the twenty-sixth floor to the basement. Yet, she still felt an edge of despair.

Paris glanced around, blinking to clear her vision as her surroundings came in and out of focus. Faraday, in her arms, appeared to be doing the same thing, like they were both waking from a dream.

She turned her head to find the fireplace crackling slightly, a small dying fire in the hearth. Looking the other way, Paris found the structure she most recognized in this space—a large, ornately carved desk. Behind it, with his back toward her, was the man she almost always found in this space.

She thought, based on his slumped appearance and lifeless figure, he might be asleep…or worse. Paris shook off her worry and cleared her throat.

Thankfully, this made the man come alive, meaning he was. Then he jumped, probably because he hadn't expected someone to suddenly appear behind him in his shut office. Saint Valentine turned around in his chair and faced her, a look of surprised pride and also weary dread on his face. It was strange to see two completely opposite reactions in one expression, and yet they were there.

Finally, after taking in the sudden appearance of Paris and Faraday in his office, the leader of the FGA nodded. "So you must have visited the twenty-sixth floor, and it brought you here. I can't deny it any longer. The biggest problem in this place is me."

CHAPTER NINE

Saint Valentine's Office, Matters of the Heart, Fiftieth Floor, FGA Tower, New York City, New York, United States

Remarkably, Saint Valentine looked worse than the last time Paris saw him, and that had only been a few days prior. His cheeks were more sunken, giving him a hollow appearance. Under his eyes, he wore heavy purple bags that made him appear almost zombie-like.

Had he lost some of his silver hair? Paris wondered. It definitely was more salt than pepper now.

To the leader of the FGA's credit, he was still as impeccably dressed as ever in a high-quality black suit with a red rose in the lapel. However, it hung off his shoulders more than usual, indicating he'd lost some of his muscle mass.

"Saint Valentine," Paris said, hurrying over with Faraday in tow. "Are you all right?"

She reminded herself the man just admitted to being the biggest problem at the FGA, so he definitely wasn't okay. She had meant, did he need something immediately, like a doctor?

When he drew in a breath, there was a rattling noise in his throat. "I'm dying, Paris."

She shook her head, unable to accept this. Instinctively she held Faraday closer for comfort. "I can help you. I know people, powerful people. There has to be a way."

He held out his withered hand, shaking. "Sit, please."

Without hesitation, Paris lowered into the chair, releasing Faraday, who jumped up on the surface of the desk and looked over the man in front of them, concern written in his gaze.

"As you've learned by now, the FGA is a living and breathing structure," Saint Valentine began through wheezing breaths. "What happens to the organization directly affects the building. When certain departments excel or as in the case of Advanced Love branch, it deteriorates."

Paris and Faraday both nodded.

"Well, the ultimate source of power for the FGA is held within the person responsible for it—its leader." Saint Valentine pointed to himself. "That's me, of course. When the organization is strong, then so is its leader. The important point here isn't that I'm dying."

"The FGA is dying," Paris gasped.

The feeble man bobbed his head in agreement.

"With it, it's taking you," Faraday guessed.

"I'm afraid so," Saint Valentine answered. "The concern shouldn't be about me. It's that the company is dying, and without it, love will suffer. Its enemies will take over, and I fear it won't be long before it's at an all-time low. You know the consequences of that."

"The planet will die too," Paris stated.

He nodded again. "There are always those like you and the Beaufonts who love without abandonment. I'm afraid it isn't enough. There's a domino effect when it comes to love, or rather, the loss of love. Heartbreak spreads like a disease when we're not in a position to protect and stop it."

"If the FGA dies, then with it goes the opportunity to defend love from our enemies," Paris said, thinking of Jackson Zelle and all the others who have warred against love, afraid of their own hearts.

"What can we do?" Faraday asked, vibrating with emotions, much like Paris.

Saint Valentine remarkably laughed at this, although that sent him into a coughing fit. "You have done so much. It is only through your efforts that the FGA has survived this long. If not for you, then Jackson Zelle would have destroyed this place from the inside out. Our other opponents would have torn us apart." He glanced around at his heart-shaped office, which Paris now saw was muted in color in comparison to the last time she saw it. "To survive this, there are a few things we must do."

"Stop us from going bankrupt," Paris guessed.

"I wish that money could fix all our problems," Saint Valentine answered. "Unfortunately, our financial status is more a symptom of a bigger ailment. I've made a lot of mistakes, and that's evident now."

"You can't blame yourself for trusting Jackson Zelle," Faraday offered.

Saint Valentine offered him a tired smile. "That's exactly what a leader has to do, take responsibility. I did trust Jackson Zelle, and he used his power within this company to set us up for financial suicide. Since he left, things have spun out of control. I was so afraid of the mismanagement of the Advanced Love branch that I didn't do anything. Now, I fear it's been stagnant for too long. How many long-term marriages broke up because it wasn't there to save people? How many didn't marry because there were no fairy godmothers to encourage them? These questions have become more numerous in my head as I come to terms with my impending death. Like an addict who looks back from their death bed at all the times they used, all of those occasions contributing to their ultimate demise."

Paris shook her head, unwilling to accept this. "There has to be something we can do. Things can't be so dire for you or the

FGA. I'll have funding soon. I'm managing the Advanced Love branch. We can turn things around."

"I want that to be true," Saint Valentine replied. "Timing is critical. The board is ready to sell, and there are buyers. They won't be good for the organization, I fear, and it will then be out of the fairy's hands. It will be conglomerations that want to profit from love, which will be its ultimate downfall. Mother Nature warned us from the beginning that to make profits from love would be to destroy it."

"This is a corporation," Faraday argued, shaking his head, obviously confused.

"Only for structural reasons," Saint Valentine explained. "It was meant to maintain balance, but to think about the bottom line first, would be to lose sight of our mission. Love makes money, no doubt about it. That's not why we foster it. To create love on an intrinsic level, it can't be about money."

"So I'll get the funding source," Paris said. "That will give us the means to save the FGA and provide budgets to departments to create and nurture love. I just need a little more time."

"There's something else, though, and I think it's the reason the love meter is down dramatically."

Paris had been so busy with everything, including her own wedding, that she'd forgotten to check the love meter recently. "What is it?"

"That's just the thing," Saint Valentine answered. "I'm not certain, but something is attacking love on a very dangerous level."

"Jackson Zelle," Faraday guessed.

"He's probably set the foundation for this a long time ago."

Saint Valentine appeared so crestfallen suddenly. "I fear that by the time we learn what is going on, it will be too late."

"We can't give up, sir," Paris said. "I stopped Jackson Zelle from destroying his hometown. Agent Jasper is researching Zelle Corp. I'm sure that during my time fighting Tomár, Jackson Zelle was putting things into place. He might have won a few battles and be ahead of us, but we're going to win the war. However, to do that, I think we're going to have to take some chances. Ones you haven't been willing to do in the past."

He arched an eyebrow at her, curious.

"I'm saying that instead of being conservative with the Advanced Love branch, I need to push it full force," she replied. "We have nothing to lose at this point."

"We have everything to lose," he argued, motioning to the Matter of the Heart office.

"Yes, but if we don't act fast and radically, we will fail regardless," Faraday offered. "At least this way, we know we gave it our best effort."

"Advanced Love handles the most important of relationships," Saint Valentine began. "The ones that most affect the love meter. If you're not careful, you could destroy us faster than if we did nothing."

"I could also save us when we're headed over a cliff right now," Paris countered. "Let me try this, sir. Let me try to save the FGA...you..."

He drew a breath and then pushed away from the desk. With a great effort, he got to his feet. "Very well, then. For now, we must go and fight those within our borders. It's time for your very first FGA board of directors meeting. I'm sorry to say, but you're about to meet those who most want this place handed over to the enemy, where it will surely die."

CHAPTER TEN

Board Room, Forty-Ninth Floor, FGA Tower, New York City, New York, United States

Since taking a squirrel to a board meeting with a bunch of stuffy old sticks in the mud was probably not going to make Paris look like the professional she wanted to be seen as, she sent her squirrel to help the IT department with Isha's new idea. With Faraday's expertise, the new website functionality would be operational within the hour, if not sooner. It was a brilliant idea, and Paris wondered why no one had thought of it sooner.

Paris was tempted to have a shortbread and see if it gave her some bright ideas to help the FGA. However, if she didn't deliver an even ten cookies minus the two for testing to Ivy, she wouldn't get the wedding planner referral. Also, she thought it was better to show some faith in herself right then, believing she could fix these problems rather than rely upon a magical solution.

Subfar was working on a funding solution and would have something in time. Paris had permission to start pushing the Advanced Love departments now. She could make big changes. That meant she could make big problems, but she also reminded herself there was only farther down to go if she didn't help the FGA go up.

Things couldn't possibly get worse. Saint Valentine was dying, and it was because the FGA was dying and taking love along with it. As the old saying went, desperate times called for desperate actions, and Paris was ready and willing to push things.

Never having been to the forty-ninth floor where the board of directors met, Paris halted upon stepping off the elevator. If the FGA Tower mimicked the emotions of a department, then the board was full of mystery and oddities.

The forty-ninth floor only allowed entry of those invited by the board or Saint Valentine. Therefore the elevator dropped its transports off straight into the board room. There was no reception area or lobby of any sort. No hallway or entryway. Just one big room cloaked in darkness and definitely mystery.

"It's beautiful," Paris whispered to Saint Valentine, clutching her arm, needing her support to help him with every step. She worried that if she wasn't there, even his ornately carved cane, which was also his magical instrument, wouldn't hold him up. With every step, he wobbled and seemed pained, making Paris' heart hurt for the leader of the FGA. This was just the incentive for her to fix things and crush Jackson Zelle.

"It is full of the oldest magic related to the fairy godmothers," Saint Valentine related in a hoarse voice. "The board was the first thing Mother Nature appointed upon starting the organization to protect and promote love. At that time, she elected seven individuals to make decisions on behalf of the FGA, with one Saint Valentine to lead them. He had veto power, but they could override it by a two-thirds vote."

"Much like our United States government," Paris said, noticing the figures bathed in shadows sitting at the long rectangular table.

"Well, it all came from somewhere."

"The seven individuals," Paris continued. "Much like the seven families, both mortal and magician, meant to represent the House of Fourteen for magic."

"Yes. It is a powerful number supposed to align an organization with balance," he explained.

Paris nodded, taking in the strange space. It reminded her more of a library than a meeting area. The board room was two stories, with the second level accessible by a spiral staircase at the back. The second floor was just a balcony that went around three-fourths of the room and was an extension of the book shelves that lined three walls.

The fourth wall was a floor-to-ceiling aquarium full of vegetation and large and small, colorful fish. The glass was framed by beautiful blue curtains, and the reflection of a giant chandelier radiated off the surface. A shark swam dangerously close to the glass as though it was going to burst through before swerving and continuing back in the other direction.

Paris couldn't believe that a huge aquarium sat there on the forty-ninth floor. However, there was an anti-gravity chamber on the forty-eighth floor that used to be devoted to the finance department, so she shouldn't be that surprised.

The crystals of the chandelier reflected off the glass of the aquarium and the large baroque table below it in the middle of the room. Around it were other items one would find in an old library, like a free-standing globe in a large stand. There were also clusters of leather upholstered armchairs, statues, and large plants.

Paris directed her attention to the figures seated quietly at the table. She couldn't see them well in the dimly lit space, but the eerie reflection of blue from the aquarium and chandelier overhead told her they were all staring at her and Saint Valentine as he hobbled into the room and approached the head of the table.

She helped him to his chair, pulling it out for him. Then she stood and looked around at the faces—some of them ones she recognized and most she didn't.

There was one woman who she did recognize, but she hadn't seen in quite a long time. She was the first one to speak, looking directly at Saint Valentine as he took a seat.

She pointed at Paris accusatorially. "You don't realize that you're dying because of her."

CHAPTER ELEVEN

Board Room, Forty-Ninth Floor, FGA Tower, New York City, New York, United States

Paris sucked in a breath, narrowing her eyes at the woman who had made her time at Happily Ever After College difficult. Virginia Montgomery had used her influence and power as a board member at the FGA to get things she wanted at the college. Unsurprisingly, Becky, one of Paris' old employees, was her daughter and just as insufferable. Paris had wrongly thought she was done dealing with the Montgomery family, forgetting they were entrenched at the FGA.

"Agent Beaufont isn't the reason I'm dying," Saint Valentine argued, unflustered. "That is because the FGA is failing."

"Because you appointed an untried fairy godmother to an agent role, breaking traditions," Virginia Montgomery countered rudely. "Women are meant to be fairy godmothers, not agents and certainly not directors."

Mae Ling, on the far side, at the end of the table, leaned forward. "You'll excuse me if I dare to disagree with you and ask what evidence you have to support such claims."

Virginia, in her powder blue fairy godmother gown with its

pink sash, pointed at the far wall of shelves. Her hair was gray, how it turned anyone who wore the robe became, taking on the look of a grandmother even if the person wasn't quite old. "Read our history. It tells you that women, the nurturing ones, were meant to make matches as fairy godmothers and men, as leaders, were meant to direct us."

"That's the history it tells," Mae Ling argued, looking very different in her all-black loose-fitting clothes and short dark hair. "It doesn't state it has to be that way. Just because something was always one way doesn't mean it must always be. Change is how we evolve."

"Change is the way we break the things that have always worked." Virginia Montgomery, who loved pointing, directed her finger back in Saint Valentine's direction. "Is it by coincidence that our leader of the FGA is dying and has made so many radical changes? He elected a woman to an agent position. Then another to a director position. Then there are all the changes related to the modern era before that."

Saint Valentine cleared his throat, gaining the attention of everyone at the table. "I'll remind you of the timeline and that the FGA was faltering before I made these radical changes. I read the writing on the wall that if I didn't start doing things differently, we'd sink faster. I want to believe my way of doing things has kept us afloat longer than if I had gone with the status quo of our ancestors."

"Virginia is right, though," a man beside the old fairy godmother with a sour expression said. He, like all the board of directors, was elderly, gray, and crotchety looking. "You're dying, Saint Valentine. This means the FGA is dying. We must do something about it before it's too late."

Paris was furious they were talking about Saint Valentine dying so casually, and on top of that, the FGA. She stared across the table at the only other familiar face she knew—Agent Barney

Jasper. He directed his gaze to the chair next to where she stood, giving her a pointed look.

Taking the hint, Paris pulled out the heavy chair and took a seat, her eyes shifting to Saint Valentine, who appeared to be thinking, rather slowly.

"Your solution is to sell the company we've all vowed to protect," Saint Valentine finally said, each word painstakingly slow.

"One must know when to cut their losses," the man countered. "If there is nothing to do for the company, to save it, then it would be better to make a profit, split it evenly and move on."

"I'm as sad as any of you that the FGA is failing. My family has been on the board of directors since the beginning. We've invested everything into this organization. It's for that reason that I'm not going down with this ship. A smart person jumps well before."

"A captain goes down with his ship," Saint Valentine stated.

"Your life is linked to this organization," another man said, his face mostly covered in blue shadows from the light of the aquarium. "I'm sorry for you, but that's the commitment you made when you took your role as Saint Valentine. Every leader has known the risks, but none until you have had to face it."

"This is about love," Saint Valentine said, banging his fists on the board room table. The sound was feeble and weak. "How can you quit when you know what we stand to lose?"

"Because we can walk away with our heads held high now," Virginia Montgomery said through gritted teeth.

"You want to walk away with money in your pocket," Saint Valentine fired back, more energetically, fueled by anger.

"The company is valued at over one hundred million dollars," the man in the shadows stated. "If we sell now, we walk away with that. If we wait, stocks will plummet, and we will go bankrupt, maybe overnight. We have to sell while we can."

"Some despicable company who exploits love will buy the FGA," Saint Valentine stated. "How will you sleep then?"

Virginia Montgomery sighed, leaning forward. "We all care about love. That's why we're here. Someone sailed this ship into uncharted waters, and now the rest of us are trying to salvage it." She cut her eyes to Paris, a rude look on her face.

It was taking everything Paris had to just sit there and listen, but that's what her instincts told her to do. This was her turn to learn. To listen. To understand the challenges Saint Valentine was facing. Only then could she help him to fix them, and that's exactly what she intended to do.

"Sometimes you have to sail through unchartered waters to find treasure," Saint Valentine declared at once, smiling fondly at Paris. "I stand by my decision. I think the decisions of the past put us in financial hardship. I think that resisting the modern world for so long has caught up with us. I believe pivoting to embrace change will save us, but we can't jump ship before that happens. A captain knows when to hold on and weather the storm. I truly believe if we just stand firm, we will come out the other side to the dawning of clear skies and a stronger crew."

"With all due respect," the man beside Virginia said. "You must die when this place goes down. I get why you have to keep the faith. The rest of us, we don't have to see ourselves falter to financial ruin."

"So it *is* about money, then," Saint Valentine seethed.

"The FGA has paid me handsomely for decades, as it has every board member," the man answered proudly. "I don't see why I should walk away with nothing at this point. I've devoted my life to it. I work to support love, but I don't work for free."

Virginia Montgomery nodded. "If we wait to sell, we lose the company and our shares. I vote that we sell now, once we find a buyer, before it's too late."

"But…" Saint Valentine choked on the word.

"Whether we sell and the FGA trades hands or it goes bankrupt, you're going to die," the man on the far end of the table said firmly. "You're linked to the fairy godmothers, and they will be no more once the FGA is traded. We sell the name, the building, and the brand. The rest will be dissolved, along with Happily Ever After College, which will no longer be necessary."

Inside, Paris was screaming, "Noooooo." She wanted to yell aloud. To argue. To be heard. To tell these morons why they were wrong. She stayed frozen, not wanting to make more trouble for Saint Valentine. Just watching him battle the board of directors was enough to break her already fractured heart. How could she lose him and the FGA and the fairy godmothers? Where would she go? Where would any of them go? Now she was seeing first-hand how Saint Valentine was at the mercy of the board, trying to explain that love was worth the sacrifice to people who only cared about money.

"So we leave it to the vote," Virginia Montgomery began. "All those in favor of finding a buyer for the FGA for the price of one hundred million dollars?"

Around the table, one by one, hands went up until there were seven in the air. There would be no vetoing a unanimous vote by Saint Valentine. There was no use. He'd been outvoted.

Soon, if Paris didn't have the money, the FGA would be sold, and her life with the fairy godmothers would be over. Even sadder was that Saint Valentine would be dead.

CHAPTER TWELVE

Fairy Grounds Coffee Shop, First Floor, FGA Tower, New York City, New York, United States

After the conclusion of the depressing board of directors meeting, Paris just wanted to go up to the rooftop of the FGA Tower and yell. She couldn't believe the board had voted to sell the company. Now it was a race to hope she could get the money to save the company before an investor or another corporation bought the organization.

Instead of finding catharsis on the rooftop, Paris decided she needed to use her time most effectively. That meant doing a lot of things she didn't want to. First, she had to deliver the Smarten Up Shortbread to Ivy at Fairy Grounds because, as much as she hated to admit it, her friends were right.

Her wedding could positively affect the love meter, and she was going to do everything possible to help love—even if the FGA was going to be lost. They'd go out with a bang.

Second, Paris had to quit avoiding taking the reins of the Advanced Love branch. She had to quickly get down there and take over and start directing. That would mean actually recruiting and leading projects. Unlike how Saint Valentine had advised her earlier to be conservative in her approach, Paris was going to dive in head first.

Third, Paris had to push Subfar to come up with a viable strategy and fast. No more researching for the right approach. Instead, she needed a lot of money, and she needed it right away. She'd figure out how to make it sustainable when she could. She needed approximately one hundred million dollars. Then the FGA would be saved, and hopefully Saint Valentine too.

Paris hoped it wasn't too late for the man. She reminded herself that this wasn't just about money. This was, as Saint Valentine would remind her, inevitably about love.

So Paris swallowed down her pride and went into Fairy Grounds with the Smarten Up Shortbread.

She strode over to the counter where the pixies were arguing about if an apple cake and a carrot one were baked at the same time, they'd taste like each other.

"It's true," Ivy said to another pixie, the pair floating in the air, their wings flittering. "If you bake them at the same time, the carrot will have a nutmeg flavor. The apple will taste like cream cheese."

Paris wanted to point out it was impossible science to start with. It was even more impossible for one of the cakes to come out tasting like the other one's frosting that went on after baking. She decided the educational lecture would fall on deaf ears.

Instead, she held up the box of Smarten Up Shortbread. "I have something for you, Ivy."

The pixie with pink wings jerked her head in Paris' direction. Then her eyes widened, and she screamed in response.

"Go and put cream in the butter," she barked at the other pixie.

"Why?" the other pixie asked, confused, as they normally were.

"Because how else are we going to cream the butter!" Ivy yelled, pointing to the kitchen.

She waited until the other fairy had disappeared before turning back to Paris.

Handing over the box of Smarten Up Shortbread, Paris said, "You realize that creaming the butter isn't achieved that way, right?"

The look that Ivy shot her told her she should probably allow the pixie to believe whatever she wanted.

"I didn't want anyone to know I was getting these," Ivy said, snatching the cookies from her and looking them over. "Are you sure they work?"

"There are two brainless idiots on the third floor who are probably working for NASA by now, so yeah, it will work for you." Seeing the pixie's face blossom red with anger, she smiled sweetly. "Because you're so much smarter than those ladies. I bet you'll be recruited by…Space X."

Ivy shook her head. "I have no interest in working for Disney World."

"Right," Paris said, drawing out the word. "So why is it that you want to be smarter all of a sudden?"

Ivy sighed. "Well, I know it's weird, but no one comes in here for our coffee."

"No." Paris pretended to be surprised.

Ivy shot her an irate look. "We are known for our scones, but that's it. I'm not sure if it's true, but I've heard a rumor that the FGA might get sold or something."

Paris chewed on her lip, fuming that the rumor, which was true and hopefully not coming to fruition, was spreading. "Go on."

"Well, I think it would be good to expand our business potential," Ivy continued. "So we need to learn to make cakes and frostings and cookies and—"

"Coffee," Paris interrupted, earning her another annoyed look. "Ivy, can I offer you some advice as a successful business owner of a restaurant?"

The pixie stared at her.

"Well," Paris decided to continue. "At the FGA, we're in the business of love. We're not trying to make people anything but in love. To have and hold, you know. You're good at scones. Really good for those who like that kind of thing. Just do that for all your worth. Sometimes less is more. Does that make sense?"

Ivy scowled and shook her head. "That makes no sense at all. Less is less. I may not be able to do math, but if I have one, that's less than two."

Paris rolled her eyes. "Math is hard. What I'm trying to say is—"

"Terrance!" Ivy yelled.

Paris tilted her head to the side, wondering what this strange outburst by the pixie was about. Maybe they were playing a weird knock-knock joke, and Ivy forgot the first part. "Terrance who?"

"Terrance is the name of the wedding planner," Ivy answered, buzzing around in the air. "You got me the cookies, and I'll tell him you've been referred to him. That's all you're getting from me."

"Cool, cool, cool," Paris said, trying to keep her calm. "Can I get a number or location or place to find this Terrance?"

"Roya Lane!" Ivy yelled and then zoomed for the back room with the cookies in hand.

"Cool, so I just run around Roya Lane and ask for a Terrance," Paris said, shaking her head. "How hard can that be?"

CHAPTER THIRTEEN

Advanced Love Department, Level One, Basement, FGA Tower, New York City, New York, United States

Paris would hunt down this Terrance, the best wedding planner in the business, when she went to Roya Lane later to meet up with Subfar. Hopefully, the Protector of Wealth had good news for her because, at this point, she was desperate.

Paris even considered going to her pseudo-uncle, King Rudolf, and asking him for the money to save the FGA. However, at her core, she didn't believe Saint Valentine would allow it. This place was owned and operated by fairies, not fae—which were a subset of the fairy race. Still, they were very different types with different interests and skill sets. Having fae owning the FGA would create a whole host of new problems.

No, the way to get the one hundred million dollars had to be through Subfar. She'd gone to all the trouble to track down Sherlock Holmes just for this purpose. The great detective, with King Rudolf's help, had followed the clues to find Subfar. Paris couldn't give up yet. She'd resolved the conflict between Subfar and Subner so they didn't kill each other. There was no turning back now. She just had to hope it all worked out before it was too late.

If the FGA Tower responded to the vibrations of a department and the building changed accordingly, then her current departments were definitely in sad shape. As Paris entered the basement of the building, she consoled herself with the fact that at least the lights were on. It wasn't much of a consolation, though, since the place probably would look better in the dark. At least then, one couldn't see the mold stains on the ceiling or the rotting carpet or the scorch marks on the walls from a previous fire.

"Oh, there you are," Faraday squeaked when she stepped off the elevator, holding her breath to prevent herself from vomiting.

Did it smell worse than before? Paris thought her employees had been down there cleaning up. She reasoned there were only three of them, and they didn't appear to be the brightest bunch.

They had helped her in Piney Woods Hills to pass out the antidote to nihilism and done it very efficiently, so they weren't a lost cause. She didn't think she would have saved the town without their help. Now she just needed to turn them into a stellar team that created a massive amount of love in advanced relationships—overnight. No biggie, she thought with a morbid laugh.

"How did it go with the website?" Paris asked, pinching her nose.

The squirrel nodded to this gesture, obviously bothered by the smell too. He probably got more of it than Paris, both by being a squirrel and being so close to the floor, which was no doubt riddled with mold and dust and who knew what else.

"It's up and running already," he replied happily. "It was a brilliant idea Isha had, and everyone wondered how we hadn't considered it before. The fairy godmothers have always been proactive at creating love in strategy but rarely do they look for ways to troubleshoot problems in relationships. The tele-eventor alerts to potentials more than problems. This has started a hunt looking into relationship therapy and seeing if they can help there. At least we know those are areas where people are seeking help."

"That's totally brilliant," Paris said, relieved to have some good news. "It makes a lot of sense and just shows how much low-hanging fruit we've had that we didn't realize."

"It's true," he chirped. "The love meter alerts us to levels of love. In the past, when low, you've used your detective skills to determine the problem and fix it. Those are usually high-level problems. I think we can really impact love by helping people on an individual basis."

"I hope so," Paris offered. "So lovers go onto the website when they have a problem and, what, fill out a form?"

"Then we can dispatch a fairy godmother, depending on which department it falls into."

Paris smiled. "It is the simple things that can make a difference."

"The only issue we have now is communication at this point," Faraday explained. "We need a way to get the word out there."

"Sounds like a way that I can help," Paris replied. "Now that I have the authority to move fast with my departments, it gives me the initiative to hand it to my employees."

She looked around at the broken cubicles and furniture spread around the open area. "Only question is, where is that ragtag bunch?"

CHAPTER FOURTEEN

Advanced Love Department, Level One, Basement, FGA Tower, New York City, New York, United States

It didn't take Paris long to find her three employees. She just had to follow the sounds of chimes and monks chanting.

Paris groaned, looking at Faraday as they discovered the ragtag crew sitting on the floor of a mostly clean room. It was small and cleared of furniture and didn't smell like mold or feel like death. "Why do I have to deal with hippies so often?"

"It must be something you did in a past life," Agent Ron Opal said, cracking an eye at her, similar to how Jenny had when Paris and Faraday interrupted her meditation. The way the three were sitting in lotus position with their eyes closed and hands resting on their knees, they were definitely meditating.

"Yes, I must have murdered many a hippie, and this is my karma," Paris joked, squinting in the darkened room.

"If you encountered open-minded, free individuals often," Ron began, his thick mustache covering his mouth as he spoke. "Or hippies as you call them, then maybe the universe is telling you something. It was Adyashanti who said, 'The paradox is that when resistance is fully accepted, the resistance disappears.'"

Sissy, who looked both like a preschooler sitting on the floor and an elderly person who couldn't get up, opened her eyes. "What we resist persists, as they say."

Ron nodded, his shaggy white hair falling over one eye. "Yes, it was Guy Finley who said, 'On the other side of resistance is the flow.'"

Misfit opened her eyes, her dark, curly hair already covering one of them. "It was Marilyn Manson who said, 'When all your wishes are granted, many of your dreams will be destroyed.'"

Paris tilted her head in confusion regarding the strange emo fairy godmother. "What does that have to do with hippies or resistance?"

"It doesn't," Misfit answered. "I just wanted to join the discussion, and I like that quote."

"Well, here's a quote for you, said by Agent Paris Beaufont," the halfling said, her hands on her hips. "If my employees don't get off their butts and stop meditating during work hours and clean up this place, as they were told to do, then they are fired."

Ron pushed up to his feet, groaning. "I think for that to be a memorable or helpful quote, it needs brevity and poetry."

"And a little less bitchery," Misfit added, also standing up before offering a hand to Sissy.

"I think a good quote should add some inspiration to the world," the small fairy said.

"I'm all for inspiring," Paris muttered dryly, looking around at the bare space. "How can I inspire you all to fix this place? One room won't do. Really all you did was clean one room."

"We were just finishing with this one," Ron explained. "We pulled up the carpet, cleaned the walls, cleared out the furniture, and we were cleansing the energy before moving on to the next office."

Paris sighed. "Well, thankfully, I've enlisted the help of a magical renovation expert, so I won't need to use your time on this stuff anymore. Which is good because I'm putting you all to work on real tasks that are going to heavily affect the love meter."

"I thought you were supposed to take it slow and observe," Ron argued. "No big sweeping changes or radical decisions that could make big effects."

Paris sighed, nodding. "Yes, but that's before I learned it's worth the risk. The FGA is in trouble. It would be better to do big things and chance it. Hopefully, what we do is positive for the love meter, but if not, well, then we're going down regardless."

"That sounds serious," Ron said, looking concerned.

"It is," Paris said, mimicking his expression. There was no point in sugarcoating things at this point. Her employees needed to know how serious this was. "Agent Opal, you can't lead fairy godmothers unless you have some for your departments."

"Yes, the Long Distance and Fifty-Plus Years of Marriage departments are currently operating at zero."

"Put in a call to Headmistress Willow Star at Happily Ever After College," Paris began, formulating a plan as she spoke, not having thought about it beforehand. "Ask her to send you over as many of her top students as she thinks are qualified to skip the final project and graduate early."

His mustache twitched with surprise. "That's very unorthodox to put fairy godmothers into the field before they've completed their training."

"Desperate times call for unorthodox measures," Paris declared.

"That's not how the quote goes," Sissy corrected.

Misfit smirked. "My ex-boyfriend used to say, 'Desperate times call for desperate music.'"

Sissy shook her head. "No, it was William Shakespeare who said, 'Desperate times breed desperate measures.'"

"William Shakespeare also told Paris she dressed funny but then searched the globe for her," Faraday offered, flicking his puffy tail.

Everyone looked down at the squirrel.

He shrugged. "It's a long story for another time."

"Does your friend do drugs?" Misfit asked Paris, pointing at Faraday.

She shook her head. "No, and he's telling the truth about Shakespeare. We worked together on writing Romeo and Juliet, but it's not that interesting of a story. I'd rather we center our energy on creating modern-day love."

"Maybe she does drugs," Misfit whispered loudly to Sissy, staring at Paris.

"I'm thinking about it," Paris interrupted, returning her attention to Agent Opal. "As I was saying, have the Headmistress send you over her best and brightest fairy godmothers in training. Then send them straight out into the field to start nurturing long-distance relationships and long-lasting marriages. Do things better and with more gusto than before."

He scratched his head. "How you suppose I do that?"

"Well, I have a friend in the Casual Romance department who might be able to help," Paris answered, still thinking on her feet. "Go up and talk to Isha and ask her for advice. I bet you could find ways to help unite long-distance lovers, and that would really swing the love meter. I wish we had money because then we could fly many of them to see each other and that would be great. We need to think of creative solutions, and Isha is our gal for that until the spell she's under wears off."

"Sounds good to me," Ron said. "That gets me thinking. I can offer my dude ranch for weekend stays to couples married for a long time. Tell them they won it for being so committed to each other. I will need employees to go and find them and tell them."

"Great idea. Good thinking, and thanks for the donation. It's stuff like that which will turn things around and get us going in the right direction."

He nodded, heading out the door right away, ready to get to work.

"What would you have me do, boss?" Misfit asked. She was wearing baggy jeans and black combat shoes and a shirt that said, I only came here to piss you off.

Paris brightened, grateful that her goth employee seemed eager to help. "You work in the Heartbreak Recovery department, and we've just launched this new feature on the website for the FGA." She pointed at Faraday. "The IT department can get you up to speed on how it works, but I want you to craft a press release and have it sent out. Really blanket the newspapers and online media sites with this new resource. Then monitor it and see what comes in and how we can help. There's something that's affecting the love meter, according to Saint Valentine. Something specific. If history has taught me anything, Jackson Zelle and his new corporation are probably behind it. So look for a thread that is consistent."

Faraday nodded. "Yes. Before he turned his hometown nihilistic. He's also used entertainment and music to try to spell lovers to break up. This is a man who crafts strategies and uses resources he knows lovers go after."

Misfit narrowed her eyes. "Spelling music and abusing it is just wrong. If that man is doing something to harm love and create heartbreak, then we're going to take him down."

Paris clapped her hands together, and the fairy godmother smiled. "Good. Misfit, go up to the IT department and find a workstation. Have someone up there run you through the website and work on a press release. I want one out immediately."

"What about me?" Sissy asked, smiling up at Paris. It was strange since usually, it was the halfling who was shorter than everyone else. The woman was wearing poufy pants like she was Jasmine from Aladdin and a shirt with entirely too many ruffles.

"You're in the Soul Mates Department," Paris began, chewing on her lip and thinking, not having worked out a plan yet. "I know finding those matches is complex and time-consuming work."

"It's true," the fairy godmother replied. "I have to consult star charts and moon cycles and Chinese zodiacs and—"

"Let's try a more scientific approach," Paris interrupted, an idea occurring to her. She turned to Faraday. "You have a way of measuring vibrational frequencies in people, correct?"

"Yeah, I perfected it on you," he answered. "Which is why you were getting those strange headaches for a while."

"Not cool, Squirrel," she muttered. "I'm going to gather that soul mates vibrate at the same frequency."

"Which is impressive since the spectrum is quite large," Faraday offered. "I'm sure you're right."

"So we bypass all the grunt work of finding soul mates by taking the data from the tele-eventor," Paris began, talking faster than she could think. "Then cross-examine that with a digital report of frequencies that are close in range. It should tell us who are soul mates from a small test pool. Even if we match only a few soul mates and bring them together, it will have large effects on the love meter."

"That's brilliant," Faraday stated proudly. "Have you had any shortbread by chance?"

Paris laughed. "No, I'm just really motivated, and sometimes that's all it takes to break through the wall and find new ideas."

"Speaking of breaking through walls," Faraday began, pointing to the main area. "I think Clark is here."

Paris sighed with relief. "Good. Renovations can begin. You all create love, and I'll work on creating a place for you and all the new fairy godmothers to work."

CHAPTER FIFTEEN

Advanced Love Department, Level One, Basement, FGA Tower, New York City, New York, United States

Uncle Clark was understandably wearing a look of pure horror when Paris greeted him by the elevators. He had his hands pressed into his suit pant pockets as if afraid for them to touch anything in the department's space. Paris didn't blame him.

"Thanks for coming to help," Paris said, hugging her uncle. "I know you're busy with all that you have going on."

He shook his head, seemingly in a daze. "It appears that you need my help here. I can't even believe this place is in the FGA Tower." He pointed to the ceiling. "Up there, it's so..."

"Clean," Paris offered as a howl echoed down the corridor that led to offices, supply closets, conference rooms, and the kitchen. "Oh, and not haunted."

Clark nodded as though this made perfect sense. "A ghost could be helpful."

"You know, I wouldn't have believed that before," she began, "but after my last mission, going to Haunted Harbor and learning they aren't harmful and can offer knowledge, I think you might be right. I should probably have a meeting with that ghost and pick his brain."

"That's a good idea and a novel approach," Clark offered. "They might know things about the history of the FGA and Advanced Love branch that will save you time or trouble. Or maybe even who you can trust or not trust here."

"Like who killed him," Paris said, the realization suddenly occurring to her. "I bet it was Jackson Zelle." She sighed. "Finding out that man is a criminal isn't new information."

"This ghost might be able to offer something else regarding this branch."

"Apparently, he's an old director by the name of Agent Tourmaline."

"It's worth investigating when you have a chance." Clark revolved in one spot, taking in the space. "So, what is your vision for this floor? We can't just glamour it to look better. It's going to need to be magically demolished and renovated from the ground up."

"I'm not sure about design, but let's strive for functionality first," Paris answered. "I'm hopefully about to have a few dozen new employees, and I need a place for them to work as efficiently as possible."

"So feng shui will be important," Clark muttered, his hand on his chin as he thought. He cut his eyes to Paris. "Don't tell your mother I said that term. She'll make fun of me."

She laughed. "I promise. You're right. I want the space to have a nice flow. Not in the way that hippies want flow, though. It should promote good vibes and creativity and also motivate fairy godmothers to work."

"All good goals," he agreed. "First, we need to do some demolition."

Holding out his hand to her, he smiled. "This will go faster if I can borrow your magical powers. I'll direct the operation as a magical renovations expert, but I'm going to need to draw on your energy to make this happen quickly. Otherwise, this could take a while."

Paris wrapped her hand around her uncle's and smiled, grateful for his expertise and willingness to help. "Of course. Thanks for offering to do this."

His blue eyes twinkled—the Beaufont trademark color. "My pleasure. I believe in what you do and want you to have what you need to be successful and create and nurture love. I know you're great at it. If it wasn't for you, then I wouldn't have taken a chance to pursue Stacy."

"She makes you happy, doesn't she?" Paris observed.

"She does, and although she's hesitant to jump head first into anything, I think she will in time."

"Well, of course you would attract a woman who was careful," Paris teased.

Uncle Clark grinned bashfully. "Yes, I tend to be cautious and very deliberate myself. She's a mortal who has her hesitations about the House of Fourteen, even though she was raised there by her aunt."

"Then she probably knows firsthand how crazy that place can be," Paris said, glancing down at her hand still in her uncle's.

"She does," he affirmed, squeezing her fingers. "Are you ready to tear this place up and build it back anew?"

Paris grinned, excited and nervous at the same time. She was grateful she was making strides and hoped they saved the FGA rather than bring it down faster.

CHAPTER SIXTEEN

Advanced Love Department, Level One, Basement, FGA Tower, New York City, New York, United States

The demolition project felt more like they were doing an incredible art project than tearing apart the first level of the basement. Watching the carpet get ripped away by invisible forces was satisfying. The walls were taken down to their structural beams, and all the plaster was stripped away.

All of the furniture was broken into pieces and sent in shipments up the elevator to the lobby. There it would be carted off to the dumpsters with the carpet and walls. Nothing in the basement was salvageable, but it also meant a fresh and new beginning.

When Paris and her uncle stood in the bare and open basement, she felt a strange peace sweep over her. This first level was a blank canvas, full of potential.

Noticing Clark slump a little, Paris spun to face him. "Are you okay?"

He feigned a smile. "I'm fine. We did a remarkable job and faster than I would have ever imagined." He held up her hand, still in his. "I knew you were powerful, but to feel it, well, was incredible. You're a battery of energy."

She blushed. "It was just so cool to see the place taken apart like that. It fueled me."

"Speaking of which. I'm going to need internal and external fuel before I continue."

Releasing her hand, he slipped his into his suit pocket and retrieved two protein bars he'd no doubt made himself. They appeared to contain oats, nuts, and dried fruit and were probably chock-full of nutrients. Her mother would have called Uber Eats for nachos.

Handing one of them over to Paris, Uncle Clark pointed to the elevator. It chimed as though signaled by his gesture. "There's the fuel I need for the next phase, on cue."

"What is it?" Paris asked, watching as workers carried large crates into the now empty and bare space.

"Materials for the renovations," he explained. "I'm going to do it all using magic, but you can't create walls and paint them without…"

Paris glanced at the crates, studying them. Then she guessed. "Plaster and paint."

He nodded and pointed at another box. "There we have wood for constructing furniture. In the other one is rock for projects. Also, there's glass and fabric. I'll have everything to create the renovation."

"Uncle Clark," Paris argued. "the FGA doesn't have any money. I can't afford this."

He shook his head. "Like I said, I owe you. The world owes you. This project is on me."

Paris blushed with emotion. "Thank you. I don't know if I can even express how much this means."

He grinned at her. "Again, you've done so much for me. Even if it was just a gentle nudge, your meddling in my love life changed everything for me."

"Well, I'm glad I did," she said. "While you're trying to thank me, do you have one hundred million dollars you want to donate to my cause to save the FGA from bankruptcy?"

His eyes widened in alarm. "I don't think so."

She laughed. "Worth a shot." Pointing at the crates, which were now stacked like a new wall beside them, Paris grinned with giddiness. "So this is all you need to renovate the space?"

He nodded, taking a bite of his homemade bar and chewing. "Yes, and I'll need your powers again, so eat up. That will make it go faster." Clark pointed to the bar in her hands she'd forgotten about.

Paris unwrapped the protein bar and took a bite, enjoying how chewy the bar was. It would be a good thing to give to someone when she needed them quiet, she thought with a laugh. After finishing the bar in another two bites, she swallowed and wiped her mouth, turning her attention back to her Uncle Clark, and saw he was done too.

"Thank you," she said, feeling her energy returning.

"You're welcome. Now, just tell me what color you want the walls, what type of carpet and furniture, and I'll have it done."

"Do you have any sample books?" she joked.

He shook his head. "No, but I'm excellent at figuring out things based on what you describe and picking the best for the space."

"Okay. Let's see. This is the Advanced Love branch," Paris muttered, mostly to herself, thinking. "Under that umbrella are Long Distance Relationships, Soul Mates, Heartbreak Recovery, Long-Lasting Marriages, True Love, and Second Chance Love, just to name a few."

"So the space should be warm and feel secure to promote the types of relationships it helps," Clark suggested.

"It should feel like the foundation of the FGA since, in essence, it is. That's why we are in the basement."

"What if it mimicked the elements of the Earth then, to show foundation?" Clark ran his hand horizontally through the air, and under their feet, turquoise carpet appeared, shimmering like they were standing on the surface of the ocean.

Paris glanced down, amazed as the entire huge space was instantly covered in plush carpet. Of course, one of the large crates was empty now. "I like it."

"To further the theme, we do the walls in wood to represent the trees." He swept his hand vertically, and one by one, all the exposed walls were covered in a light oak wood that contrasted nicely with the ocean blue carpet.

"This feels right," Paris said, smiling. The crate next to her caved in, suddenly empty of materials.

"Then we bring other elements in with wrought iron and glass workstations," he continued, pointing to the far corner where a modern desk was both warm with metal and cool with glass, appeared.

"That looks good in the space," she observed, astonished at how fast it was coming together.

"Great," Clark stated. "Now we'll just need more workstations, chairs, some plants, artwork, and of course, lighting."

Paris grinned, grateful it was all happening so fast, although she felt the energy quickly leaving her again and would need to replenish it. "I'll work with the IT department to get computers. I'm certain Mae Ling has to be easier to work with than Agent Josh Emerald, who I nicknamed Agent Jerk Face, I believe."

Her uncle snickered, shaking his head. "You are your mother's child, aren't you?"

"Hey, it's a trick Aunt Sophia taught me," Paris explained. "When we reduce our villains down, using name-calling, we make them seem less sinister."

Clark was amused. "Oh, the Beaufont women and their strategic and sometimes juvenile ways."

"It works!" Paris said as the elevator chimed, gaining both

their attention. Paris had lost track of time with all the renovations and had no idea if an hour or several or a day had passed.

"Whoa, the love of death metal," Misfit said, her eyes wide with astonishment as she strode into the space that was completely different from before. She halted, looking back at the elevator suddenly before glancing at Paris. "I did get off on level one, right? Of the basement? I didn't think the others were viable yet."

"The others are probably worse than this one."

"Was," Clark added.

"Right, worse than this one was," Paris amended.

"Dude, boss, you did all this over the last few hours?" Misfit asked, looking around.

Paris pointed to her uncle. "The magical renovations expert deserves all the credit."

He shook his head. "Without borrowing your powers, this would have taken me much, much longer. We still have a lot left to do."

"It's awesome." Misfit turned around in a complete circle, taking in everything.

"You like it?" Paris asked proudly. "We came up with the design together, trying to mimic—"

"Earth," Misfit interrupted, nodding. "I like the use of all the elements. You just need some plants and lighting and maybe a stone waterfall."

"Good idea," Paris remarked, liking the idea.

"Then we'll get back to it." Clark offered his hand.

"Before you do," Misfit cut in again, coming closer, "once we sent out the press release, the FGA website was flooded with requests for help from lovers." She held up an electronic tablet for Paris. "I think there's something you need to see."

CHAPTER SEVENTEEN

Advanced Love Department, Level One, Basement, FGA Tower, New York City, New York, United States

The FGA website had been flooded with submissions from those looking for help from love right after the media coverage and press releases. The brilliant idea from Isha was already working and offering so many opportunities to help people. With Faraday's help, the IT department was able to create a form with categories that made it easy to determine where each submission should go.

It made sense that the FGA should be opening their "virtual" doors, so to speak, and asking lovers what they needed help with. These were the simple solutions the company had missed out on early on because they were always so focused on big-picture things. The board, Paris was well aware of since her time at Happily Ever After College, liked the idea of focusing its time, energy, and resources on making matches associated with fame and fortune.

The mindset of the old fogies stuck in tradition was that spending fairy godmother's efforts making matches with famous

individuals, royalty, and those in the public eye was more important than focusing on the average Prince Charmings and
Cinderellas of the world. The influx of submissions asking for
help proved there was so much more they could be doing at
the FGA.

Matching a king with a queen and having a lavish publicized
love affair and wedding made the love meter swing positively,
but Paris loved the idea of fixing everyday people's problems too.
Relationships were hard, and each day there were new challenges
for the mom who stayed up late and during the day worked all
the time and the partners who never saw each other because of
circumstances.

Boyfriends and girlfriends were always struggling in little
ways, and helping them navigate their relationships could lead to
big wins. Most importantly, it could keep people together so they
had long-lasting romances. Over time, that would positively
affect the love meter in big ways.

Paris read over the report Misfit had given her. It all seemed
so strange and coincidental. It also seemed like a problem that
had Jackson Zelle's name written all over it.

"It's all brides-to-be affected," Paris said, looking up from the
tablet.

"Yes, the submissions of concerns all are from grooms, who
say their fiancés are sleeping all the time. At first, just a bit more
than usual, but with every passing nap, they sleep longer and are
harder to wake up. Seems coincidental, don't you think? Can it
just be the women are exhausted from all the wedding planning?"

Paris shook her head. "I know firsthand it's a lot, but something tells me there's a reason brides-to-be have been targeted."

Uncle Clark lowered his chin, regarding her with a serious
look. "I don't like the irony that you're newly engaged and your
nemesis, who is very strategic and calculated, knows that."

Paris felt sudden dread. "Yes. He's coming after me, isn't he?"

"Love, too," Misfit said. "Because you can't have a wedding with a comatose individual, although I once tried."

Paris and Clark both exchanged confused looks before shaking off the weird fairy godmother's statement.

"I need to do more research on this," Paris began, formulating an idea. "There has to be a certain common place that brides are being spelled to be sleepier. I'm guessing magic is behind this."

"It's a good guess," Clark agreed.

"Thankfully, I've got the name of the best wedding planner in the business," Paris replied. "That's a good place to start, but it's going to take me away from this." She indicated the partially renovated space.

"I can finish it on my own," Clark assured her. "It will just take me longer."

Paris pulled Amantis from her holster, the round blue gem on its end glowing with power. "This serves as a battery too, and it's currently full. It's my magic, so you should be able to draw from that to help you."

"Great idea." Uncle Clark took the wand. "Although I usually wouldn't use a wand, especially someone else's, in this instance, it makes sense."

"Okay, and I'll go dig around and see if I can't find out how these brides are getting put under a sleeping spell," Paris said, heading for the elevator at once, spurred by a new mystery and mission.

"Maybe they all ate a bunch of bad apples like Snow White," Misfit joked.

Paris paused. "You know, you might be on to something."

The strange fairy godmother shot her a surprised look. "I don't much care for fruit, but I don't think an evil witch gave all these women bad apples."

"No, but someone who wants those who are happy and about to embark on love that will positively affect the love meter would," Paris countered. "I'm guessing that somehow, someway, these Snow Whites of the world have been given something that will put them to sleep. Something tells me it won't be a prince's kiss that wakes them up."

76

CHAPTER EIGHTEEN

Roya Lane, London, United Kingdom

Paris thought the first thing she'd need to do upon stepping through the portal to Roya Lane would be to locate a man with only his first name. Once she got her bearings on the cobbled road, she had another mystery to solve. The sounds of screams echoed from down the lane, where a cluster of people was gathered.

Paris glanced behind her where the Fantastical Armory stood at the end of the street. That's where she thought the most logical place was to start finding Terrance, the wedding planner.

The last time she had a mystery to solve, Papa Creola had been very helpful. It wasn't that she thought he'd changed for good and would be a wealth of answers, but she was hoping maybe he'd softened. Or this time, Mama Jamba would supply information. After all, this was a case related to love that affected her planet.

However, Paris wasn't banking on the hope that Father Time and Mother Nature were handing out information all of sudden since that had rarely been their way. She might get a hint or two.

The shouts from the other side of the lane stole Paris' attention. There was definitely a commotion going on, and it seemed to be intensifying. Paris told herself it wasn't her problem, and she had to stay focused on her current mission. She told herself there were enough people seemingly involved. She tried to convince herself she should avoid drama rather than run in its direction.

Then someone yelled and Paris sighed, knowing what she had to do.

"Stand aside. King Rudolfus Sweetwater is here to save the day!" her pseudo-uncle's voice rang out from inside the crowd.

"Good," Paris muttered to herself, turning for the Fantastical Armory. "Rudolf is on it. I can focus on something else."

"Come here, pretty little puppy," she heard King Rudolf sing, his tone a little on edge. "No one is going to hurt you. I just want to check your tags and see who you belong to."

Paris squinted at a tiny little dog standing in the middle of the road, shivering with fear. Animals, well, nonmagical ones, weren't usually on Roya Lane, but then again, there was also pretty much everything on the magical street at any given time.

She couldn't deny her curiosity was piqued by the commotion, but Paris shook it off and started for the Fantastical Armory.

"Easy now, wolfy," King Rudolf sang, his tone pleading. "There's no reason to worry. I just want to check your little dire wolf tag. Then I can get you back to the pack you belong to. Or the troll or gnome or whatever strange creature owns you."

Paris froze. "Dire wolf," she whispered to herself, picturing a giant black wolf in the middle of Roya Lane, surrounded by people.

"That's it, little guy," King Rudolf said, loud enough for Paris to hear down the road.

"Little guy." Paris laughed, often amused at how the king of the fae misconstrued things.

She was once again going to leave the problem in King Rudolf's capable yet clumsy hands when a loud growl rocked the cobbled stones under her feet. Shouts echoed in the distance. People went running, fearing for their lives and the threat of a mysterious dire wolf.

CHAPTER NINETEEN

Roya Lane, London, United Kingdom

The ground continued to rumble under Paris' boots as she ran toward Roya Lane and the strange drama going down. As she ran in the direction of the commotion, others were running the other way, fleeing with looks of panic.

When Paris broke through the thinned-out crowd, she expected to find her uncle facing a massive beast, defending himself. She didn't expect to find the king of the fae standing in a fighting stance in front of a chihuahua-sized dire wolf.

The people around them were on edge with trepidation but also curious about what would happen next. There were roughly a dozen or so people enclosing King Rudolf and the tiny black wolf, who had his teeth bared and appeared madder than hell and ready to attack.

Paris encouraged the circle of people back, thinking it would be best if they could dial back the drama. Then a resolution to this strange situation could happen. Most didn't appear ready to give up their front row seat to the action, wanting to see if the king of the fae got attacked by a rabid little wolf.

"What's going on here?" Paris asked in a hiss at her uncle's back.

He glanced sideways and smiled widely at her, like he wasn't facing off with a tiny threat, ready to rip out his jugular. "Well, hey there, my favorite halfling with demon blood."

Paris laughed, knowing her uncle had three halfling children, but none of them had demon blood, so he could say that. He probably liked her more than his children, the Captains, because she didn't say things like, "Money please!" to him in reply to his affections.

"What is this about?" Paris asked, noticing that King Rudolf wasn't trying to shield her from the creature. Instead, he held out his arms and moved to the side as if making her a target.

The small black wolf growled, looking around the crowd. Drool slipped down from its teeth as it hunched down low as though about to pounce on one of the onlookers.

"Well, nothing for you to worry about, my freaky little genius," he answered casually, although he kept a fighting stance as he traversed the circle, his arms outstretched and his gaze darting to the people around them, gawking with amusement at the spectacle.

The wild animal pivoted to face the king as he strode around the throng of people. However, the creature appeared to be the one leading the hunt rather than focusing on the king himself. Now that Paris was watching, it was Rudolf who kept throwing himself into the line of sight of the rabid wolf.

"This is my friend Noff," King Rudolf began, nodding in the direction of the tiny purse wolf that shouldn't be such a threat, and yet, its attitude and intimidation were impressive. "We're not sure how he got here. Just appeared from another world or something."

Paris drew in a breath. "I can't say I'm surprised. This is Roya Lane."

"He was barking up a storm and growling and yipping at anyone who went near him."

"Well, he's afraid," Paris pointed out.

He shook his head. "He was sent here from somewhere for a job."

"How do you know that?" Paris asked, intrigued.

King Rudolf motioned with his head in the wolf's direction, the animal having pivoted to face a different area of the crowd, sniffing and studying the people around them. "Look around his neck. There's a collar."

Paris narrowed her eyes, trying to see what her uncle meant. Dangling from the wolf's neck was a shiny little object. "Is that a key?"

"Yeah, apparently, Noff is the key."

"To what?" Paris asked, watching as her uncle moved into the animal's line of vision again.

Rudolf pointed in the direction of the dog, who growled and snapped worse than ever. The king pulled back his hand suddenly as though the dog might attack. "According to that collar and tag around his neck, his name is Noff, and he's the key."

"Again, to what?" Paris questioned, trying to encourage people back as the wolf appeared to be getting more aggressive by the moment.

"According to the key around his neck, he was sent to stamp out foolishness," King Rudolf explained.

Paris squinted in confusion. "A miniature dire wolf was put on Roya Lane to stamp out foolishness? Why?"

"Hard to say," the king replied, jumping over several feet to block the line of vision where Noff was currently bearing down, growling at a man. "There happens to be a lot of fools on Roya Lane, and I'd prefer that no one get hurt. We're all works in progress, right? It's not these people's fault they're idiots."

Many around the fae protested the insult.

King Rudolf turned around and waved his arm. "Hey, you all know that I'm the biggest dumb face in the lot. Fortunately, I also have superior looks and a chivalrous nature that counteracts my lack of brain cells. Most of you can't rely on your winning smile or grace to offset your idiocy."

To the fae's credit, Noff didn't appear interested in killing him and ridding the world of his foolishness. Although he kept studying those in the crowd and every now and then appeared enraged by a person, he also didn't seem ready to attack anyone. Still, the small wolf kept sniffing and inspecting, on the prowl for the foolish one among them.

"I knew you'd be fine when I saw you arrive, Pare," King Rudolf continued. "Which is why I'm not defending your honor. I hope you don't mind."

Paris regarded the menacing but tiny wolf for a moment. Noff didn't seem interested in her. He didn't even seem to notice she was there. "Well, good. I'm glad he doesn't regard me as a fool."

"It appears he's still deliberating on these buffoons."

This was met by more protests from the crowd. They were interrupted by the sudden appearance of Ramy Vance as the store clerk burst onto the scene, his arms wide and his eyes buzzing with excitement.

"Did someone say baboon?" he asked, smiling ear to ear. "I love monkeys!"

At the abrupt appearance of the shopkeeper, who was lovable but not bright and definitely didn't have many redeeming qualities to counter his foolishness, Noff spun around, growling and ready to attack.

CHAPTER TWENTY

"I said, buffoon, not baboon, you dim wit," Rudolf stated as Noff hunched down low, growing louder than ever.

"So there isn't a baboon around?" Ramy asked, looking at those in the crowd. "You sure one of the guys isn't an ape or a chimpanzee or other kind of monkey?"

Paris closed her eyes for a half beat, shaking her head. "Monkeys aren't apes or chimps."

King Rudolf was trying to move in between Noff and Ramy, but the dire wolf was fast and sidestepped him. Paris, not trying to be a coward but definitely not seeing the point in being a hero here, stepped back. She knew exactly where this was going. Whereas she admired King Rudolf for wanting to defend the innocent and mortal people of Roya Lane, she didn't see the point in defending the immortal Ramy, who was prone to accidents.

"Oh, look, a cute puppy," Ramy sang, smiling at the dog and kneeling. "Are you lost, little guy?"

"Ramy-Cans," Rudolf warned, stepping back beside Paris, having come to the same conclusion as her. It wasn't worth either of them messing up their pretty faces to save a man who could regenerate and couldn't die...easily.

"Hey, dogs love me," Ramy argued, squatting down low and clicking his tongue at the animal. "Isn't that right?"

The dire wolf snapped and jumped forward, baring its teeth only a few feet from the man.

"Not this one," Paris instructed.

"Yeah, he does seem to have gotten up on the wrong side of the wolf bed," Ramy said, leaning back but not moving, undeterred.

"Ramy-Cans," King Rudolf said again cautiously. "Just get back, and you won't die today."

The shopkeeper shook his head. "Oh, you think this angry little guy is going to best me? He's all bark and no bite. I've been taken down many a time, but by bulls and crossbows and buses. Not chihuahua-like wolves."

"Ramy-Cans," Rudolf urged. "I think you're underestimating this small creature. It was sent to—"

The fae didn't get to finish his warning because right then, Noff shot forward and straight for Ramy's throat. The man dropped to his backside and rolled, the rabid wolf making quick work, attacking him all over. The pair were like a cartoon fight, rolling and kicking up dust. Screams echoed from the blur of movement as the two appeared as one.

Paris turned her eyes away, not wanting to accidentally see blood or violence or anything to do with the demise of Ramy Vance. She'd already seen the man's death too many times. Although she knew he'd most likely be back to annoy the world another day, she still never got used to the fact he died so often.

It was almost like he'd asked for it.

CHAPTER TWENTY-ONE

Fantastical Armory, Roya Lane, London, United Kingdom

Paris was still shaking off the blurred images of the tiny dire wolf ending Ramy when she entered the Fantastical Armory. Strangely enough, Mama Jamba and Papa Creola were both dozing in their pink armchairs at the front of the shop.

With sudden alarm, Paris rushed over. "No, not you too. Are you both spelled to sleep as well?"

"They are gods who created this planet, the constructs of time and space, and oversee all," Subner mumbled from the far side of the shop. "Do you think they can be spelled the same as flimsy mortals?"

Paris turned to face the sullen man who, as usual, was sitting behind the glass counter full of oddities, weapons, and artifacts. In front of him was an open book and on his long pale face was an annoyed expression. He wore it well. It matched his greasy black hair that partially covered his face.

Having grown accustomed to having Subfar, Subner's twin brother, around, it took Paris a surreal moment to assimilate that they were very different people. They looked so much alike in appearance, but the way they behaved was totally different.

Subfar was almost pleasant to be around and spoke in an animated fashion. Subner, in contrast, was like sitting on a pin cushion, and he talked like he had the energy of a bored sloth.

"I'm guessing no, then," Paris remarked, turning back to studying the pair who definitely seemed fast asleep, although she never remembered seeing them asleep. Not like this anyway. There had been an occasion where Papa Creola would close his eyes, but Paris thought it was so no one would bother him.

Mama Jamba often spoke of needing a nap, but Paris thought it was the goddess trying to act as mortal as possible. She loved pretending to be a Dallas socialite with her big bluish hair and velour tracksuit. Her current iteration of Mother Nature seemed more for her amusement than to create a strong presence in the world.

They were a very strange pair, indeed, hence the weird and wonderful world they'd created.

"The answer is a definite no," Subner muttered, pretending to be focused on his book. His attention skipped to Paris every so often. "Those two can't be spelled to sleep. Believe me; I've tried."

"You have?" Paris asked, confused. "Why?"

"Because sometimes I could use a break and the one thing they don't offer is breaks," he answered.

Paris laughed at this. "Yeah, that's definitely true. I swear, it's always back-to-back missions with these two."

"They don't let their best rest, knowing the needs of the world don't take breaks either," he offered matter-of-factly.

Paris paused and regarded the Protector of Weapons for a moment. She couldn't be sure, but it sounded like he'd just complimented her. She shook off the notion and angled her head at the pair. "So they both decided to take naps then?"

"They are playing possum," he corrected.

"What?" Paris gawked at the man behind the counter, thinking he had to be messing with her.

He didn't reply, just kept pretending to read his book.

Turning around, Paris glanced at Mama Jamba, who had one eye cracked. She pressed them shut all the way suddenly. A loud snore popped out of Papa Creola's mouth.

Paris shook her head. The two sleeping gods were acting like little children more than anything, pretending to be asleep.

Walking over to where Subner was stationed, Paris asked, "Why are they acting like they are napping?"

"Because they have lived a long time and are amused by silly things," he answered.

"I guess. Well, maybe then you can help me with something—"

"I can't," he interrupted.

"You don't even know what I'm going to ask."

He looked up at her with an arched eyebrow.

Paris sighed. "Fine, you probably do know what I was going to ask. You probably know how to find the wedding planner, Terrance, who is somewhere here on Roya Lane. By 'can't,' you mean 'won't,' which is pretty much par for the course."

"I'm sorry."

"You're sorry?" she asked, confused, never having heard the elf say anything remotely close to an apology. "You're sorry that you won't help me with a simple question to find a man?"

He shook his head, glancing back at his book. "I'm sorry that I was rude to you after you helped reunite Subfar and me, resolving our dispute."

Paris stood quite still in silent disbelief. Was this a joke? A trick? Was Subner trying to take down her guard so he could finally lure her to her death as he'd always desired? It didn't make sense.

He finally sighed. "After you gave him my sword, Originalis, to give to me, to remind me of who we used to be, I was ungrateful and unkind. I insulted you and your intentions. For that, I'm sorry."

Paris considered him for a long moment. "I'm sure seeing

your brother after all that time brought up a lot of strange emotions for you."

He slammed his book shut. "Oh, for the love of the angels! I try to be civil, and you have to go off and psychoanalyze the situation. You can't take the apology and bit of gratitude I've offered you and move on, can you? You Beaufonts are the worst. The very worst!"

After his very melodramatic speech and the most emotion he'd ever displayed, the elf got to his feet and stormed for the back room of the Fantastical Armory, slamming the door behind him. Paris shook her head, wondering if she should be more surprised that Subner apologized or he yelled. Both were outside of his normal character.

"Well, I'd say that went fairly well, wouldn't you, Papa?" Mama Jamba asked behind her.

When Paris turned around, Mother Nature didn't appear at all asleep or sleepy, just mischievous like the Cheshire cat.

CHAPTER TWENTY-TWO

Fantastical Armory, Roya Lane, London, United Kingdom

"So you were playing possum?" Paris asked, turning to face the pair, sitting tall in their pink armchairs, both looking rather alert. "Is it because you have been around since the beginning and have to find clever and new ways to amuse yourselves?"

"A good nap is always refreshing, wouldn't you say?" Mama Jamba asked, pursing her lips at Papa Creola.

The skinny hippie with his long brown hair pulled back in a low ponytail nodded. That day he was sporting a tie-dye shirt that read: Alice never wondered a land without getting lost and finding a friend. Papa Creola gave her a sly expression. "It can be."

That seemed like an ominous reply, Paris thought. "So are you two playing the Sleeping Beauty game because brides all over are finding themselves napping an exorbitant amount of time? Also, could it be true their sleepiness could be the potential downfall to their upcoming nuptials, as I suspect, because who wants to marry Snow White if she's not awake to clean their house?"

"She's good, isn't she, Papa?" Mama Jamba asked the man.

That day she was wearing a navy blue tracksuit with bright red sneakers.

He shook his head. "Pick a reference. Either it's Sleeping Beauty or Snow White. It can't be both. They are two very different stories."

"Not that different," Mama Jamba argued in a sing-song voice.

"I'm not sure that's the point here," Paris cut in. "So you both are aware that brides all over are falling victim to an extra dose of sleepiness."

Mama Jamba shrugged. "Most struggle to sleep. I don't see that being a little sleepy is a problem."

"It is if you were so sleepy and progressively so with each nap that after a while, you didn't wake up."

The old woman threw her hands up in the air. "Oh, for crying out loud. Why don't you just hand over the secrets to the universe and be done with it."

"I didn't tell her anything she didn't already know," he argued.

She lowered her chin, regarding him with hooded eyes. "Before you said you were helping her because the case was complex and full of mystery."

"It was," he agreed. "She still had to go to those two very different places, the extremely blissful one and the hateful one, and find the parts of the antidote on her own."

"Unraveling the riddle around it is key too," Mama Jamba told him sternly.

"Fine." He sat back. "I won't help anymore."

"Good," she chirped, glancing at Paris. "Now, what do you need?"

"Well, your help, but it appears I'm not going to get it."

Mama Jamba nodded adamantly. "It's best this way. We're not enablers."

"I get it," Paris said. "If you wouldn't mind pointing me in the direction of where I can find Terrance, the wedding planner, then I'll start the hunt for answers on this Snow White mystery."

"Terrance?" Mama Jamba asked, seeming to think. "I don't know a Terrance." She glanced at Papa Creola. "Do you, by chance, and my memory is just failing me?"

"It is," he said at once. "He can be found in a treehouse overlooking Roya Lane. On the opposite side from this shop."

"Papa!" Mother Nature scolded, sitting up more.

"What?" He held up his hands innocently. "You said you didn't remember. I was jogging your memory."

"I was being purposefully withholding," she said. "You just agreed not to help her anymore."

"Once you start, it's fun and rewarding," he said. "Then it saves me all the work of figuring out how to wrap things in a riddle. I think direct communication can benefit everyone."

"Oh, phooey, you know nothing at all, old man."

"There's a treehouse on Roya Lane?" Paris asked, thinking. "I've never seen one before. For that matter, I've never seen a tree here."

"Well, you don't see things until you're told to look, dear," Mama Jamba offered. "That's how my children are wired." She glanced fondly at Papa Creola. "Remember the Native Americans just staring and staring at the shores, not even seeing the ships crossing the waters in front of them?"

"They didn't know to look for them, so they just kept seeing what they expected to see."

"That's very confusing," Paris said. "I was raised here pretty much and went out and observed the lane every day. How could I not see a tree?"

"You didn't expect to find one here," Mama Jamba answered. "What did Uncle John always say to you?"

She thought for a moment. "He used to say it would be nice to get to some place that had trees and nature at some point."

"Because you were stuck here to protect you," Papa Creola explained. "Therefore, that wired you to think there were no trees here."

"Not to mention that you needed the referral to see Terrance, who owns the Treehouse," Mama Jamba added.

"Oh, well, I think you could have led with that," Paris muttered.

"It's a double-pronged explanation though, dear," Mama Jamba said. "If you had the referral but didn't expect to find a tree here, you still wouldn't. Now you've been told, and you have the referral." She directed her periwinkle gaze to Papa Creola. "You see why I don't tell them anything? They just say you should have told it to me this way."

"They are stubborn. I'll give you that."

"Okay, so I go to the end of the lane and find a treehouse—"

"*The* Treehouse," Papa Creola interrupted Paris.

"Okay, I find the Treehouse, and then I find Terrance. Hopefully, he'll help me find out what's happening to brides. He is in the best position to understand the market and where and how they could be spelled. I'm sure he deals with brides all day long. I am a bride, so I guess I should have him help me too."

"You shouldn't," Mama Jamba stated plainly.

"I shouldn't?" Paris asked, confused. "Why? He's the best wedding planner in the business."

"You don't want the best wedding in the world," Mama Jamba countered. "You want your wedding, and you're only going to be happy with the one that fits you."

"Everyone will be watching," Paris argued. "This is an opportunity to create a huge impact on the love meter."

"There are other ways," she said. "At the end of the day, if you have the biggest, seemingly best wedding in the world to make others happy, then you'll be miserable, and it won't work. The ends don't justify the means and vice versa. Be true to yourself. You have many talented people all around you. Have them help you to create the wedding you'll love, and it will make so much magic in the world the meter will explode that day."

Paris smiled, grateful for the advice. It was what she needed to hear. "Well, thank you."

"Go and have Terrance help you with the other stuff," Papa Creola said in a rush before Mama Jamba could scold him. "Otherwise, all those Snow Whites are going to sleep forever, and love will be in trouble."

CHAPTER TWENTY-THREE

Roya Lane, London, United Kingdom

It seemed more than strange to Paris that there was a tree-house on Roya Lane. She didn't even know there was a tree. The bit about needing the referral to Terrance, the wedding planner, explained that well enough. There were a few strange shops like that on Roya Lane that required invitations to appear.

The fact there was a tree she hadn't seen made her wonder what other things were there on the magical lane she didn't see. A troll could be sitting on the top of the Rose Apothecary building, dangling his feet, and Paris may not know it.

The part about knowing about something did make sense. Paris had often heard that the phrase "See it to believe it" was false. In actuality, one must believe in something to see it. Paris had been told since she could remember there were no trees on Roya Lane.

Since her only childhood memories were from there, the first five years of her life erased to protect her, she hadn't seen a tree. Only in pictures later in her childhood. Then she remembered the first time she saw one at Happily Ever After College and quickly jumped into it to avoid being trampled. It was how she'd met Hemingway, and the rest of it, as they said, is history.

So Paris could believe the very strange idea there was not just a tree but a treehouse on Roya Lane. Finding it, she thought, would be fun. She'd never been in a treehouse before, and the idea was intriguing, especially after her recent trip to the Redwood Forest. She just hoped it didn't turn her into a hippie. She couldn't stomach a repeat of that.

After passing the Rose Apothecary and not finding a troll on the roof, Paris came to the far side and the end of Roya Lane. She was about to conclude that Mama Jamba and Papa Creola had lost their minds or were playing a very rude joke on her when she spied the canopy of a large oak tree stretching up behind the shops.

Moving to the far side of the cobbled road, she pushed her back up against the brick wall behind her and looked up to take in the strange sight in front of her. It was unreal. It had always been there and she hadn't seen it, just like the Glowing Orchid shop that only appeared by invitation.

The Treehouse was definitely real as Paris stared up at the top of the huge green tree, filled with leaves and branches and built all around it—a shop. It was quite cute with its bungalow style, complete with shutters and plantation blinds in the windows.

The Treehouse was sage green, blending into the tree. The trim was brown, looking like branches. Now that Paris had seen the building, she couldn't unsee it.

Although it was set behind the row of shops, it was definitely there, like a second story.

There appeared to be a ladder that went up the large trunk to the center of the shop. The tree was stationed behind the shops, its base unseen.

"So the question is, how do I get to this treehouse?" Paris asked aloud, talking to herself.

Paris considered scaling the shop in front of the Treehouse

and jumping to the ladder along the trunk. Something told her it wasn't the way up. For some reason, she didn't think most brides-to-be were adept at climbing buildings and leaping through the air to get to a wedding planner.

She had heard that brides became quite insane when it came to planning the big day. Paris had no intention of becoming a bridezilla. Now that she had permission to have the wedding she wanted without the obligation to do things for the benefit of others, Paris was going to have a subtly elegant day full of love and sincerity and fond memories.

That's all she really wanted. What was wrong with that? Some wanted to be a princess on their big day. Paris just wanted to marry her best friend.

Thankfully it didn't appear that Paris was going to have to Spider-man her way onto the roof of the shop in front of the large tree. She spotted a narrow alleyway between the two shops in front of the Treehouse.

Looking over her shoulder, afraid she might be followed, Paris checked she was alone before slipping through into the dark passageway. Going into a wedding planner's shop wasn't a place Paris wanted to be spotted if she was honest. It always seemed like a place where rich daughters of aristocrats named Buffy hung out, planning a wedding before they even had a ring on their finger or even an eligible bachelor in their grips.

Also, if her hunch was correct and Jackson Zelle was targeting brides in another attempt to squash love and get revenge on the FGA, then he might be watching for her to thwart his efforts. Paris thought she was right about the evil entrepreneur based on the hints Papa Creola had given her.

She didn't know why he was suddenly being more helpful, but she wasn't complaining about it. Maybe in his extremely old age, he was growing soft. Or maybe it was just his and Mama Jamba's new good cop slash bad cop routine. She could understand them having to do things to keep themselves from getting bored.

The dark alleyway that led to the back side of the shops and a more open area was dangerously narrow. It was like this wedding planner Terrance was saying brides must be a certain size to see him and get married. That seemed rude.

She decided to reserve judgment until she met the guy. He was the best in the business, and there had been many hoops she'd had to jump through to get to him. She hoped he was just a creative guy whose talents were so exceptional he had to be choosey about the clients he took.

Sucking in a breath, Paris spied the open area ahead as she slid between the two narrow brick walls. When she was on the other side, she finally understood what it was like to feel claustrophobic. It was such a relief to be in the open air and not pressed between two walls, tightly pressing her in between them.

An extra bonus and a much-needed reward was to find the base of the giant oak tree in the small courtyard area behind the shop buildings. The grassy area was nicely manicured with fun little statues of fairies and gnomes and woodland creatures scattered around the trunk of the tree.

To further test the athletic abilities of the bride seeking the wedding planner's help, the ladder up the trunk was a series of boards nailed into the bark. There were roughly twenty rungs in the ladder, and they led to a trap door centered at the base of the Tree House.

Drawing in a breath, Paris prepared herself for the climb. The physical tasks weren't what had her nervous, though. It was this illustrious character who worked in a mysterious treehouse that had been hidden from her all of her life on Roya Lane.

CHAPTER TWENTY-FOUR

The Tree House, Roya Lane, London, United Kingdom

Never having been into a treehouse before, not having had the typical childhood, Paris didn't know what to expect. When she pushed open the hatch door, she definitely didn't expect to poke her head around to find fine furnishings and an impeccably decorated space, attention shown to every detail.

She quickly realized she probably should have. This was the shop that housed the best wedding planner in the business. It was just that things she'd seen and read about treehouses said they often contained comic book collections, stashes of sweet treats, and usually a spider or two. The Tree House didn't have a single one of these things as far as Paris could tell.

"Oh, good, there's my three-thirty appointment," a man's voice said behind her.

Paris craned her head around, still poking through the trap door. Staring down at her was a guy dressed in a button-up shirt and slacks, wearing a pursed expression. His short curly brown hair was pushed back, and the look on his face was full of annoyance. His hands were pinned on his hips, and he didn't at all look about to welcome her warmly into the space.

"Hey there," Paris said, feeling awkward looking up at the man for their first greeting. "I'm Paris."

"I'm INCREDIBLE!" he boomed on the last word, throwing his hands up into the air. "Get up here already. You're now late. BY A WHOLE MINUTE."

Paris' eyes widened, but the strange low inflection followed by high volume did its job, and she scrambled up the rest of the ladder. Ungracefully she crawled out of the trap door and rolled onto the floor, looking up at the strange character glaring down at her.

He was still regarding her like she was a purse dog that piddled on the rug. "Is that how you make introductions? Because if so, then we're sending you to finishing school."

Paris wanted to laugh and also crawl into a corner and cry. She didn't know how this strange man was having this effect on her. As he stared down at her, one eye bulging and the other squinting, she made a note of the crazy heavy in his gaze and decided not to mess with him. Terrance was scarier than most of the monsters she'd faced, and that was saying a lot.

Fumbling to get to her feet, Paris made a few unsuccessful attempts before rising to her full height and looking up at the wedding planner. "Hiiiii…I'm Agent Beaufont." She extended her hand to him and forced a smile that hopefully covered her fear.

He shook his head, not taking her hand. "You've been touching ants and trees and who knows what else. We're past introductions. You already know who I am. Now tell me, WHAT DO YOU WANT?"

Paris' eyes widened. She wasn't sure whether to try to talk to the diabolical man or to throw him out of the Treehouse and save the world from his craziness. She didn't get a chance to make a proper decision because he spun around and marched toward a table, glancing at booklets of fabrics and samples of every sort.

Now that she could look away from her feet and not at the floor, the office was nice, even fancier than she'd thought before.

Black chandeliers with a dozen candles each hung overhead. The furniture was all starkly white. The rugs covering the hardwoods were zebra prints. The only accent color anywhere was a pop of pink—a lamp, a vase, a throw pillow. It all came together to make a great classy office area.

"You need the wedding of the century," Terrance said, singing the last word melodramatically. He thumbed through a book of swatches on an elegant table. He jerked his head up, throwing both his hands to his sides and his face flushing red. "I'm not even that oooold."

Paris sucked in a long breath, having heard that if you practice deep breathing, the screwball person you're facing will too. *Whatever it took to calm crazy pants down,* she thought. "I have good news for you. You don't have to plan my wedding."

One of his eyes got larger, and the other squinted more. "Now you give me a job, and then you take it away!"

"No, it's just that I have an even more important task for you," Paris said in a low voice, employing the tactic Sherlock Holmes used. He was always soft-spoken to calm people and ensure they were quiet to hear what he had to say.

"What is it?" Terrance asked. "Why am I not planning YOUR WEDDING?"

Oh, wow, Paris thought, trying to figure out what other strategies she had for defusing bombs. "So the thing is, as you must know from the referral, I'm a directing agent at the FGA."

"I know everything!"

"Right," Paris said, drawing out the word. "As an agent for the Advanced Love branch, it's come to my attention that brides are being targeted as an attack, and I think I know who is behind it."

"What?!" Terrance exclaimed, throwing his hands in the air. "Why is this the first that I'm hearing of this? How? Where? I repeat, what?"

"As an agent for—"

He waved her off. "We've already been through your little

spiel about being an agent for the FGA. I get it. You're a big deal. Momma put you through college."

"Uncle John, actually," she corrected.

"You went to the fancy dancy college because your pockets run deep."

"To stay out of jail," she amended again.

"Just tell me why, as the most respected wedding planner in the business, how do I not know that my clients are being attacked?" he asked, turning to face her, threading his arms.

"Well, the person who is behind this, most likely…I mean, he's been coming after love and the FGA, and I just became a bride, so it goes to reason he'd come after me too—"

"Others might find your speculation cute," he interrupted. "I bet they may even think it means that you clearly work things out, considering every possible angle. You know what?"

Paris lowered her chin, preparing herself for the response. "What?"

"I DON'T CARE!" he yelled, his fists by his side and his face like that of a toddler acting out. "I want to know what's going on, and I want to know now!"

"Fair enough. I'll make this quick and painless."

"Then go back in time to five minutes ago and start again," he cut in.

She laughed at this. "All right, Jackson Zelle has made it his ultimate mission to take down love and the FGA with it. From what I've learned, opening up national channels to lovers going through turmoil, men are complaining their brides-to-be are sleeping a lot more than they should be and progressively more so than usual. Then I went and visited Mother Nature and Father Time, and they confirmed this. So our job is to find out exactly how Jackson Zelle is spelling brides into sleeping, much like Snow White, and what his end goal is here."

"Mother Nature," Terrance said with a smile. "How is that old so-and-so? Is she still pretending not to give a damn and then rocking a look that only she can pull off?"

"Every single day, no matter what," Paris answered dryly.

"As for this Jackson...oh, no, I won't call him that. He's going to be Mr. Baddie, and I don't like people who are bad or end their name with an 'ie,'" he sang in a nineteen-twenties accent. "Anyway, there is magitech that could induce sleeping, but there are a few ways it can get into the heads of brides. As for how I think I know exactly where they are getting these messages."

"Where?" Paris asked.

"Well, I haven't been in the public sector for a while," Terrance answered. "I don't have to go and hobnob with commoners anymore since my services are only by referral. When I used to have to reduce myself to talking to the Plain Janes and Everyday Emilys of the world, I saw firsthand how brides got inundated with information."

"Has anyone ever told you how humble you come across?" Paris said.

"No one ever would say that!" he boomed, pulling out his phone and scrolling through it.

"So this way, you think our brides could be getting spelled," Paris began. "What is it?"

"Well, I don't know," he said, concentrating as he tapped on his device. "I think I know where we need to look."

"Where?" Paris asked, her heart suddenly beating fast.

"I'm finding the next one," Terrance answered, chewing on his lips, his eyes narrowed on his phone.

"One?" Paris asked, worried what this could mean. What was she getting herself into?

"If you know someone who is tech savvy, then have them join us," Terrance instructed. "I'm guessing that if this Mr. Baddie is inducing sleep, he's using advanced technology. Sounds like a real Evil Queen you made enemies with. I'm guessing finding out how will be the easiest solution. Figuring out how to stop him, well…unlodging the apple from Snow White's throat won't be easy."

"I like that you went with the metaphor," Paris muttered, pulling out her phone and sending a message to Faraday. "I have someone who can help. Where do I say for them to meet us?"

"In Nashville, Tennessee. It's the city where the next event is located," he answered.

"Event?" Paris asked, looking up with trepidation. "What kind of event?"

A glint of victory flickered in his eyes. "We're going to a bridal conference."

CHAPTER TWENTY-FIVE

Bridal and Wedding Expo, Fairgrounds, Nashville, Tennessee, United States

"Someone please shoot me now," Paris said, standing in the center of the huge convention of crazed brides.

"I know," Terrance said beside her, looking around at the various booths with disgust. "Look how many people are wearing polyester." He covered his face with his hands. "This is why I refuse to work with the general public anymore. People just don't know how to dress themselves."

"Your new friend is interesting," Faraday said, peeking his head out of the large black handbag she'd agreed to bring him in. Since bringing a squirrel to a bridal expo seemed too unorthodox, they had to come up with options for Faraday. It was either he hung out there, pretending to be a purse dog, or she magically put a chihuahua disguise on him, and he pranced around like an actual dog. Since he didn't want to be a dog, and she'd had just about enough of them after the Ramy incident, this was an easy decision.

"You have no idea," Paris muttered to the squirrel. "This is him dialed down."

"I *mean*, I can respect that you wear that whole black leather get-up, but I *hope* that's pleather, and you *didn't* kill a cow for that outfit," Terrance went on, getting himself worked up, alternating between talking and yelling every several words. He pointed around at the crowd. "Because these people are *killing* me with their fashion choices."

"Don't you have a zebra rug in your office?" Paris challenged.

"It was mostly dead when I found it," Terrance replied. "I did it a favor. Now it's epic in my shop and not just prancing around that safari land in Baton Rouge."

Faraday blinked up at Paris. "This guy is supposed to be able to help us? Is he going to taxidermy me afterward?"

"As if!" Terrance yelled, swerving around and looking down at the squirrel. "Squirrels make the worst fashion statements. I once had a boyfriend who got me a shirt with a squirrel on it. You can guess what happened to him."

"You murdered him in a dark alley?" Paris asked.

Terrance nodded. "That's right. I dumped him!"

"Cool, cool, cool," Paris said dismissively. "So we're here to find out how brides are being spelled to sleep all the time and progressively more often. You think it will be a vendor or something that's catering to brides?"

"It makes sense," Terrance answered, looking around at the crowd of excited brides all talking rapidly, giving their list of demands to different industry experts. There was so much going on in the huge space. Each booth catered to a different part of the big day: dresses, invites, cakes, DJs and bands, favors, honeymoons, and so much more.

Paris wanted to puke. She hadn't been cut out to be a fairy godmother, but she'd grown to respect what they'd done. After finishing her education, she became a manager for the FGA because she was a holistic and logical thinker. Still, after all this time, she didn't understand romcoms, ballads, or weddings.

What Paris understood was how she loved Hemingway—with

all her heart. The rest just felt so contrived, but that was why she was good at her job. Paris didn't get distracted by emotions like the other fairies. She didn't get swept away in feelings. Paris saw things for what they were.

Right then, she saw a lot of starry-eyed brides who were intoxicated with the dream of having a big day. At one booth, women were tearing each other apart to get dibs on this year's top veils. Across the aisle, brides were fighting over a raffle prize to enter for a chance to win a horse-drawn carriage. All around, it appeared that drama was the result of this event meant to offer wedding day options to brides.

"At least all these brides appear to be awake and alert," Faraday stated.

"Yes, they haven't been spelled yet."

"Oh, they've been spelled all right," Terrance seethed, staring around.

"They have?" Paris asked, confused. "By what?"

"By bad marketing!" Terrance exclaimed, throwing his hands down and hunching forward. "Amy, it doesn't matter if that tiara is discounted. It looks hideous on your big head!"

Paris stared in shock between the wedding planner and the red-headed woman he had yelled at. The woman froze, put down the fake-diamond-encrusted tiara, and ran off. "Ummm...do you know that woman?"

"No, but she knew I was talking to her," Terrance replied.

"So you just call them all Amy?" Faraday asked from the purse.

"I call them whatever comes to my mouth," Terrance said through clenched teeth. "They're all about to be called by worse names."

"I can't help but think that we're losing sight of the mission," Paris imparted, trying to keep her calm. Terrance definitely made her blood pressure rise. "We need to search for a booth that could be spelling brides. It could be anything, but it's something that caters directly to brides based on the submissions from fiancés."

"Don't even get me started on grooms," Terrance said, throwing his arm across his forehead like he might pass out.

"I'm not," Paris said matter-of-factly, deciding it was best to ignore the diva of all divas. She looked down at Faraday. "What do you think? Could it be a cake company that's sending out samples the brides tried? Or maybe it's a florist? Or a make-up company? Something that's specifically interacting with brides."

"How about a wedding planner website?" Faraday asked, looking up at her.

Terrance laughed loudly, getting even more attention from those around them. "Those sites are the worst. You think you can create a bunch of Pinterest boards of what you want and get online referrals from vendors, and that replaces a brilliant mind who can make magic happen on your big day?"

"Noooo," Paris said, her voice full of uncertainty.

"That's right," Terrance declared. "The Knot, the Ball and Chain, the Bullet have all tried to replace what I do. Who knows better than me that you can't have silk table napkins with a seashell theme?"

"You do," Faraday answered, doubt in his voice.

"That's right!" Terrance exclaimed. "A website can't tell you that."

Paris looked down at her squirrel, knowing he was the only sane person around her right then... and wasn't a person. She was alone as far as her species went. "Why do you think it could be a website wedding planner that's spelling brides?"

He pointed to a huge booth on the far side of the convention area. "Because of that."

Paris and Terrance turned their gazes the way he was pointing, and both their mouths dropped open.

"Oh, dear," Paris remarked, surprised at how on the nose the name of the company was.

Terrance yelled, his face red, "How dare they?"

CHAPTER TWENTY-SIX

Bridal and Wedding Expo, Fairgrounds, Nashville, Tennessee, United States

"I know," Paris said, vibrating with adrenaline.

"I mean, really," Terrance said, spit flicking from his mouth. "Really, people! Do you know nothing about color combinations? Blue and yellow? What, am I at a football game?" He pointed to the signs over the booth and turned to Paris in absolute horror. "Don't even get me started on the typography. Is that font supposed to be Papyrus? What type of fairy tale are they trying to sell?"

"One involving sleeping," Paris said pointedly, nodding to the slogan on the banners along the table. They read: "Beautiful as the light of day. Fairest of all. Let us make your day a ball."

Terrance turned back around, taking in the sights around the large booth. There were numerous women dressed as Snow White, and around them were actual gnomes dressed up like the dwarves from the storybook tale. Surrounding them were tons of happy brides, having conversations with the staffers, taking cards regarding services, or being ushered to the back for a "Free consultation."

Striding over to the table, Terrance picked up one of the cards and read it: "Snow White's Wedding Services. Let the dwarves work for you. Visit: SnowWhiteRelaxes.com"

He jerked his head up and regarded Paris with angry eyes. "You don't think this is how brides are being spelled to sleep, do you?"

"Well, it feels a little on the nose," Paris remarked. "Papa Creola and Mama Jamba pretty much said it was something like this. I think they've been giving me a lot more clues than usual."

"Well, I'm going to this website and checking it out," Terrance seethed.

Faraday shook his head from the purse. "I'm guessing it's a spell meant to target brides, which means it won't work on you."

Terrance nodded and shoved the card at Paris. "You go and check it out. Better yet, go back there and get a consultation."

"No," Faraday interrupted before Paris could answer.

"Faraday is right," Paris said, taking a deep breath, trying to make sense of everything. "I can't be put to sleep. I need to fix this."

"That's not what I was meaning," Faraday said tersely and nodded ahead. "I was saying, no, be quiet before you attract the attention of those goons."

Paris and Terrance both froze, turning to take in the figures they hadn't noticed before and were definitely out of place at a wedding convention. If Paris hadn't had suspicions about Snow White's Wedding Services before, she definitely did now.

CHAPTER TWENTY-SEVEN

Bridal and Wedding Expo, Fairgrounds, Nashville, Tennessee, United States

By goons, Faraday wasn't exaggerating. Stationed around the large booth attracting a lot of interest from brides-to-be were men in black suits with earpieces. They were no doubt security goons.

"Why would a seemingly regular and innocent wedding service need so much security?" Paris asked.

"Or any security at all?" Faraday questioned.

"Not to mention they give it a whole unwanted Men-in-Black feeling," Terrance imparted. "I mean, pick a theme. Are you fairy-tales, or are you hunting aliens?"

Paris shot the wedding planner an annoyed look. "I'm going to need you to focus more on what's actually going on between the lines here. We have to figure out if this company, Snow White Wedding Services, is owned and operated by Zelle Corp."

"More immediately," Faraday cut in, "we need to figure out how they are spelling brides. If they are doing it here, how wide-spread are their efforts?"

Paris held up her hand, feeling like she was managing a circus of clowns. "Back up. Like Sherlock Holmes, we deal in facts. The question first is if this wedding service is spelling brides. I get it's a coincidence with the whole Snow White motif, but we don't have any proof yet."

"How about that?" Faraday asked, pointing his paw in the direction of a group of brides exiting the booth, ushered out by a Snow White in costume. They were all shaking their heads and yawning as though trying to dispel sleepiness.

"Hold up a second," Terrance interrupted, stepping forward and holding up a hand of protest. "I can attest, having attended enough of these overstimulating events, which are full of too many women in perfume and competing vendors vying for attention, these expos can be exhausting."

"How about that?" Faraday offered, pointing in another direction.

Paris and Terrance turned to follow the way he was indicating. They both narrowed their gaze on a slew of women sitting on a bench against a wall, all dozing, their heads nestled together, using each other for support to hold the group up.

"Again, planning a wedding is so much more work than anyone knows," Terrance countered. "They probably have been on their feet for hours, and they'll return to a fiancé who wants dinner and attention and the whole nine yards."

Just then, a pair of older women passed by, coming out of the Snow White Wedding Services booth. "I don't get why they are so popular with brides," one woman said to the other. "My daughter just raves about the website, though. Well, she was, but she doesn't do much of anything anymore. Just sleeps all the time. I told her I think she has a parasite."

"What about that?" Faraday asked with a knowing look.

Paris gave Terrance a look of serious concern. "We have to investigate."

"Yeah, we do," he replied. "Wedding services aren't supposed to put brides to sleep. The wedding night is supposed to do that!"

CHAPTER TWENTY-EIGHT

Bridal and Wedding Expo, Fairgrounds, Nashville, Tennessee, United States

Now that Paris was paying attention to the booth, she noticed that inside the area, there were numerous tables stacked high with samples. That's not what caught her attention. It wasn't the many Snow Whites sitting across from excited brides, explaining what services the online wedding planners offered either. It wasn't even a strange sight to see all the women dressed like princesses.

The strange thing was the flashy commercials broadcasting on the many screens all over the booth. They, from everything Paris could tell, explained how the site helped brides to find the best vendors, organize and schedule everything in one place, and most importantly, make dwarves do all the work for them—or rather, an internet service. If Paris wasn't nervous about the site being part of a more sinister device meant to spell brides, she would applaud its genius. It was one-stop shopping.

"We should check out this wedding service and lay low so we don't attract the attention of those goons," Paris said, indicating the security team who were appraising the many individuals flocking to the booth.

"No, we can't do that," Faraday argued.

Paris paused and looked down at the squirrel in the purse she was unaccustomed to carrying around since she usually only carried a wand and a bad attitude. "The goons are probably just to keep us from getting behind the scenes or stealing information. It's totally Zelle's style, but we will be careful."

"The goons have probably been told to keep an eye out for you, especially," Faraday countered. "Jackson Zelle isn't stupid and will know you'll be investigating once it comes to your attention that brides are affected. I remind you that you have. That's not why you can't look into their wedding services, is it, Terrance?" Faraday glanced at the man for backup.

"Yeah!" he exclaimed, getting attention from a group of women from a neighboring booth. "You said you weren't on the hunt for a wedding planner and weren't allowing me to do your wedding. Therefore, you can't go over to this dastardly competitor!"

Faraday huffed. "No, that's not the reason."

"I mean, I'm Terrance!" he continued, throwing his hands in the air, not having heard the squirrel in the purse. "I'm the best wedding planner on the planet. You didn't even want me. How do you think that makes me feel?"

Paris covered her face, embarrassed for the grown man who was starting to cry.

"Terrance!" a woman yelled from nearby. "Terrance is here!"

There were several screams from around the conference. Several women rushed over, bombarding the flamboyant man at once. Paris backed up even though he gave her a pleading look that said, "Save me."

"Oh, no," Paris mouthed. "You're on your own."

He was immediately engulfed by a sea of screaming women,

all of them asking for his advice on the latest and best wedding trends.

"One at a time! This is why I don't deal with the public! You're like a bunch of hungry antelope," Paris heard Terrance yell over the horde of crazed women.

She snickered, looking over her shoulder at the Snow White Wedding Services booth. It was quickly emptying of interested brides, many of them spilling out at the announcement that Terrance was there.

Now there were fewer people congesting the many tables, she got a peek at many of the computer monitors displaying ads for the wedding planner services website. The information flashed in quick succession, a series of images that kept her attention for longer than she would have expected.

"Hey, this would be a good opportunity to get a consultation with one of those Snow Whites," Paris said, pulling her gaze from the booth with great effort and glancing down at Faraday. The squirrel swam in and out of her focus for a moment before righting itself. It was a strange sensation but brief enough that she dismissed it immediately.

"No, that's what I was just saying before your new guy went all drama queen on us," Faraday said bitterly, suddenly appearing on edge.

"That's just the thing," Paris argued. "He's created the perfect diversion for us. We can get in there, and I'll let you loose. You can check out things behind the scenes, away from the prying eyes of the goons. I'll pretend to ask those women in black wigs questions, and within the hour, we'll know exactly how Jackson Zelle is spelling brides. We need that information to stop him. Just like when we stopped him from spelling his hometown to be nihilistic."

"Paris," Faraday said, waving his paws in front of her face. "What have you been looking at?"

"Why?" Paris asked, pointing over her shoulder. "I've just been checking out the booth. Like I just said, we need to go and investigate it."

"Paris, I don't know what you think you've just said," Faraday stated, his eyes wide with urgency. "You're not making any sense. You're just saying a bunch of slurred words and staggering around like you're about to…fall asleep."

Paris straightened. Looked around. Saw a sea of people morph into a sea of blurry colors. She opened her mouth to protest, but all that came out of her mouth was gibberish, and then she realized that's all she'd been spouting before but was too incoherent to realize it.

Looking down at her best friend, she sobered up suddenly. "I need you to get me out of here and now."

CHAPTER TWENTY-NINE

Faraday had never seen Paris like this. She was talking to him like she was drunk. He'd never seen her that way. She knew she wasn't. The bride-to-be was clearly spelled.

She'd just spoken to him like she was making complete sense, but nothing she said was coherent.

He nodded, giving her a reassuring look, and pointed at a rail connected to the Snow White Wedding Services booth. "Hold onto that for stability. I'm getting us out of here. That means I've got to go rescue our ride."

Paris looked around. Stumbled. Then reached for the railing, nearly missing it, her vision blurring.

Faraday poked his head out of the large purse in the direction of Terrance. He was still surrounded by women, although by the sounds of it, he was doing his best to offend each and every one of them and get away.

Faraday would have just abandoned the obnoxious wedding planner, but they needed his help. Paris was in no condition to portal them back to the FGA Tower. Based on her current condition, she'd probably have them in China. Then she'd settle in for a nap, and Faraday would really be stuck.

Glancing up at Paris, he gave her a deadly serious look. "Don't. I repeat, don't go anywhere. Don't talk to anyone, and don't look at anything in the Snow White Wedding Services booth. Just look at the floor and wait for me to return."

She yawned loudly and nodded.

"Don't go to sleep," he urged, jumping out of the purse and bounding for the crowd surrounding the wedding planner.

Scurrying under high heels and boots of varying colors, Faraday weaved through the legs of the women until he got to the center of the crowd. The women were so busy asking Terrance questions that none of them noticed the rodent until he was yanking on the man's pants, urging him to look down. He didn't.

"No!" Terrance yelled to a bride. "I don't care if it's a winter wedding. You don't allow your bridesmaids to carry poinsettias. What, do you think you're marrying Santa Claus or something?"

"I-I-I just thought," the woman stuttered.

"Oh, as for YOU," Terrance began, revolving in another woman's direction. "Destination weddings happen in Hawaii or the Bahamas. Don't tell your family that you're having a destination wedding at the Holiday Inn in Kansas City and expect them to pay for it or attend. I won't even stop at a truck stop in the Midwest, let alone go to a wedding there!"

Several women ran away crying, probably afraid the wedding planner was about to turn his wrath on them. Faraday wasn't sure which ones he felt sorrier for, the women or Terrance, who had been accosted by the mob.

"Terrance," Faraday said, tugging on his pants again.

"Oh, this is for all of you bad decision makers," Terrance continued, pointing around at the crowd. "If you play country music at your wedding, then don't call it classy. Call it what it is. A RODEO! You might have woken up one day and decided you wanted to listen to things that rot your brain, but why do you think you can force it on other people?"

A few more women burst into tears and ran away. Faraday couldn't figure out whether this man was the worst on the planet or the best. He was mesmerizing to watch in action, like poetic chaos.

Looking over his shoulder, Faraday caught sight of Paris swaying by the Snow White booth. He couldn't play it safe any longer. Deciding to be bold, he dug his claws into Terrance's leg, piercing his skin.

The scream that came from the man's mouth made all the women around him jump back. Many took notice of the squirrel attacking the wedding planner. They might have helped Terrance, but thankfully, he was quick on his feet.

The man's eyes widened, darted to Paris nearly asleep, and then he swooped down and picked up Faraday at once. He was quick and must have assessed the situation at once. Like Faraday was a teacup poodle, he put him under his arm at once and petted his head gingerly.

"That's a squirrel!" someone yelled.

"Oh, my God!" A woman exclaimed. "He attacked Terrance."

"There's a rodent in here!"

Calmly Terrance shook his head, continuing to pet Faraday. "This is a Japanese Zitch-Poo, a new breed of dog. They are all the rage in New York." He put his nose next to the squirrels. "I was wondering where'd you'd gotten to, Humphrey. I missed you, my little guy."

"Humphrey," Faraday mouthed, his mouth close to the man.

"Well, although I wish I could help you ladies more from ruining your lives, I've got to get going. Humphrey and I have an appointment to get manis at the Ritz Carlton."

The crowd dispersed. Diplomatically and without drawing more attention to themselves, Terrance waved the women away, continuing to pet Faraday like he was a puppy. When the brides were mostly gone, unhurried, Terrance made his way over to Paris, who was slumped against the railing.

"You're asleep," he nearly yelled in her face.

She blinked at him. Giggled. Pointed at Faraday. "Your gerbil is cute. Does he do tricks?"

Terrance looked around. "What spelled her into this state?"

"I don't know," Faraday said in a rush, angling his head to the door. "We have to get out of here, though. I need you to take us to that hallway and portal us."

"Fine!" Terrance yelled, putting his arm around Paris and leading her out the door. "I swear, this is the last time that I save your butt today. You're definitely getting my bill for this."

"What Paris is doing will save your business," Faraday argued.

"That's true," Terrance acquiesced when they rounded the corner into a mostly deserted maintenance hallway. "I won't bill you for this, Agent Beaufont. I am going to find out what spelled you."

He held up his hand and created a portal before shoving Faraday into Paris' arms. Then he waved her to walk through. "Go on now. That will take you to the FGA Tower. I have access to portal there because I'm me."

"Aren't you going with us?" Faraday asked, feeling Paris sway as she held him in her arms.

He shook his head, pointing over his shoulder to the conference room. "I'm going back and finding out what's going on. Then we will bring down these jerks who think they can turn my customers into a bunch of comatose individuals." Terrance pointed to Paris, his gaze on Faraday. "Figure out how to wake her up. Then we use it on the rest."

"Okay, thanks." He tugged on Paris' jacket. "Step through the portal. Please. Before you fall asleep."

"Okay, you silly gerbil," she said in a slurred voice and stumbled through the portal just before she fell over and went into a deep sleep almost at once.

CHAPTER THIRTY

Bridal and Wedding Expo, Fairgrounds, Nashville, Tennessee, United States

Terrance was livid. Some jerk had waltzed into his territory and thought they could take over. Worse, they didn't even appear to want to help brides not make bad decisions.

From what he'd deduced, picking the brains of the women who had gathered around him, the Snow White Wedding Service charged a one-time yearly subscription to their online service of one thousand dollars. It appeared the poor brides got little service for their money and instead a lot of time to rest. Terrance was going to figure out exactly how this Jackson Zelle was spelling the brides. Then he was shutting the whole operation down.

The only thing Terrance hated more than evil villains who went after love were bicyclists. *I mean, those people were the worst,* he thought as he strode back into the busy convention space.

Those spandex-wearing fools woke up randomly one day and decided they were going to be a general pain in the ass to society. They put their "Share the Road" signs on the back of their helmets and then rode shoulder to shoulder on their bikes with their skinny buddies to the coffee shops.

From there, they all gushed over how many emissions they saved the Earth that day, all while they patronized a company with a carbon footprint bigger than a giant methane-producing cow.

"People are the worst," Terrance said, bullying his way into the Snow White Wedding Services booth. He angled around several of the gnomes dressed as dwarves.

"Sir, this booth is for brides," a few said.

"I'm the biggest bride!" he exclaimed, waving them off and navigating around them.

"Sir, can I help you?" one of the Snow Whites asked, coming over and offering a disingenuous smile.

"Not unless you've got six-pack abs and your name is Victor," he replied, finding a free computer.

Sliding down in front of the monitor playing a commercial on repeat for the Snow White Wedding Services, Terrance clicked a few buttons. He knew the shortcuts to find what he needed to in these situations.

Glancing over his shoulder, he ensured the gnomes and the Snow Whites were leaving him alone. Thankfully his rude demeanor had worked on them. It was a routine he'd perfected that ensured he got the space to do what he needed, which in this case, meant hacking into the back end of this operation and finding out how and with what they were spelling brides.

Feeling victorious, he turned back around to find three of the security guard goons standing around him on the other side. They all three stared at him.

The first slipped his jacket back and showed a weapon in his holster.

The second cleared his throat and said, "Are you Terrance, the world-renowned wedding planner?"

"What if I am?" Terrance asked, making to stand but seemed

to meet a brick wall. He turned to find two more guards blocking him from the other side.

His heart racing, he turned back around. "I-I-I'm nobody… Seriously."

"Then, Nobody," the third security guard said with a mischievous grin. "We're going to need you to come with us."

Terrance screamed. Spun to race away. The other guards grabbed him and pushed him back. He was enveloped at once by a throng of security, and he didn't think they wanted wedding advice. He didn't think he'd be seen ever again. Unless that squirrel woke Paris Beaufont up and she rescued him.

CHAPTER THIRTY-ONE

Advanced Love Department, Level One, Basement, FGA Tower, New York City, New York, United States

"Do you think if you shine that light in my eyes long enough, you'll keep me awake?" Paris asked Faraday as he held a penlight up and shone it straight into her open right eye.

"I think that if I don't figure out how you were spelled, then you're going to go back to sleep, and it will be even harder to wake you up," he answered as the others studied her with concern from the other side of the room.

Paris was lying on the floor in one of the offices Uncle Clark had finished remodeling. It had the turquoise carpet and wood-paneled walls but no furniture yet. Apparently, once she and Faraday stepped through the portal to the FGA Plaza that Terrance had opened for them, she'd passed out at once.

Although he felt guilty about it, Faraday was forced to leave Paris lying in the middle of the plaza while he retrieved Agent Ron Opal and Uncle Clark to get Paris. They'd carried her to the basement, but not until many fairy godmothers spied her "passed out." The rumors were probably circulating wildly around the FGA about what was wrong with Paris.

"I'm fine," she said with a forced smile to her employees and Uncle Clark, standing in the doorway.

"She's not," Faraday corrected, flashing the penlight into the other eye. "If you go back to sleep, it will strengthen the spell. I've got to figure out how to keep you awake. However—"

"What?" Paris asked, sensing the tension in his voice.

"I need to work on an antidote for you and then one that will work on all the other brides."

"We will keep her awake," Misfit offered, indicating Sissy and the others.

"Of course we will," Uncle Clark said, coming over, looking concerned.

Faraday glanced up at him. "I need your help with something. I can't work without equipment and supplies, and since you're doing all this renovating, I'm hoping you can fast-track a sleep lab for me, pushing it to the top of the list."

"Yes, that should take priority. Do you think you can counteract the spell? How did this happen?"

"I think it was induced by powerful magitech," Faraday speculated, putting a blood pressure cuff on Paris' arm. "It seems to only work on certain candidates."

"Brides-to-be," Clark guessed.

The squirrel nodded, taking Paris' blood pressure, which was weird since he was, in fact, a rodent. "The inventor of the magitech spell must have determined something specific about brides that allowed them to be targeted."

"Like they are all crazy and obsessed with a single day?" Misfit asked.

"Like they are bossy and think everyone should drop everything for their big days?" Sissy asked.

Paris yawned, shaking off the sleepiness trying to end her. "I'm none of those things."

Misfit crossed her arms and smirked. "No, but you're not a real person as far as we can tell."

"Yeah, you're like a strange nontypical woman," Sissy stated.

"You two are a bunch of fairy god-monsters," Paris teased.

"That's true." Misfit laughed morbidly.

"I was thinking most brides will have an elevated blood pressure," Faraday said, pulling the cuff from Paris' arm. "They also will be highly anticipatory and have several other factors that an advanced magitech could hook onto for spelling."

"So you think that I was spelled by watching something displayed in the booth?" Paris asked, not able to think of any other way she would have been affected.

"Yes, probably some subliminal programming."

"Are you saying that Paris' blood pressure is high?" Clark asked, leaning forward and looking at the notes Faraday was sketching out in front of him.

"It's higher than her usual high levels," Faraday answered, and then catching the concerned look on her Uncle's face, he added, "Her demon blood makes it so she has an elevated blood pressure normally. Nothing to worry about. I monitor it regularly."

Paris yawned again, smiling at her employees. "Isn't he such a good squirrel?"

"He's a weird one," Misfit answered.

"So, what can you do to combat this subliminal programming spell?" Clark asked, still looking very serious, as usual.

"That's why I need this sleep laboratory," Faraday answered. "I need to run some tests on Paris. If I can monitor her brainwaves, then I can compare them to her baseline readings from prior studies."

"When did you take readings of my brainwaves?" Paris asked.

"Pretty much during all your various activities," Faraday replied. "Awake, asleep, resting, concentrating, using magic—"

Paris shook her head. "That's just weird."

"That's what I said," Misfit said.

"Coming from her, that's concerning," Sissy teased.

Clark pursed his lips, worry heavy in his eyes. "The worry

here is breaking the spell before it causes you to sleep permanently."

Paris shook her head. "Yeah, and I had awful dreams when I did sleep."

"Probably related to the magitech spell." Faraday continued to write notes.

Clark stuck his hands on his hips, deadly serious as he stared at the squirrel. "Can you fix this? Or do I need to call Alicia to help?"

"I can, but call Alicia anyway," Faraday muttered, scribbling notes fast. "She's a magitech expert and can help. If I can isolate the parts of the brain affected, then I can create a signal that rewires it."

"That will stop inducing sleep?" Clark asked.

"It should," Faraday answered. "Then I amplify the signal and broadcast it worldwide to undo all those affected by this stimuli."

"So that's the question," Paris said through another yawn. "Where are women getting spelled? Surely it can't be just at wedding expos."

Faraday nodded to the card he'd taken from the booth. "I'm guessing it's there, but I'll have to do some research."

Paris cut her eyes to the card and nodded. "Of course. There have to be some stimuli on their website, SnowWhiteRe-laxes.com."

CHAPTER THIRTY-TWO

Advanced Love Department, Level One, Basement, FGA Tower, New York City, New York, United States

Paris had never much cared for death metal, and being extremely sleepy hadn't changed that. The music blaring in her head through the earbuds was making her feel like she was being assaulted. The singer screamed rather than sang. The guitar squealed, and the drums sounded more like a chaotic storm rather than a beat.

Pulling the earbuds out, she glanced at Faraday, who was in the corner, studying the website SnowWhiteRelaxes.com for clues. He had his back to the wall, so the screen wasn't visible to anyone else, just in case others were susceptible to the sleep-inducing spell.

"I don't think this is working," Paris remarked.

"Why? Are you about to fall asleep?" Faraday asked, looking up suddenly.

Paris shook her head. "No, but I want to kill myself."

"Isn't that band amazing like that?" Misfit remarked.

"Amazing isn't the right word for them," Paris replied dryly, pushing up to her feet. "There's got to be other ways to keep me awake."

Sissy grabbed her hand and dragged her out of the small office. "We'll do laps. That will wake you up."

Paris glanced over her shoulder at the squirrel. "Good luck figuring out what's causing this and finding a way to cure me. I'm going to go be walked by a fairy god-monster."

"I'm close on the trail. Hopefully, Terrance finds something too. I'll have a report and solution within the hour."

Misfit popped up to her feet. "I'll go hide in various places and jump out to scare you when you're walking the department space."

Paris laughed. "Or you could try telling me jokes. Humor is just as stimulating as fear."

"Fear is so good for your soul," Misfit argued.

"Love. It's love that's good for the soul," Sissy corrected, tugging on Paris again, but it was like being pulled by a Guinea pig.

Walking was a smart idea, and they had the perfect space for it. Uncle Clark had only gotten around to making one workstation in the large open department space, which meant the rest of the newly renovated space was completely open. Setting off to the right, Paris yawned.

"Knock-knock," Sissy said, pulling on her hand.

"Who is there?" Paris replied.

"Underwear."

"Underwear, who?"

"Ever underwear you're going," Sissy answered.

Misfit, who was trailing behind them, groaned. "You're going to make her pass out from jokes like that."

"Got a better one then?" Paris asked.

"Yeah, did you hear about the goth kid with dyslexia?" Misfit asked.

Paris shook her head.

"He sold his soul to Santa," Misfit stated dryly.

Paris shook her head. "You two are getting this put on your performance reviews."

"Yeah, what about your reviews, boss?" Misfit asked. "We can call you 'the computer' and say it's because if left unattended, you go to sleep."

A laugh popped out of Paris' mouth. "That's not bad."

"What isn't bad?" Uncle Clark asked, poking his head out of the large office where he was working.

"Oh, my employees are telling me jokes to try to keep me awake," Paris explained. "How's it going with the sleep lab?"

"Not too bad," Clark answered. "I took all of Faraday's specs, and I'm just trying to get things right. Apparently, he's going to need some pretty advanced things to broadcast a signal to fix all the brides. I've admittedly not built a sleep lab before."

"Which is where I can help," a familiar voice with a thick Italian accent said behind them.

CHAPTER THIRTY-THREE

Advanced Love Department, Level One, Basement, FGA Tower, New York City, New York, United States

"Aunt Alicia," Paris said, wishing she sounded more excited to see the woman before her and not like she was slurring her words and about to fall asleep.

"Paris," the magitech scientist said, striding over and looking at her. "You've been spelled to sleep, I hear."

Paris nodded, blinking. Each time her eyes closed, they felt like they could stay like that longer. "Yes, but Faraday is going to fix me. Then he needs your help building the ray gun or satellite or whatever to project the signal to fix all the other brides who are affected."

"Which is why I'm building this sleep lab for him." Clark indicated the area behind him.

"Good, we'll need that for testing the strength and more." Alicia went over, hugging Uncle Clark, the man who used to be her husband when they were pretending, so the Beaufonts didn't lose their position in the House of Fourteen. Paris' childhood was very complicated and involved a lot of people jumping through a lot of hoops.

Now Aunt Alicia was with the man she loved more than any other. He just so happened to be one of Paris' favorite people in the world—her Uncle John.

"This is a lot of material you have here," another familiar voice said from behind the tall stack of crates on the far side of the large department space. Paris hadn't noticed how high the crates were stacked until Bermuda Laurens poked her head around the side, having been inspecting the boxes. "Do you think you have enough in here to also build a lab for me?"

"For you?" Clark asked, confused.

The giantess nodded. She was not dressed in her usual safari outfit or Sunday church dress. Instead, the no-nonsense woman was wearing a white lab coat over slacks and a button-up shirt, looking very clinical. "Yes, I was with Alicia when Faraday called her. We were working on the half mortal, half magician fertility research. We're going to need to complete that if she and John are going to have offspring."

Paris beamed at her idea, excited she and Uncle John were trying to have offspring. It was for practical reasons since John was a Mortal Seven and the last Carraway alive. When he was gone, there would be no one to replace him on the council for the House of Fourteen. They also wanted to have a child for impractical reasons—to spread love and happiness.

"You need a lab?" Clark asked.

Bermuda nodded. "I will. It will be a place to conduct research and have everything in one place. I've been considering other places, but being down here and seeing how much open space there is, it makes sense."

"Well, it is the Advanced Love branch department space," Paris corrected. "It's supposed to give my fairy godmothers a place to work."

"Don't you have five levels?" Bermuda questioned.

"Yes, but this is the only level being renovated currently."

"Isn't Advanced Love about nurturing important relationships that would significantly add to the love meter?" Bermuda continued her questions.

"Well, yes," Paris answered.

"Wouldn't a magician and a mortal having a child who represented new beginnings and possibilities do that?" Bermuda asked.

Paris didn't answer. Instead, she turned to her Uncle Clark. "After you create the sleep lab, can you create a fertility clinic in one of the other office areas?"

He shrugged pleasantly. "I don't see why not."

"Then I'll be close by to help Faraday with this project," Alicia said to Paris and then looked to the giantess. "It's not too far to do the experiments for your research."

"Great," Paris said through a giant yawn. "I'm just going to sit down and close my eyes while you all get to work on these labs."

"Don't even think about it," Faraday called from the far side of the space, hurrying from the office where he'd been working. "I think I have a solution to fix you, but I'll warn you, it's going to hurt…quite a lot."

CHAPTER THIRTY-FOUR

Advanced Love Department, Level One, Basement, FGA Tower, New York City, New York, United States

"What do you mean the cure will hurt," Paris challenged the squirrel. "Getting spelled to have a sleep disorder didn't."

"Well, it also doesn't hurt when most people contract diseases," Faraday argued. "The actual ailment hurts, and the cure often does too."

"He's right. There are many diseases where the cure is worst at first, but it's worth it. You don't want to be in pain, but you also don't want to be in a coma forever."

"You know, you're surprisingly a voice of reason sometimes," Faraday offered to Misfit.

"Often, I'm a ray of sunshine," Misfit said, peeking out from under her dark hair, her black eyeliner making her appear sweetly sinister.

"I'm sure," Faraday said, turning his attention back to Paris. "I know it sounds avoidable, but I don't think it is. The alternative is to take longer to find a different solution."

She leaned back on the wall, yawning and feeling herself recede into the world of sleep where all was well.

"AND!" Faraday yelled to wake her back up.

Fingers snapped in front of her face.

Paris startled back to the waking world, standing upright.

"As I was saying," Faraday continued, as Misfit continued to snap in front of Paris' face before narrowing her eyes at her. "We don't have the luxury of time. I've found a solution. Better yet, I've found the cause or at least who I think is behind this. Even better yet, I've tracked this person down. There are only three different scientists who could be behind such advanced magitech."

"Wait," Paris said, shaking away the cobwebs in her brain. "I thought Jackson Zelle was behind this. It seemed like something he'd do."

"He probably is," Clark remarked. "He most likely employed this scientist."

"Didn't Agent Barney Jasper say that many of the résumés for the IT director position were stolen by Jackson Zelle when he fled the FGA?"

Paris' eyes widened. "That sneaky little devil."

"He definitely is," Alicia said, having jumped right in and started taking notes. "That means we have to find this scientist."

"That's what I'm thinking," Faraday began. "I can cure Paris, but only because we're in close range. With your help, Alicia, I think I can build and amplify a signal that goes out and cures brides who have been spelled."

"We have to stop the person who has the know-how and magitech to do this," Sissy said, sounding very adult for once. Very logical too.

"Exactly," Bermuda stated, having been observing from the sidelines. "Because you can cure, but that does you no good if you don't shut down the entire operation."

"Okay, so we have to track down this scientist," Paris said with conviction. "Faraday, send me over the information you have on the possible suspects, and I'll have him found."

"I'll get your sleep lab created." Clark moved for the room he'd been renovating for such purposes.

Faraday gave Paris a meaningful look. "None of this can happen until we fix you. Are you ready to undergo the cure?"

She nodded, not sure what he meant by painful, but prepared to do whatever it took not to fall victim to a sleep filled with nightmares.

CHAPTER THIRTY-FIVE

Advanced Love Department, Level One, Basement, FGA Tower, New York City, New York, United States

"You're going to feel some pressure," Faraday instructed, scurrying between several computers he had set up on low tables in the makeshift sleep lab. Paris was stationed close beside them, stretched out on the carpeted floor.

"Is this like when the doctor says it's going to be a slight pinch and it's more like a stab?" She laughed, knowing how ridiculous she must look.

Electrical nodes were connected to her head, ready to broadcast a signal that would "correct" her brain. This was the individual cure for the sleep spell put on her through the magitech at the wedding expo by Snow White Wedding Services. To fix all the brides affected all over would take something much more advanced.

"No, this is going to feel like pressure at first," Faraday said, concentrating as he checked settings and connections between the wires and the machines. "Like your head is in a helmet."

"Oh, that doesn't sound so bad," Sissy offered sensitively, watching from the corner.

"It's going to grow in intensity until it's quite intense," Faraday continued. "Don't panic, but it might feel like your head is in a vice grip."

"That sounds cool," Misfit imparted, stationed beside the other fairy godmother.

"Don't you two have things to do?" Paris urged, annoyed.

Misfit shrugged, looking bored. "Most of the complaints coming in from the website are around how women are sleeping all the time, ignoring their fiancés."

Sissy smiled, wrapping her finger around one of her gray pigtails. "The frequency scanner to help pair soul mates is in the works but taking time to get going. It's in the research and development phase."

"It's true. It should be up and running soon," Faraday affirmed, flicking his tail as he handed a device to Alicia, who was acting as his assistant for this project. It was funny to think the polished woman with a Ph.D. in magitech was assisting the squirrel, but few were smarter than him.

"Okay, well, go and find the ghost in one of the back rooms," Paris ordered. "Find out what he knows about the Advanced Love branch or Jackson Zelle. Or just make friends with him and see if he'll stop howling so much. It might freak out the new fairy godmothers."

"I like the howling," Misfit said. "It gives the place character."

"The fact that you like it means the new employees won't," Paris said. "Try not to scare them when they get here. I'm sure Ron will have them here soon."

"Not scare them?" Misfit asked. "Like I would do that. Oh, by the way, my pet tarantula, Lucifer, is loose somewhere down here. Keep an eye out for him, would you?"

Paris tensed, turning her head both ways on the floor and wishing she was anywhere else after learning that information. "Say what? Does he bite?"

"Only if he's provoked," Misfit answered.

Paris let out a sigh of relief. "Okay, well, I won't do that. I'm just lying here."

"Oh, and blondes," Misfit added. "I taught him to bite blondes."

Paris tried to sit up, but the wires attached to her head made it difficult. "You what?"

Misfit shrugged. "Sorry, it was before you, boss. Usually, blondes make me want to puke. You're all right."

"You're fired," Paris threatened.

"Yeah, right." Misfit waved her off, turning to Sissy. "Want to go and make friends with a ghost?"

"Not really," the other fairy replied. "I also don't want to stay here where there's a loose tarantula."

The pair left Paris with Faraday and Alicia and possibly an angry spider that would profile her and attack.

"How do I always inherit employees who challenge my patience and sanity?" Paris joked, thinking of how much work Holly and Isha had been in the beginning. They were still a lot of work but also competent, especially after the Smarten Up Shortbread.

"I'm going to ask that you not move," Faraday said, peering down at Paris from a stool at a workstation where he'd settled, ready to start the procedure.

"Says the squirrel who isn't on the floor with an arachnid," Paris muttered, trying to breathe through the tension.

"Hey, remember when we were in Egypt, and you made friends with that spider in Hathor's temple?" Faraday offered.

"Mrs. Clicks," Paris said with a laugh.

"I'm sure Lucifer will like you, even if he's been programmed to bite blondes," Alicia said thoughtfully.

Paris smiled at her aunt, grateful she was there and helping. "Let's hope so. Although his namesake doesn't fill me with a lot of hope."

"Okay, we're going to get started," Faraday said, focusing on the screen. "Go ahead and give it to her, Dr. De Luca." He was calling the magitech scientist by her maiden name, although she was married to Uncle John now.

Alicia kneeled and pressed a soft foam ball into Paris' hand. She offered a compassionate smile. "I'll be right here."

"Thanks," Paris said, holding up the ball. "What's this for?"

"The pain," her aunt answered. "It's going to be more than intense. This is going to be extremely painful, I'm afraid."

CHAPTER THIRTY-SIX

Advanced Love Department, Level One, Basement, FGA Tower, New York City, New York, United States

At first, Paris didn't know why Aunt Alicia had given her such an ominous warning. The pain wasn't at all that bad. It made Paris wonder if her demon blood made her threshold for such things higher. Then it hit her, and it was unlike anything she'd ever experienced.

The sensation started as gentle pressure, and then nothing about it was subtle or soothing. It felt like Paris had stuck her head in a vice grip and it was seeking to smash her skull like a watermelon.

In her fist, Paris flattened the foam ball at once. She screamed so loud that she was certain they could hear it on the floors above. She twisted and convulsed.

"Restrain her!" Faraday exclaimed. It was such a strange order to hear him give. It made him sound like a mad scientist. Even stranger was that he meant the order for Paris.

Then in a world of bizarre things, Paris felt her aunt's hands on her shoulders, pressing her down, seeking to keep her still.

Paris was stronger and instantly worried that she'd hurt the woman before her, who was trying to help. Something inside her was tearing to be let loose. To fight. To escape the pain that was making her brain feel like it was about to explode.

"Breathe, my love," Alicia encouraged, her voice soothing and instantly reminding Paris of her humanity.

She wasn't a crazed demon that needed to fight to survive. She was a woman. A person who had been spelled, and this was fixing her. She just had to endure the agony a little longer.

Sucking in a giant breath, Paris felt a tiny bit of relief, but it was quickly followed by what seemed like a blunt force. It was like she'd been struck. The only hands on her were Alicia's, and they were holding her down and providing comfort.

Still, it felt like an anvil had crashed down from the ceiling and pummeled her straight in the forehead. Stars blurred her vision. The pain was so much that Paris thought she was going to bite her tongue and draw blood. She was vibrating from the electrical force convulsing through her.

It had started at such a low voltage, but in the sane part of her brain, she knew it was electricity making her brain feel on fire. It made her teeth shake in her mouth so hard she thought they'd fall out.

Her eyes bulged and watered. She smelled smoke. Hair burning. It was her, she knew, but was in too much pain to worry. She wasn't worried in the least. Faraday wouldn't be doing this if it wasn't necessary. Aunt Alicia was still there, although she wasn't holding her anymore.

It made Paris feel safe knowing she was close and Faraday was in charge. The pain was lessening, which was another relief. The buzzing that wasn't just in her head lessened too.

Everything had started with such a jolt of pain that Paris hadn't registered all the strange things. The buzzing. The electrical pulsing. The vibrating. The blood in her mouth.

Feeling still for the first time in what felt like hours but could only have been minutes, Paris tested her hands. She reached them up to her face. They were shaking.

She nearly punched herself in the face when she went to touch it, feeling something tickling her under the nose. It was in her ears too. She felt wetness and pulled her fingers away to find blood.

Her nose was bleeding. She guessed her ears too. It could be tears she felt in her eyes. What had happened to her in order to fix the sleeping spell? This cure was too much, and no others could go through it.

Aunt Alicia, who swam in and out of focus, appeared with a towel. "I'll clean you up. You just rest. You've been through a lot."

Paris opened her mouth to reply. Made to sit up. Her head felt like it was full of lead. Unable to hold onto consciousness any longer, Paris closed her eyes.

The last thing she heard before she was swept away into dreamless sleep was Faraday consoling Alicia.

"It's okay," the squirrel said, sounding tired. "It's fine for her to sleep now. She's cured."

CHAPTER THIRTY-SEVEN

Advanced Love Department, Level One, Basement, FGA Tower, New York City, New York, United States

"I don't ever want to go through that again," Paris said when she awoke an hour later. She felt like she could sleep for days, but after the scare of the Snow White spell, she didn't want to risk it.

"I don't ever want to put you through anything like that again," Faraday agreed, hopping over to her and checking her over.

She caught a glimpse of a bunch of bloody rags just as Alicia swept out of the room with them in her arms.

Paris felt her nose and then her eyes and ears.

Catching sight of this, Faraday gave her a sympathetic look as she sat up. "The cure was…a lot…."

"It didn't feel like a pinch." Paris laughed at this, but that hurt her head, so she stopped immediately.

"For anyone, that would have been excruciating," Faraday stated. "The fact that you maintained consciousness is incredible. I'm just so sorry I had to put you through so much."

"That can't be the solution for fixing all the brides who have been spelled," Paris said, feeling breathless. She was grateful when Aunt Alicia returned with a glass of ice water. "Thanks."

Faraday shook his head. "No, I agree." He glanced up at the other scientist. "We must find a different counter spell using magitech. I would have taken the time with Paris, but—"

"I couldn't risk it," Paris interrupted, wanting to cut off his guilt immediately. "You fixed me, right?"

"I also gave you a nose bleed and more in the process," Faraday said.

"It's okay," Paris told him. "Now I'm better and not feeling like I need to nap constantly, which means I can help find a better solution. There's got to be one, right? You were going to create a signal and amplify it. Was it like the one you gave me?"

He nodded, looking lost and frustrated at the floor. "I realize now it won't work. I mean, I knew it wasn't going to be a pleasant experience for you, but if I knew it was going to be like that, I hope you know I'd never have subjected you to that."

"Stop," Paris ordered. "You did what you had to, and now I'm better and can help you. So we just have to find a better solution to fix everyone. You can still use the amplifying solution, right? You just have to innovate it."

Faraday glanced up at Alicia. "Do you think if we have the original coding then..."

The magitech expert was already nodding, starting to pace. "Yes, if we have it, then the signal we build can be a reverse of the original one, and it won't have to rewire."

"Yes, that's what I had to do to Paris," Faraday admitted.

"You rewired my brain?" Paris asked. "Can I still tie my shoes?"

"Probably," Faraday answered with a snicker before looking back at the pacing woman. "Even with the original coding...."

"You're going to need something to amplify the signal," Alicia again supplied, finishing his sentence. They were cute when they worked together. "I've been thinking about that. There are a few places where we can find what we're looking for, but…."

"It's not going to be easy if it's one of the places I'm thinking of." Faraday was the one who completed her sentence then.

Paris glanced back and forth between the pair. "It's cute that you two know what you're talking about, but I'm wondering if maybe you'll clue me in. I did just have my brain melted, so I'll need you to boil things down to basics. Scratch the boiling reference. Just explain to me what you're talking about."

Alicia paused. "We're going to need a very specific type of magitech to make the signal with the counter spell work."

"Okay," Paris chirped. "Can we get it off Amazon Magitech? At the Fantastical Armory? Where?"

"There are a couple of places," Faraday answered. "None of them are safe locations. They are…"

"A result of a blast of electromagnetism," Alicia continued when the squirrel seemed unable to.

"Like a lot of it," Faraday added.

"It's the huge influx of the radiation that caused electronics to take on such magical properties," Alicia explained.

"Great," Paris said, taking a sip of the ice water and enjoying the refreshment. "So I'll stop by there, and we'll get whatever it is that you all need."

"It will be a bit more complicated than that," Faraday argued. "These sites are usually pretty deadly due to the high levels of radiation. The magitech, it's downright dangerous."

Alicia nodded. "Many of the sites have been sectioned off and put into quarantine status."

"So we have to break into this place," Paris muttered, knowing it would get complicated.

"Most likely," Alicia agreed. "Faraday and I will have to determine which one will have the parts we need for the signal."

"Okay. What can I do in the meantime?" Paris asked.

"You have to go and find the scientist Jackson Zelle had create this Snow White spell," Faraday urged.

"Right," Paris replied. "I take him down so he can't spread his treachery anymore."

"Not exactly," Alicia countered.

Paris tilted her head to the side. "Say what?"

"We are going to need this person," Faraday explained. "They know the exact coding used in the spell, which if we're going to avoid fixing brides the way we did you, we need that information. That's the only way that we can rewrite things so that we broadcast a signal that undoes the spell."

"Okay, so I have to track down this scientist and abduct him from Jackson Zelle," Paris said mostly to herself as she ran through the checklist of tasks ahead of her. "Then I have to convince them to help us, probably in exchange for amnesty. Once that's done, we can go off to Radiation Ville and grab this part. Is that right?"

Faraday looked up at Alicia, a question in his eyes. She nodded. He smiled.

"Yeah, that's about it," the squirrel replied.

"Great." Paris got to her feet. "You all find the place for this part. Fare, send me the information on the potential people this scientist could be. I'll put my best detective on the case."

CHAPTER THIRTY-EIGHT

Crying Cat Bakery, Roya Lane, London, United Kingdom

Paris was grateful to find Sherlock Holmes without too much trouble. Her brain still didn't feel like it was working properly just yet. Since the man didn't carry a cell phone and refused to share his future whereabouts, she had to detect where he was going to be. Thankfully she thought it was close to his snack time.

"I have a case for you," Paris said after entering the magical bakery on Roya Lane and sliding into the seat next to Sherlock Holmes, who was eating a piece of coffee cake. She suddenly realized how hungry she was after her "procedure." Holding up her hand, she waved at Lee, the assassin-baker behind the counter. "Can I get a slice of what he's having?"

Lee shook her head and turned around, striding for the back.

"Cool, cool, cool," Paris muttered, returning her attention to the detective. "I should have expected that answer, really."

He looked her over in the way he did that felt like he was boring into her soul. "You've been through an ordeal."

"I had my brain rewired, but it wasn't as bad as this one time that some hippies braided my hair."

He didn't seem to think this was as funny as her. "You have a case for me. Is it related to this rewiring that you had done to your brain?"

"Yes," Paris replied, pulling the files that Faraday had given her from the inside of her jacket and putting them on the table, sliding them over to Sherlock Holmes. "I need you to first decide which of these three scientists is most likely to be the culprit behind our current criminal behavior delivered from Zelle Corp. Then I need you to track him down. I don't think he's just going to be taking calls which is why I think it will involve detective work."

"He's been working on something for Jackson Zelle?" Sherlock asked, finishing his coffee cake.

"Yes, which means he will probably be paranoid, believing that the FGA will be looking for him."

Sherlock Holmes dusted off his hands. "I have to figure out who the person is based on what?"

"Well, these are the three top magitech scientists in the world who specialize in sleep spells," Paris explained. "We need to determine which one is our guy."

The great detective nodded. "It makes sense that you were spelled using magitech related to sleep now, based on your appearance."

Paris picked up a spoon and checked her reflection. "What's that mean?"

"It means you look tired," Lee answered for the detective, striding over with a red muffin on a plate. She slid it down in front of Paris, looking proud of herself.

"What's that?" Paris pointed to the pastry. "I asked for the coffee cake. As you said yourself, I look tired."

"That's because you've lost a lot of blood," Lee said, pointing at the red pastry. "That's a beet muffin. It will help with your anemia."

"Thanks," Paris said, grateful she had such weird and observant friends. "Oh, hey, Lee, while you're here—"

"I'm always here," she interrupted. "I work here."

Paris laughed. "Yeah, but I meant while you were giving me your attention, which I don't think I'll keep long."

"Not if you keep talking," the baker retorted.

"What I was saying was that I was hoping you'd make my wedding cake."

"For what?" Lee asked, quite seriously.

"For my wedding," Paris muttered dryly.

"Who are you marrying?" Lee questioned, her hands on her hips.

"Hemingway. You know the guy I've been with for a long time now?"

"Name doesn't ring a bell," Lee mumbled, thinking. "Does he have red hair?"

"No."

"Is he fat?"

"No."

"Is he short?"

"No."

Lee threw her hands up in the air. "Well, I guess we've never met."

"You worked with him when I opened Little Pleasures," Paris explained. "The horticulturist with dimples and a nice work ethic."

"You're marrying the farmhand?" Lee asked.

Paris laughed. "He likes hard work and takes care of the farm and house."

Lee nodded proudly. "You have him nicely trained. I hope he has your meals on the table when you return home from your accounting job."

"I'm an agent for the FGA," Paris corrected. "No, Uncle Clark usually feeds me."

Lee shook her head, glancing sideways at Sherlock Holmes. "This one and her men. I hope you don't do her laundry."

"I work the cases she assigns me," Sherlock Holmes replied.

"Because she's got you under her thumb."

"Because they are interesting, and after all this time, I've seen just about everything. Not when it comes to the cases related to FGA business."

"So, will you make my wedding cake?" Paris asked, picking up the muffin.

"No," Lee said at once. "Now that I know you're getting married, I also know you're the reason I'm short twelve dollars today."

Paris took a bite of the muffin, finding it surprisingly good, even containing beets. "Please explain this logic."

"Well, every morning, Terrance, the wedding planner, comes in here and buys an Everything but the Kitchen Sink bagel and a cup of coffee," Lee explained. "My prices are high in an attempt to discourage business. So that sale, which should be about six dollars, is double that. Anyway, he didn't come in today. Since trouble follows you and anyone associated with you and you're getting married, I'm guessing you dragged him down with you."

Paris halted chewing. Swallowed her bite dry. Shook her head. "Terrance is missing? Is that what you're telling me?"

"Yes, and I'm not a detective, but when did you see him last?" Lee asked.

"Recently," Paris admitted guiltily.

"That's what I thought," Lee said. "I knew you'd be behind this."

"It's not my fault," Paris argued. "He's the one who decided to stay behind. He wanted to spy around and get more information. I bet those goons got to him."

"Paris Beaufont got to him first," Lee said. "I swear, we all are risking our lives being around you."

She gawked, putting down the muffin. "It's not my fault. I just have a dangerous job, and it puts me in crazy places. I'm not to blame. Sherlock, tell her I'm not to blame."

The Englishman offered her a pleasant look. "I stick around because your life is interesting and always offers me a challenging and rewarding mystery."

Lee laughed. "See there. You're the cause. You're the reason Terrance is missing."

"Are you sure he's actually missing?" Paris asked. "Maybe he just didn't feel like coming by."

"Right, after a dozen years of never missing a day, he decided to cut the carbs," Lee muttered dryly. "Yes, I went over to his treehouse. He left yesterday and hasn't been back since."

"That was when he left with me," Paris said, looking down at the table, suddenly consumed with worry.

"Will this scientist know where Terrance is being kept?" Sherlock Holmes asked, the voice of reason.

Paris thought for a moment. "He might. He'll know more than what we know right now. I mean, we suspect that Jackson Zelle is behind all this, but we don't have any proof. Our best bet is to find this scientist. He's the one behind this Snow White sleep spell business. Then hopefully, we can get him to talk, and he'll know where Terrance is."

"Okay, then I'll need to determine which of these candidates is the most likely to be your scientist." Sherlock tapped his finger on the files.

"Do you have enough information to narrow down who it can be?" Paris asked.

"Someone who is motivated to create a spell which targets brides," Sherlock Holmes began, ticking off fingers on his hand. "Someone who will work for Jackson Zelle." He lifted another finger. "Then someone who is obsessed with fairytales. I think I can figure it out based on that personality profile."

"Then you'll track them down for me?" Paris asked, hope filling her chest.

"Yes, and I'll let you know when I'm close. Then you should be ready to swoop in and apprehend."

Paris smiled, grateful for the great detective's help. She couldn't do this without him. There was just too much to do. Paris needed all the help she could get.

CHAPTER THIRTY-NINE

Fantastical Armory, Roya Lane, London, United Kingdom

Although Paris needed to figure out how to counteract the Snow White spell, she also had other concerns. Even if she fixed this problem, if the FGA went down because of finances, then she would too. Therefore, she couldn't forget that currently, the board of directors was looking for buyers for the company.

Also, Faraday didn't know where the part was he needed to boost the signal for the device he and Alicia were building. Therefore, Paris was in limbo, waiting for Sherlock Holmes to locate the scientists and for Faraday to tell her where they needed to go next for equipment.

With the time to spare and a desperate necessity for funding to save the FGA, Paris met Subfar at the Fantastical Armory. The Protector of Wealth had a plan that could help save the FGA, and it could work based on the sped-up timeline.

"It's risky, though," Subfar explained as he pushed a stack of papers he brought with him across the glass countertop at her.

"Losing the FGA is what I'm facing," Paris stated. "I can do risky."

"It's not just risky in that you might lose a lot of capital,"

Subfar offered, pushing an errant piece of hair behind his ear. "There are many ways this can go wrong."

"She's going to mess it up, most likely," Subner cut in, sitting on his stool, reading his book and eavesdropping—all his usual activities.

"It's ever a wonder that I would ever fail with such endearing support like his." Paris indicated the Protector of Weapons on the other side of the shop full of oddities.

It was strange to look at him, somewhat polished and with an expressive face, and then compare him to his brother nearby. Subner was plain and unkempt in contrast, and his face mostly wore a sullen look.

Subner scowled at her, back to his old ways of abusing her after his apology regarding her help with Subfar. "Your sarcasm makes you even more intolerable as if that was even possible."

"I happen to find it delightful," Subfar said with a laugh. "It takes great wit to pull off such comments so quickly. I hope that your child has your intelligence."

Paris cut her eyes to Mama Jamba and Papa Creola sitting at the front of the shop, always listening. It was Mother Nature who pushed Paris to accept any terms that Subfar insisted upon for his help.

She had, and now she'd promised this man her firstborn child. However, Subfar definitely didn't know that as a halfling, she couldn't have children. What was evident based on the knowing smile Mama Jamba was giving her right then was she knew the truth. Of course she knew. That woman knew everything, even if she didn't share most of it.

"Yes, let's hope the child has all parts of Paris," Subner muttered dryly.

Subfar nodded passionately. "Yes, I would like it to have her strength and power."

"Her ethics," Subner added.

"Then, of course, her attractiveness," Subfar said with a laugh, glancing at his brother. "We wouldn't want the child to take after us, would we?"

"Looks aren't everything," Subner seethed, cutting his eyes to Paris.

She averted his gaze, realizing he must know her secret too. It was ever a wonder that Subfar didn't know she couldn't have offspring, but he had been sheltered for a long time.

He also didn't seem as well versed on all subject matters like his twin. Instead, he was narrowly focused on things like wealth and getting what he wanted. In the case of the deal he made with Paris, it was an heir to take over for him if anything should ever happen to him. Paris reasoned this made sense.

Subner had Wilder as his assistant, who he had appointed at the time of his birth. It seemed that Subfar was going about picking his would-be replacement in a different way.

"So this plan that you have that's risky," Paris said in a rush, glancing at the stack of papers Subfar had pushed in her direction. "What is it?"

"Well, I would be your benefactor," Subfar began, pulling the first page off the top and showing her a set of graphs. "I'm happy to supply you funds as you buy up stock, but you have to do it under your name and exactly when I tell you."

"I'm following you so far," Paris lied, her head swimming as she took in the various charts and graphs and the sea of numbers. She was obviously still recovering from her brain melt.

"She's lying and doesn't understand the true implication of what your plan entails," Subner cut in as though he was invited to the conversation.

The Protector of Wealth nodded good-naturedly. "It's not that explicit based on the information I'm showing you. Although this is a fast-tracked plan based on projections and also well-educated suspicions on my part, it will take some time. It will also take your trust, Paris. Although I'll hold your hand through most of it, you inevitably have to make the transactions, or the money won't be yours, which is key."

"You're going to have to do more than hold her hand," Subner criticized.

Paris rolled her eyes at him and directed her attention to the nice brother. "Okay, boil this down for me."

Subfar nodded, picking up a pen and pulling another piece of paper from the stack. "As your benefactor, over a set amount of time, I'm going to loan you this amount of money." He pointed to a figure on the next page that contained a lot of digits.

Paris jerked her head up, looking at him. "I need to have a sustainable income. Although that's a healthy amount, it isn't what I had in mind."

"I'm loaning this to you and instructing you how to invest it," Subfar explained.

"I told you she wouldn't understand this," Subner muttered. "Try something simple like one plus one, but she might still struggle with that."

"Okay, so I take that money and do what with it?" Paris asked, ignoring the Protector of Weapons, which was a skill she'd perfected.

"When I tell you, you're going to buy stock, but only in one company," Subfar answered.

"One company?" Paris asked. "Like Apple or Google or Facebook?"

Subfar shook his head. "I understand clearly your mission and what you need to do on multiple fronts. I've been watching the market. More importantly, the future money resides in the people who have it. So I've been watching people and the ones that will most affect you and the FGA. When I tell you, on your own, you must buy a specific amount of stocks in this company."

He slid the page off the stack to reveal a new one and pointed to the center of the page. Paris read the name of the stock and jerked her head up. She wasn't sure if the name meant what she thought.

Subfar was grinning. "Smart, huh?"

"Why would I do that?" Paris asked, shocked that he would have her purchase stock in that company of all companies.

"Have you ever heard of short-selling stock?" he countered.

Subner chuckled darkly. "You're talking complex financial theory with a person who relies on her phone to tell her what the weather is outside. Consider enabling her and doing this all for Paris."

She scoffed at the grumpy elf. "I only look at the weather to find out what the weather is going to be in the future. I can look out a window." She glanced at Subfar. "No, I skipped the finance classes at Happily Ever After College."

"Well, I've taken the guesswork out," Subfar explained. "As the benefactor and advisor, you're going to buy stock when I tell you to. It must be in your name, though. Then you're going to sell it at my command. Again you'll buy back the stock at precisely the right time. If you follow my lead, then at the end of a few very precise transactions, you'll be worth…"

He slid another piece of paper off the stack and pointed the tip of the pen at a very large number. "You'll be worth that amount of money."

"Bu-but I need to have a sustainable income," Paris said, her mind boggled with all the numbers and strange ideas related to Subfar's risky strategy.

"See, she's stuttering like a monkey," Subner cut in again. "Maybe you should help her learn to speak first. Baby steps."

"If you take the money you earn shorting stock as I advise you to," Subfar continued, ignoring his brother, "then you can purchase as many companies as you'd like, and they'll provide your sustainable income. It's about taking a large sum of money and making it a larger sum of money."

"It's about getting powerful and taking over," Mama Jamba imparted, listening from her armchair beside Papa Creola's.

Paris gulped, feeling very nervous about this strategy. It was definitely risky. It felt weird too. She had the Protector of Wealth advising her. What could go wrong, she reasoned.

"Okay, so when do we begin?" Paris asked, shaking off the tension in her chest.

"Soon," Subfar answered. "I've installed an investment app on your phone. All you have to do is wait for messages from me. I'll tell you when to buy stocks and transfer the funds to do so to your account. You have to do it exactly when I say. This all depends on the timing of several hundred transactions at precisely the right time. So when you see a message from me, drop everything and do as I instruct, buying or selling exactly the amount I tell you."

Paris nodded, not sure what all this meant but knowing she just had to go with it. "Okay, no matter what, I'll drop what I'm doing and take your message and follow it."

"Unless you're in the john," Mama Jamba offered. "A lady shouldn't be expected to do financial transactions then."

"Right," Paris said, drawing out the word, never surprised at how weird these conversations got.

"Oh, and dear, while I'm thinking about it," Mama Jamba began, smiling at her. "Book an appointment with Jeremy Bearimy at the *Silk Armor*. He books up well in advance, but I told him to fit you in."

"For what?" Paris asked, confused, although it was par for the course at this point.

"For your wedding dress," Mama Jamba answered. "He makes the best dresses of all time."

"Oh, right," Paris said. "I hadn't really thought much on that since I've got to wake up brides all over the place and now be a stockbroker."

"Once you wake up the brides, you're still going to have a

wedding to plan," Mama Jamba informed her. "Since you're not using Terrance, you'll need to start doing some of the work."

"Well, first I have to rescue Terrance," Paris argued. "Then I'm not using him. Maybe I will since I guess I got him abducted."

"He got himself abducted," Papa Creola corrected.

Paris arched an eyebrow at the man. "So he has been taken?"

Mama Jamba shot him a punishing look before glancing at Paris. "No, even after you rescue Terrance, he's not the right one to do your wedding. Oh, but I know who can do your flowers. They are the best in the business, and they've agreed to do them."

"Who?" Paris asked, suddenly excited and intrigued.

Mother Nature grinned and pressed her hand to her chest. "Me, of course."

CHAPTER FORTY

Crying Cat Bakery, Roya Lane, London, United Kingdom

No, the case that Agent Beaufont had given to Sherlock wasn't a murder mystery. It was more like police detective work. Sherlock Holmes also believed it wasn't going to be as straightforward as it seemed. Nor would it be without adventure, investigation, or mystery—all things Sherlock craved.

"I dropped everything and rushed over as soon as I got your call," King Rudolfus Sweetwater said, hurrying into the Crying Cat Bakery, not wearing any pants, his shirt half-buttoned, and his usually perfectly styled hair a mess.

"Were you sleeping?" Sherlock asked the fae, shaking his head and keeping his eyes up so as not to see Rudolf in his boxer shorts, which looked ready to make an accidental reveal.

Rudolf laughed loudly. "Of course not. Look at the time. What kind of bum do you take me for? I was conducting court at the fae headquarters. It's my people's opportunity to tell me their wants, problems, and concerns of all types."

"You were dressed like that?" Sherlock questioned, indicating the less-than-put-together look the fae was sporting.

"Well, no," Rudolf answered. "I was dressed impeccably until some rude fae threw a vat of pig's blood on me and tried to have a fist fight."

"Where were your guards?" Sherlock asked, horrified.

The king laughed. "It was my guards. They wanted a pay increase and said it was overdue and tried to overthrow me using force. I told them if I had to start fearing them, they were definitely out of a job." He scoffed. "They did themselves no favors by acting brutally except to prove that I didn't need them at all. So I fired the lot of them."

"Do you think it's safe for you, a king, to have no guards?" Sherlock asked.

"Absolutely not," Rudolf answered at once. "I'm certain all those guards of mine will want my head after all the names I called them. Not to mention, they know my routine, have keys and access to all the doors in the kingdom, and are all expert fighters."

"You should probably find a small army to replace them," Sherlock advised, glad he didn't have the same problems as the king.

"I'm already on it," Rudolf sang, glancing around the bakery until he located the owner. "Hey, Lee, will you be my personal bodyguard when I'm at my palace?"

"You got it, boss," she replied back at once, saluting.

"Well, there you go," Rudolf said, waving a hand at himself and instantly changing clothes, meaning he was now wearing appropriate attire. It included white cashmere pants and a lavender silk shirt. His hair was fixed perfectly in place like usual.

He snapped back in the direction of the baker. "Oh, and can we get a bottle of brandy and some glasses? My friend and I have business to attend to."

"No," Lee fired back.

Rudolf shrugged, a look on his face like, "Well, it was worth a shot." He pulled out the chair across from Sherlock's and took a seat, eyeing the open files on the table. "So what do we have going on? A string of unsolved homicides? A stealthy burglar who steals priceless gems? An art thief? A national security threat? What delicious mystery do you have for me this time?"

"We have to find a scientist and abduct him," Sherlock answered.

Rudolf turned back to Lee, working behind the bakery case. "Seriously, what do you have to drink back there? My friend here has given up on real work, and we have to mourn the loss of his spirit."

"I'll bring you what I've got," Lee consoled.

"Thanks." King Rudolf spun back to face Sherlock. "So why is it that you've taken this nose dive in your career?"

Sherlock Holmes had only really had one partner—Dr. Watson. He'd had many assist him from time to time. King Rudolf was the closest he had to replacing his friend from so long ago, although they were very different men. There was something refreshing about the seemingly dimwitted fae that brought out Sherlock's genius. It was similar to what Watson had done for him.

"There are no small cases," Sherlock began, spreading out the files so each could be seen fully. "Although some are more complex than others, it's about the end result that solving them will bring that determines its importance."

"You think finding some nerd will be of supreme importance?" Rudolf asked as Lee brought over a bottle of Veuve Clicquot Yellow Label champagne and two paper cups.

"This is all I have," Lee said, putting the open bottle on the table with the cups. "I was saving it for when my wife took another promising fall down the stairs, but she's so sure-footed lately."

"Maybe you should give her the wine," Rudolf suggested.

Lee shook her head. "No, a bottle of champagne is like a starter course at breakfast for her. That wouldn't even have her missing a step. Anyway, enjoy the champagne and if you are looking for a real mystery, find out how an accident-prone woman like her has lived so long."

"Thanks," Rudolf said, waving as a crestfallen Lee strode back to the kitchen of the bakery.

"To answer your question," Sherlock began as Rudolf filled up the paper cups from the bottle of two-hundred-dollar champagne. "I do think the repercussions for solving this case will be of supreme importance. Not only will it lead to saving many innocent women, which is almost like preventing several thousands of needless deaths—"

"So it's like we're stopping the murderer before he strikes," Rudolf said, taking a drink.

"It's like we're stopping him before he succeeds," Sherlock amended. "Also, I think this scientist will lead us to where Terrance is being held. So there will definitely be someone we're rescuing."

"He is an awful human being who annoys me at every turn," Rudolf added. "So maybe we get the scientist, find out how to save the innocent women, but just think of the wedding planner as a necessary casualty."

Sherlock shook his head. "No one dies on my watch. We're going to do everything we can to help Agent Beaufont. I think you know, Rudolf, that when saving others, even when we don't like them, we save a bit of ourselves. For men like you and me, who have a past and demons, we need all the saving we can get."

Rudolf gave him a sober look, despite the cup of champagne he'd drunk and the next he was working on. Finally, he nodded to the files on the table. "Okay, tell me the details of this case and what we're working with."

CHAPTER FORTY-ONE

Advanced Love Department, Level One, Basement, FGA Tower, New York City, New York, United States

"Please give me good news, Squirrel," Paris said, walking into the still empty department space in the basement of the FGA Tower.

"I had a really delicious roasted tomato soup with a grilled cheese, done to perfection," Faraday answered, glancing up from the computer station in the corner where he was working.

Paris glanced at Aunt Alicia, hoping she could be a voice of reason. "Can you explain to the rodent that by good news, I mean things pertaining to the very important projects I have going on and not the success of his meal endeavors?"

"I believe you just did," Alicia answered with a polite smile. "Did you have something to eat? You look to have gotten a bit more of your color back."

"I had a surprisingly good beet muffin, although I lost my appetite when I learned Terrance got abducted."

Faraday looked up from his work suddenly. "Is he okay?"

"Well, his kidnappers are awful because they haven't sent me a status report about how he's doing," Paris answered sarcastically. "So, unfortunately, I can't answer your question."

"Touché," Faraday replied dryly. "It was one of those goons guarding the Snow White Wedding Services booth at the expo, wasn't it?"

"I think so, but I put Sherlock Holmes and Rudolf on the case. They are going to hunt down the scientist behind the Snow White spell, and hopefully, that will lead us to Terrance. Currently, we don't have a way to link Jackson Zelle to anything, so we're going to follow the leads that we do have."

"Shutting down the sleep spell is key," Alicia said. "Unfortunately, there's no way to take down the website. We've tried. You really need the person behind it. It's all protected and by a very crafty programmer who knows his or her stuff."

"Then we also need to fix all the brides who have been spelled before it's too late," Faraday said, typing on the keyboard in front of him. "From my calculations, estimating on how long the website and other media have been out there, spelling brides and then adding in multiple factors...." He hit a series of keys, muttered to himself, and then decisively hit a key. "Yes, I've determined the first victims of Snow White Wedding Services will be falling into irreversible comas within approximately twelve hours, thirty-six minutes, and twelve seconds."

"I'd ask how you came to that rough estimate, but I'm afraid you'd tell me," Paris teased. "I'll trust that you did some math, along with some science, and figured out the point the consciousness of the brides would succumb to the sleeping spell."

"It's fascinating, the formula we used," Faraday began in an excited voice. "Dr. De Luca gave me the idea. You see, if you take the frequency—"

Paris held up her hand, pausing Faraday. "Remember, you already melted my brain once today. Let's just keep it to that."

"I do have good news. We located a junkyard we think will have the part we need to build the device to amplify the signal."

"Junkyard?" Paris asked. "That's where we need to go to get this special magitech?"

"Yeah, it's fenced off and really dangerous due to the levels of radiation."

"You're not selling this like you think you are," Paris joked.

"I can put a protective spell on you two that should last long enough," Alicia offered.

"You're not going?" Paris asked, hoping to have her help.

She shook her head. "I'm going to stay back and work on the device that will project the signal. It won't be complete until we get the programming from the scientist behind the Snow White spell, but everything should be mostly ready since time is of the essence."

"You have to stay to help with the fertility lab," Bermuda Laurens called from a side room, poking her head out like she'd been in the conversation the entire time.

Paris waved. "Hey, Mrs. Laurens. Glad to have you as a neighbor."

"I'm sure," the giantess grumbled before stepping back into the room.

Alicia gave her a guilty look. "This is my first priority, and I'll work on it until I can't do anymore, waiting on the part you two retrieve and the coding. However, I am supposed to help Bermuda with the fertility clinic. It is for me, after all."

"The device to fix brides actually inspired the technology to help Alicia and John," Faraday supplied. "They are building a signal in the fertility lab that broadcasts a frequency. The idea is it should make it so that the mortals and magicians it connects with it will be able to breed while affected by the rays from the signal. Very cool technology, but very experimental."

"That is cool," Paris said. "I hope it works. Thanks for your help on all of this, Aunt Alicia."

"You're welcome," she said. "As a woman who was recently a bride, this is close to my heart. Thankfully I'm not anymore, and I can work on the project without being affected. Still, it makes me angry that someone is targeting those who are so close to making a lifelong commitment to love. It's really, really sad."

"It is, but we're going to stop it." Paris directed her gaze to Faraday. "So, what's the plan?"

"There's this junkyard, and we just have to sneak in there and find a certain part," he explained. "It should be fairly easy. Mostly a scouting project."

"Okay, break into a radiation-filled junkyard and find a magitech part." Paris clapped her hands together. "I'm ready to go."

"No, you're not," Faraday stated, looking around. "You need to go and get your wand from Clark."

Paris glanced down. She'd forgotten she'd loaned Amantis to her uncle to help with the renovation magic. She did feel naked without it all of a sudden. "Why is it that I need my wand? I thought you said this was easy."

"We do have to sneak into the junkyard," Faraday explained.

"Oh, and there's the radiation," Paris guessed.

"I'll put a spell on you to protect you from that," Alicia offered.

"It's more about the things in the junkyard," Faraday said in a squeaky voice. "The fences that section it off aren't just to keep people out."

Paris lowered her chin, regarding the squirrel with hooded eyes. "What else are they for?"

"To keep the junk inside the yard," he answered. "The radiation made it come alive."

CHAPTER FORTY-TWO

Crying Cat Bakery, Roya Lane, London, United Kingdom

Sherlock Holmes had thoroughly reviewed the three candidates Agent Beaufont had given him for the potential scientists. King Rudolf had merely glanced at them and then played on his phone while polishing off the expensive bottle of champagne.

Finally, having come to a conclusion, Sherlock lowered the stack of files and glanced across the table at the fae. "Well, I know who we need to go after."

"Me too," Rudolf squealed, his voice higher pitched now he was buzzed. "You go first and tell me everything. Tell me how you arrived at the conclusion and all your detecting details. I like to learn how your brain works."

"We only had these three files to go off," Sherlock began, spreading out the reports on three very different men. "Faraday believed these candidates are the only ones qualified to create the sleep spell using magitech, which I'll admit is a very specific discipline."

"Speaking of sleep," Rudolf began, trying to get every last drop out of the champagne bottle. "My wife Serena keeps coming to bed all stressed. I tell her it's our special place and not to bring her problems to bed. She then looks at me and says, 'Where are you going to sleep then?'"

Sherlock Holmes regarded the man for a long moment before plowing on with his explanation. "As I was saying, I reviewed the files, keeping in mind the three things that had to be the common denominators for our scientist. Someone who is motivated to create a spell that targets brides. Someone who will work for Jackson Zelle. Then someone who is obsessed with fairytales. From there, after reviewing the files, I believe I figured out who created the Snow White sleeping spell based on that personality profile."

King Rudolf put both elbows on the table and leaned forward, looking interested. "You really thought this through. I love how your brain works. Tell me more."

"Well, knowing it had to be someone who was willing to target brides, I looked for a single bachelor out of the candidates," Sherlock started, indicating the files. "Of the magitech sleep experts, there are two who are single. That meant the one who was married, and it appears happily, didn't qualify to conduct such a project."

"Good. I like your reasoning. Although my wife is seemingly happily married, and she'd have me asleep all the time if the pills she slipped me worked."

Sherlock wasn't sure if the fae was joking or not and worried he wasn't. Again, he decided to ignore him. "As I was saying, the other factor is a personality that would work for Jackson Zelle. These résumés were taken from candidates applying for the IT and operations director position at the FGA. Only a certain type of person would allow themselves to be taken to the other side based on Zelle Corp's obviously sinister agenda."

"Was there a clear winner from that criteria?" Rudolf asked.

Sherlock shook his head. "Humans are tricky, and of the remaining candidates, either one could be swayed in that regard. They both appeared to need the money, which is a strong motivator. They both wanted a high-level position, so that doesn't help."

"So, how did you arrive at your conclusion then?"

"Well, like I said, the last factor was they used the Snow White theme," Sherlock explained. "I found that one of our candidates was obsessed with the science of sleep and things related to lucid dreaming."

Rudolf nodded, fascinated. "Interesting."

"The other one is mostly interested in robots," Sherlock went on.

"Well, how can you make an educated decision based on that?"

Sherlock held up a triumphant finger. "It was a small detail hidden away in one of their profiles." He picked up the file closest to him and read from an article about the candidate. "*Dr. Jessie Raven's robotics team came in first at the national tournament, making it their third decisive win. Snow White's Dwarves appear to be unstoppable.*"

"So we're dealing with a bunch of shorties," Rudolf stated, narrowing his eyes. "We'll have to keep our gazes low and our shins covered."

"The reference," Sherlock said. "That's why I think it's Dr. Jessie Raven we need to go after."

"Oh!" Rudolf exclaimed. "Well, you're exactly right. He's our nerdy guy and the one we have to go after. He's on the run and definitely going through a whole crisis over what he's done."

"Wait, you already figured out it was him?" Sherlock asked, blinking at the fae. "What do you mean he's on the run? What crisis?"

Rudolf motioned to the files. "It was too much reading for me. So I put those three names into the world wide web to see what our geeks were up to now. According to Facebook, the married guy just went on a boring cruise with his wife. Seriously, people, get an imagination when it comes to vacation."

Sherlock sucked in a breath, wondering if the fae had bested him yet again on this puzzle. "Continue."

"Then the other candidate is currently celebrating signing a book deal about a sleep study he conducted on lucid dreams," Rudolf answered. "Our third guy, his mother reported him missing two days ago."

"What?" Sherlock asked, leaning even farther forward.

"So it goes to reason that's the one who is behind this Snow White business. He went into cahoots with Jackson Zelle. Created a sleep spell for him. Then being the sad romantic he is, but living with his mother and having only the kids at the robotic school to keep him going, he started to have doubts. He was too far in to cut the cord on the project, and Jackson Zelle is too powerful and is a man who will kidnap horrid wedding planners, so they can't mess with him. Therefore Jessie Raven decided to disappear. Consequently, not only do we have to find a scientist, but we have to find one who's on the run."

Sherlock stared ahead for a long moment, shocked the fae had figured all that out and better than him. He was right. "That's it."

"Or maybe Jackson Zelle killed him, and we're screwed as far as solutions go," Rudolf added. "The only bonus to that is we can't rescue Terrance then, and he'll die. Oh well."

"No, Dr. Jessie Raven is out there," Sherlock said. "Jackson Zelle needs him. Based on what you've said and what I've read, it all makes complete sense." He started flipping through the closest file before he looked up. "It fits Jessie's personality. He's a runner. So he started the project but got in over his head, and then he wanted out. He saw what Jackson Zelle was capable of and took off, afraid of what he was doing and being a part of."

"Now we've got to track down our nerd," King Rudolf declared. "Where do we start? At the arcade? Library? Star Wars convention?"

Sherlock Holmes shook his head. "No, you always start with the places closest to a runaway. Those who run always go home."

CHAPTER FORTY-THREE

Outer Limits Junkyard, Nicholson, Alabama, United States

"You always take me to the nicest places," Paris joked as she and Faraday stood outside of a large fenced-in junkyard. The nine-foot steel enclosure was covered in barbed wire at the top, and portaling inside the boundary wasn't going to work.

"Isn't this so exciting?" Faraday asked, sitting on the top of a rusted-out barrel beside the tree trunk where Paris was stationed, hiding. The shade of the tree and the camouflaging spell helped to shield their presence from the patrolling guards. However, it was very likely the magitech security could see past the spell, so they couldn't take any chances. They'd very soon learn the capabilities of these guards.

"I don't think exciting is the word I'd choose," Paris said, studying the huge area that stretched over two dozen acres. "So what happened to this place? Why is it off limits?"

"Besides the high levels of radiation?" Faraday asked.

"Yeah, besides that." Paris looked around at the metal fence covered in graffiti and scorch marks in places. Behind it, there were towers of old rusted appliances, cars, and transportation of every sort piled high. To add to the charm, flies buzzed in several places, and the area smelled of swamp water and sweat.

"It's fascinating," Faraday began. "There was a scientist who set up his laboratory and home in the center of a junkyard—"

"Some pine for a beachfront view," Paris cut in. "Some want to live in a cul-de-sac. Or the country or in a high rise. No one ever talks about the perfectly sane and reasonable scientist whose dream is to live in the center of a junkyard."

Faraday snickered. "This guy was definitely insane. He was always tampering with electromagnetic radiation, trying to harness its energy."

"I'm guessing he didn't succeed," Paris muttered, watching as an old beat-up truck passed on the nearly abandoned road in the middle of nowhere in Alabama. Paris had always heard that Alabama was charming with its Southern hospitality and the Appalachian Mountains stretching to the northeast. She wasn't crossing off this possibility, but this backwoods part of the state that Faraday had dragged her to definitely didn't have the charm she was hoping for.

Faraday shook his head. "He thought he had everything he needed to contain the radiant energy. Not having calculated for several factors, he released a blast here, and it spread out in all directions, hitting everything in the junkyard, dosing it in huge amounts of radiation."

"Then what happened?"

"Well, the authorities swept in, fenced the area off, and found it unsafe for several reasons," Faraday explained. "What's in there can't get out. Otherwise, we'd be in big trouble."

"So, it's like its own Chernobyl, then?" Paris questioned. "Why haven't I ever heard of this place? Outer Limits Junkyard."

"Chernobyl was huge and affected a much larger area," Faraday said. "We've also learned from that incident that containment is key. The authorities couldn't risk any leaks here. They covered the whole thing up so that no one tried to sneak in there to treasure hunt."

"Which is exactly what we're going to do," Paris pointed out.

"What I need is in there, and I can't find it anywhere else. Also, our purposes are noble," Faraday argued. "Although the junkyard is dangerous with its high levels of radiation, it's also a treasure trove of incredible and one-of-a-kind magitech. Much like Chernobyl, the radiation did strange and wonderful things to the junkyard.

"Okay, so how do we get in there? Make a hole in the fence?" Paris asked.

Faraday shook his head. "That fence is meant to contain the radiation, so it's important we don't break it."

"Which means we have to get over it and bypass security without any damage or commotion? That sounds difficult."

The security consisted of drones that circled overhead, watching the perimeter. Mounted on the top of the small black drones were lasers. On the larger ones, there were guns. Paris thought they were probably programmed to shoot first and ask questions later.

"There's got to be a way in there," Faraday mumbled, thinking as he scanned the area ahead of them. "I mean, I'm a squirrel, so for me, it would be somewhat simple to find a way in. I'm going to need your help to harvest these parts, though."

"That gives me a brilliant idea of how to get in there."

He looked up at her with bright wide eyes, his curiosity piqued. Before she could explain, there was a rustling noise behind them. Tensing, they both turned, hoping it was who they were expecting and not a robot guard meant to shoot on sight.

"Hey, it's me," Aunt Alicia said, hurrying out of the thick set of trees behind them. She had on a camouflaging spell too, but they could see her, not affected by it.

"What did you find?" Faraday asked.

"The entire perimeter is heavily guarded by patrolling drones," she answered with a look of disappointment on her face.

"Was there any part of the fence that didn't look as secure?" Faraday asked.

Alicia shook her head. "They have this place locked down. For good reason. I spied just a little bit of activity on the other side of the fence when I was exploring, and the things in there, they are dangerous."

"Great, let's go junk picking," Paris chimed in with a smile.

"What we need to amplify the signal is in there," Faraday argued. "I don't know anywhere else to find these parts. I definitely can't create them. Not in time, anyway."

"Well, we can't have any women falling into comas, so time is a priority," Paris agreed. "It's bad enough what this is doing to the love meter. Losing people would be much worse."

"Then we have to go in there," Faraday declared.

"How?" Alicia asked, sounding hopeless. "I didn't see a way for a human to get past the drones and over the fence."

"Did you see a way for a squirrel?" Paris asked.

"Well, yes," she answered. "There were a few places where there were holes at the bottom of the fence. I'm guessing the authorities don't care about the wildlife getting in. Sadly, if any squirrels or mice or rats went in there, they wouldn't survive the radiation for long."

"You're going to put a protective spell on us," Paris said.

"It's not going to do you any good if you can't get in there."

"Well, what if I was a squirrel too?" Paris asked, a clever grin on her face.

Faraday's eyes widened. Alicia's mouth popped open.

"That's brilliant," Faraday gushed in disbelief.

"Can you do it?" Paris asked her aunt. "Put the protective radiation spell on and make me a squirrel? Nothing permanent like Faraday."

"Yes," Alicia said. "You won't be able to maintain it for very long."

"I don't need to," Paris remarked. "Just long enough to get through the fence. Then I can pop into human form and help Faraday get the part."

"I think that could work," Alicia mused, thinking. "From what I can tell, the guards are around the perimeter. The drones don't seem concerned with what's happening inside. Just with keeping what's outside out."

"If you spring into human form, how are you going to get back out of the junkyard?" Faraday asked.

"That I will figure out when the time comes," Paris said. She sounded reactionary when usually her style was to be strategic and proactive. They were running out of time.

Thankfully, Alicia and Faraday didn't dismiss her idea immediately.

The woman nodded, seeming to agree with the notion.

Faraday combed his paw over his chest. "It could work."

"The drones are concerned with keeping things out of the junkyard," Alicia said. "The things in there probably aren't trying to get out. Not anymore, anyway."

Paris smiled, grateful they had a plan. She gave her Aunt Alicia a sturdy look. "Okay, then. Make me into a squirrel."

CHAPTER FORTY-FOUR

Annedroid's Robotic Academy, Salt Lake City, Utah, United States

There were three possible places Sherlock Holmes thought that Dr. Jessie Raven would have run to after fleeing from Jackson Zelle and his corporation. The scientist had two part-time jobs and lived with his mother.

The first job involved working evenings as a robotics instructor with elementary and middle school kids. Since he had an advanced magitech degree, he led the competitive team that trained and went to robotic tournaments. That's where Sherlock Holmes learned the information that made him believe Dr. Jessie Raven was the scientist behind the sleep spell.

His team of kids, who had won the last few championships, were called Snow White's Dwarves. The detective pictured it as a team, composed of a bunch of geeky boys who would probably go on to run the free world.

Surprisingly, the robotic school called Annedroid's Robotic Academy was located in a busy strip mall. Often stuck in the past, it sometimes caught Sherlock by surprise how the most scientifically advanced things in modern culture were adjacent to everyday things.

A robotics academy seemed like it should be in a fancy skyscraper or on the campus of an Ivy League school. Instead, Annedroid's Robotic Academy was situated in between an Italian restaurant and a dry cleaner. The detective thought busy parents liked the convenience of one-stop shopping. They could pick up their dry cleaning, their child from training, and a pizza for dinner and only get out of the car once.

"So what's the plan?" King Rudolf asked, leaning against a building. They were across the street beside a sports bar and grill, checking out the academy from a distance. It was enough space to get a lay of the land but far enough away from the other side of the busy four-lane road.

"We need to go in there and question the staff and students," Sherlock began, scanning the area around the parking lot, full of cars and bustling shoppers. His eyes paused on a set of strange figures that stood out. He watched the three figures stationed in different parts of the shopping area.

"Do you think anyone will talk to us?" Rudolf asked.

"People in these situations never want to talk," Sherlock answered. "They are either guilty and therefore withholding for that reason. Or they are innocent and paranoid and therefore withholding. Or they are both guilty in some ways but innocent overall, and so they lie. Our job is to ask questions and observe, knowing that most likely we're not getting honest information."

"You're good at this," Rudolf said proudly.

"I have experience."

The king of the fae nodded in the direction of a man in all black, wearing an earpiece and a studious expression on his brutish-looking face. "What do you make of those guys?"

Sherlock pointed to the other two men in black suits stationed around the shopping area. "He and his companions match the description Paris gave me of the goons at the wedding expo."

"Their attention is on the robotics academy," Rudolf observed. "I bet it's not because they have kids that are attending."

Sherlock shook his head. "I think it's a good indication that we picked the right scientist and location. Dr. Jessie Raven fled from the Snow White project and Zelle Corp, and I'm guessing Jackson Zelle wants him back."

"Or he wants to ensure that Dr. Raven doesn't talk," Rudolf supplied.

"Or that Paris doesn't get to him," Sherlock added.

"Well, that's exactly what's going to happen," Rudolf said. "If those goons are watching the robotics academy, then we can't just walk in there and ask questions. That will raise their suspicions."

The detective nodded. "Yes, we're going to need a distraction."

King Rudolf grinned. "In my experience, distractions usually cause suspicions because they cause a disruption. Instead, people don't pay attention to that which blends in and just seems normal."

"The king of the fae and a famous detective walking into a robotics academy definitely isn't normal," Sherlock said.

Rudolf nodded, brandishing a toothy grin. "A couple picking up their kiddo from a school in the suburbs, well, that's totally normal."

Sherlock regarded the other man like he'd lost his mind. "You don't mean that we should…Are you serious?"

"Of course I'm serious." Rudolf put his arm around Sherlock, pulling him in close. "I think we make an adorable couple."

CHAPTER FORTY-FIVE

Outer Limits Junkyard, Nicholson, Alabama, United States

Paris squeezed her eyes shut, scrunching her nose. Anxiety and fear bounced around in her chest, and as hard as she tried, she couldn't push them away. Springing her eyes open, she held up her hands. "Wait, don't it yet."

Aunt Alicia, who was deep in concentration, lowered her hand. "Are you okay?"

"Yeah, it's just that whole not wanting to be stuck as a squirrel forever like some people."

"She means me," Faraday said, flicking his tail.

Paris shot him an annoyed look. "I think we all know who I meant, although you're not a people anymore. That's what I want to avoid."

"I'll remind you that I used advanced and powerful magic coupled with time travel," Faraday explained. "That's how I got stuck as a squirrel."

"Yeah, but it's advanced magic for Alicia to turn me into a squirrel," Paris argued. "What if something goes wrong and I can't turn back on my own?"

"Paris, I'm mostly doing a disguising spell," Alicia said,

offering her a sympathetic look. "It's more like camouflage, although you will be small, that's only because I'm coupling it with a compartmentalizing spell. You will still be you, and although it will appear that you have a tail and paws, you won't."

"Okay, so it's just a disguise," Paris said, taking a steadying breath. "That helps."

Faraday crossed his tiny squirrel arms, giving her a look of frustration. "This was your idea."

"Yeah, and it's just that Aunt Sophia does amazing disguises and transfigurations," Paris said and then quickly added, "It's not that you're not great, Aunt Alicia."

"I don't have her skill for sure," she said, not at all offended.

"Yeah, she changes Lunis into creatures all the time," Paris said, having heard the recent story of how the large blue dragon became a blue arctic fox when they went to recover Subner's sword.

"You don't have to worry," Alicia said. "I'm not doing anything quite so advanced. It's a good idea you had and will work as far as I can tell."

Paris nodded, chewing on her lip. "Yeah, I hadn't thought it through when I mentioned it, thinking it would be a true transformation. You're smart to do it as a disguise."

"A true transformation is complicated," Faraday explained. "Things can inevitably go wrong. Keep in mind, there were many complex factors associated with why I couldn't turn back, one being that I didn't have magic in this form."

"You'll still have your magic," Alicia told Paris. "Again, I'm just shrinking you and, in essence, putting a very real squirrel suit on you."

"That sounds adorable, actually," Paris related with a smile, relaxing. She closed her eyes as she drew in a calming breath. "Okay, I'm ready. Shrink me and suit me up."

CHAPTER FORTY-SIX

Annedroids Robotic Academy, Salt Lake City, Utah, United States

"I think that blue is your color," King Rudolf said, pursing his lips at Sherlock Holmes and regarding him with an appraising eye.

Sherlock picked up the blue scarf hanging around his neck and regarded it. Rudolf had magicked them some accessories to sell their disguises. "I'm not sure this is necessary."

"Of course it is," Rudolf insisted. "That tweed suit screams 'straight man.'"

"That's what I am," Sherlock said dryly.

"Well, we have to go and pick up little Billy from the robotics academy," Rudolf explained. "Those goons are going to think we're detectives looking for the same person they are unless we sell this persona. So either you embrace who Preston is, or you don't get to do your investigating."

"Preston?"

"That's your name," Rudolf told him, pressing his hand to his chest. He was now wearing a fluffy faux white fur coat and big sunglasses. "I'm Remington, but you call me Remy. Cute, huh?"

"Adorable," Sherlock said dryly, nodding in the direction of the robotics academy. "We just have to cross this street and enter that school. I'm just not sure that all this is necessary."

"If you were Sherlock Holmes, then you would march across the street looking competent and eager to get answers," Rudolf explained. "Those men, who are stationed looking around, surveying everyone who goes near that academy, would rush over and apprehend you. I can guarantee that. However, follow my lead, and they are going to dismiss you so quickly, and we'll have answers they could never get. No one wants to talk to men in black suits with earpieces." He scoffed. "Dumb goons. I bet they are the ones who abducted Terrance. I'd commend them for it if it wasn't immoral and I wasn't against such things."

"Okay, let's get going," Sherlock encouraged, holding out his arm to the road, which was momentarily clear.

Without permission, Rudolf wrapped his arm around Sherlock's and paraded him across the road. He smiled wide and sauntered like they were walking down a modeling runway.

With his other arm, he gestured broadly in the air. "I don't care what you say, darling. I won't have a cheetah print couch. The last one didn't hide any stains."

"Cheetah print couch?" Sherlock asked quietly.

"Just go with it," Rudolf said between clenched teeth. "They are watching."

Sherlock cut his eyes to the three goons stationed around the shopping area, watching. They did, in fact, have their eyes pinned on the couple crossing the road. "Well, if you insist, dear."

"I do," Rudolf said loudly, drawing out the last word. "After we get Billy from robo-camp, I think we should go get sushi. I've got a hankering for a California roll. I know it's not real sushi, but I don't care."

"Whatever you want, dear." Sherlock cut his eyes to the closest goon. He was watching their every move as he spoke into the earpiece.

"I want to go to that cute little place in Sugar House," Rudolf continued as they reached the curb.

"No!" Sherlock barked, noticing the goon tense as they neared the robotics academy. Halting, the detective turned to Rudolf Sweetwater. "We're going to that hole-in-the-wall place I like in Rose Park, and I don't want to hear another word about it."

Rudolf widened his eyes at Sherlock as if surprised he'd challenge them during their fake domestic fight. His eyes slid to the side, catching sight of the goon over Sherlock's shoulder. Finally, he softened and nodded. "Okay, dear. If that's what you want. That's what we'll do."

"Good," Sherlock said, pivoting and continuing to the storefront.

"It worked," Rudolf whispered. "I read the goon's lips, and he just said into his earpiece, 'Ignore them. It's just a couple bickering.'"

Sherlock smiled proudly to himself, surprised the tactic worked. It just proved he had something he could learn about detective work from the king of the fae.

CHAPTER FORTY-SEVEN

Outer Limits Junkyard, Nicholson, Alabama, United States

Thankfully it didn't hurt at all when Aunt Alicia used the shrinking spell on Paris. The disguising one felt like she was wrapped in bubble wrap, and a funny hat was placed on her head.

All at once, Paris' view changed. She'd gone from several feet high in the air to all of a sudden a few inches off the ground. It was a weird vantage point but also humbling.

"This is how you see the world?" Paris asked, looking around and feeling like the world was a much larger place all of a sudden. The junkyard seemed like its own country.

"You get used to it," Faraday said, looking at her from straight on. "It's good for my brain because I see things differently and therefore more scientifically."

"That makes sense," Alicia offered with a smile before looking directly at Paris. "How do you feel?"

She shook out her arms beside her, and they felt like they always did. When she flexed her fingers, it was her clawed paws that responded in front of her face. "This is weird."

"You don't really have claws, so don't try using them," Faraday offered.

Turning around, Paris took in the sight of the brown bushy tail behind her, but only briefly because it turned with her. "Now that's odd. I have a tail."

"Well, again, not really," Faraday corrected. "You just appear to have a tail. You're still you, just wearing a very real squirrel costume."

"So weird," Paris said, hoping this worked after all the effort and risks they were taking.

"Okay, so are you ready?" Faraday asked, indicating the drones patrolling the perimeter with their weapons mounted on top. "We'll run out and gauge if they take notice. I suspect they won't. Then we'll continue to the fence. Remember, you don't have claws, so I'll dig us a hole."

"You can do that?" Paris questioned. "I've never seen you so much as a bury a nut."

"Because I'm allergic," he reminded her. "I'm still a squirrel, and I have the claws and the ability, and I'm good at it. So yes, I can do it. Then we'll squeeze under the fence, and we'll be in."

"Okay," Paris said, letting out a breath.

"I'll be here in case you run into any problems," Alicia offered. "Remember, the radiation protection spell will only last a couple of hours. If you are in there too long, you'll be in danger of radiation poisoning."

"We will be fast. Just get in, turn back to normal, and then we'll find the part. What could go wrong?"

"We are going into a junkyard hit with a blast of electromagnetism where everything is now alive," Faraday said quite seriously. "So just about everything can go wrong."

CHAPTER FORTY-EIGHT

Annedroids Robotic Academy, Salt Lake City, Utah, United States

The robotics academy wasn't what Sherlock Holmes had expected. In truth, he didn't know what one would be like, never having been in such a place.

The area was full of tables with equipment for building and bringing robots to life. Not being well acquainted with this branch of modern science, the detective ignored the parts of the school he didn't understand. What Sherlock understood was humans, and so he focused on them.

Sitting around the various tables and chatting and building were children between the ages of ten and thirteen. Directly in front of the door was the main workstation, which also appeared to be the instructor's desk. Behind him was a woman with a messy bun of brown hair wearing goggles. She looked up and snorted at the sight of them.

"Who are you?" she asked, looking over their strange accessories. In contrast, the woman was wearing a plain white t-shirt, and from under the desk, Sherlock spied Converse shoes. Although the woman was probably in her mid to late twenties, she appeared to be dressed much like the kids in a t-shirt and jeans and unkempt hair.

"We're the Harpers," Rudolf said, not dropping the act.

However, Sherlock had assessed the situation and knew their disguises weren't necessary here. It had gotten them through the door. Now was the time to get answers.

He pulled off the blue scarf and wadded it up. "We're detectives, and we're looking for information on Dr. Jessie Raven."

At the mention of this name, many of the kids looked up and over.

The woman pulled her goggles off and waved the kids away. "Get the coding right on those sumo robots. We're starting the competition rounds soon."

She stood and pressed her hands down on the desk in front of her. It was filled with building blocks for robots, gears, electronics, and tools. "You and everyone else. Are you with those meatheads out there?" She nodded in the direction of the door where the goons were stationed.

"No, we're with the good guys and here to help Dr. Jessie Raven, but we can only do that if we know where he is." Rudolf snapped his fingers, and the white fur coat disappeared along with the sunglasses.

The woman raised an eyebrow. "You've got magic, just like Jessie."

"He was a magician," Sherlock stated. "You're not?"

"I work at a robot academy for kids," the woman spat. "What do you think?"

"Jessie worked here," Rudolf argued.

"Jessie worked here for those guys." She nodded in the direction of the kids at the table.

"Snow White's Dwarves," Sherlock Holmes said in a low voice.

She appeared surprised again. "You've done your homework."

"It's my job to do my homework."

"Did you hear that, guys?" the woman asked loudly to the kids, who were pretending to work but were clearly eavesdropping on the adult's conversation. "The nice detectives like doing their homework."

"I bet they don't have to memorize the names of all the US Presidents," one of the kids grumbled.

"I remember all of them, in the order I met them," Rudolf replied.

The woman spun back to face them, again surprised. "You're very strange detectives."

"Indeed," Sherlock agreed. "Who are you, and how did you know Dr. Jessie Raven?"

She pointed to a sign behind her workstation. "I'm Annie of Annedroid's Robotics Academy. Jessie was one of my best instructors. It's because of him that I got this retail space. More importantly, he took the kids to nationals the last three years and won first."

"You knew he was a magician," Rudolf said. "Did he employ magitech with his robots? Is that how he won?"

Annie shook her head. "Absolutely not. That's strictly against the rules. He always played by the rules."

Rudolf and Sherlock exchanged curious looks that didn't go unnoticed by Annie.

"He used magitech at his university job," Annie continued. "I always thought it would get him in trouble. I told him that. There are just some things that don't mix."

"University job?" Rudolf asked. "What can you tell us about that?"

"Well, I couldn't pay him enough," Annie answered, seeming to be trying to help. That part bothered Sherlock, but he needed more information. "So he had to get a job working in the sleep labs at the university. Even then, it wasn't enough."

"That's why he took the job with Zelle Corp," Sherlock said, waiting for the woman's reaction.

"Yeah, I guess," the woman said nonchalantly.

"Are you aware that Dr. Jessie Raven is missing, and that's why those men are out there?" Sherlock asked, pointing at the parking area and watching carefully for her reaction.

She pursed her lips, her eyes skipping to the side. "Those men are—"

"Raven isn't missing!" one of the kids exclaimed from the table.

"What?" Annie asked, her eyes wide.

"Yeah, what?" Rudolf asked curiously, turning to face the kids.

"He's with the other robots in the back," another kid offered.

"Of course he isn't," Annie said, shaking her head.

"Yeah, he is," the first kid said. "I'll go get him." He ran for the back excitedly. "Just wait until you see. He's the coolest!"

Sherlock and Rudolf again exchanged looks, both undoubtedly taking very different notes about the same situation.

CHAPTER FORTY-NINE

Outer Limits Junkyard, Nicholson, Alabama, United States

Following Faraday's lead, Paris took off across the dirt field between where they'd been stationed and the fence around the Outer Limits Junkyard. The squirrel halted, looking up at the sky. The drones were doing their rounds, and she knew Faraday was checking to see if they'd alerted them. The fake birds in the sky didn't pause. They kept on their patrols.

"Come on," Faraday urged in a whisper over his shoulder.

Paris nodded, feeling stranger than ever before, standing only a few inches high and carrying a tail behind her. She was pretty certain Faraday would tease her incessantly about this one at some point. She'd call him a squirrel, and he'd reply, "Takes one to know one." Sadly, he'd be right. It was humbling to be so small.

Ahead of her, Faraday dropped his front legs and bounded forward several feet. Paris followed. After several paces, he paused again, this time turning around to face her instead of checking on the drones.

"Do you think they are onto us?" Paris asked, looking around but not seeing any drones in the vicinity.

"No, but they will be if you don't shape up," he warned. "They are manned by a real person, looking through the camera. Your behavior screams, 'I'm not a squirrel.'"

Paris glanced down at her figure, which from her vantage point was covered in short brown hair. She blinked up at the squirrel. "What do you mean?"

"When have you ever known a squirrel to walk about like *homo erectus* on two feet?"

"Oh," Paris groaned, realizing she was walking like a human instead of scampering around on all fours how she was used to seeing Faraday. "Right."

Willing herself to fall forward, Paris' paws met the dirt, and she looked up, feeling like her butt was in the air, but she just looked like a squirrel. "Like this?"

"Now, just follow me and try not to look strange."

As Paris followed after Faraday to the fence, it was hard not to think she looked weird. She might have appeared to be a squirrel to others, walking on all fours. To her, she was on her hands and feet and walking like she was impersonating an animal. It felt very strange.

As the drones made their rounds, Paris was grateful not to be spotted. They just kept going on rotation.

When they came to the fence, it felt like they'd been traveling for a long time. Paris reasoned she didn't normally, or ever, travel on all fours, so the journey seemed longer.

At the fence, Faraday went to work digging, making fast work of throwing the dirt out and making a hole.

Paris glanced up at the sky, noticing a drone with lasers on its top passing over. It paused just above them and did a full rotation as though it had caught sight of something of interest.

"Fare," Paris whispered. "The drone."

He glanced up. Noticed the drone taking special interest in them. "Dig around in that patch of grass."

"It's suspicious because you're digging under the fence," she hissed.

"Squirrels dig," he countered. "What squirrels don't do is stand around and watch the other one dig. Now, look like a squirrel."

Paris sighed but did as she was told, leaping into the patch of grass close by and scratching around as if trying to find a nut or something. It was a very odd experience, but she was grateful it worked when the drone moved on after a moment, apparently being fooled.

Faraday dove for the deep hole he'd tunneled under the fence. "I'm almost through."

Paris glanced to the skies, keeping a watch for the drone. She was starting to feel tingly all over. That's when she remembered what Aunt Alicia had said about the spell.

She jerked her head in the direction where the magitech scientist was stationed. Alicia was staring straight at them, and she was frantically pointing at her watch.

"Fare…" Paris said, her tone coated in doubt.

"Yeah," he said, his voice muffled by the dirt tunnel.

"I need you to hurry."

"Why? Are you tired of poking around in the grass? Welcome to my world, Squirrel."

"Touché," she replied, feeling tingly now. "It's just the spell is wearing off. I'm about to spring back into human form before getting to the other side of the fence and right out here in the open."

The sound of the drone circling back around brought her attention up.

"Oh, and the drone is back."

CHAPTER FIFTY

Annedroids Robotic Academy, Salt Lake City, Utah, United States

Something wasn't adding up, Sherlock realized as he studied Annie's worried face. She was showing real concern for the first time, and then there were the excited kids. He glanced over his shoulder to ensure the goons weren't watching through the windows in case Dr. Jessie Raven appeared in the open. He was a man Jackson Zelle wanted, and when he surfaced, he'd be hunted. Paris needed this man to stop the Snow White sleeping spell, and that's exactly what was going to happen.

The children all cheered when a motorized sound erupted from the back room and a small robot with bird-like features marched through the opening. The kids, along with King Rudolf Sweetwater, all laughed as the robot cawed and then fluttered its wings, seemingly trying to take flight.

Annie choked on a laugh. "Oh, that Raven. I thought he was broken and not working anymore."

"Did you think I was going to get out the real Raven?" The boy who had gotten the robot materialized in the doorway.

"Well, yeah," Annie replied. "He's not working, is he?" Her question sounded very pointed.

"Not since the competition," another boy supplied.

"What's the real Raven?" Sherlock asked, his tone neutral but his interest piqued.

"I'll show you," one of the kids offered. They ran over and grabbed Sherlock's hand without his permission and hauled him toward the back. Again, Sherlock was being paraded places and handled by others touching him. Things had shifted in his life since joining forces with the FGA and Paris Beaufont and her strange friends.

"No, don't," Annie said, trailing after them, but the kid was fast and had dragged Sherlock to the back room quickly.

They halted in a crowded back room full of equipment and old parts and robots.

The kid pointed to a life-sized robot that looked raven-like. It was like a big version of the small robot they'd brought out. "That's the real Raven."

"That's the one they built to win nationals," Annie said, sounding breathless as she caught up with them.

"Why did you say for us not to come back here?" Rudolf asked, looking around the space.

"Because look how messy it is," Annie answered casually. "Since Raven left, I haven't had the help to tidy up. The kids aren't really dwarves who do chores or go to the coal mines or anything."

"We build awesome robots," one of the kids said, smiling up at her.

She ruffled his head with a grin of her own. "That you do. You do it well. Now get back to it, the lot of you. Sumo competitions start in two minutes."

The kids all yelled and ran back to the front.

When it was just the three adults, Sherlock cleared his throat as he looked around the space. "So the kids, they are okay without Dr. Raven?"

Annie shrugged. "We manage."

"Are you worried?" Rudolf asked. "He went to Zelle Corp and then disappeared."

Again another shrug. "Those meatheads hang around here all the time, watching us. I don't know what type of trouble Raven got himself into there. I wished he hadn't brought it here. That's all."

Sherlock nodded, studying the space and making special notes. "Okay, well, good luck with the tournaments. Thank you for your time. We'll be in touch if we find out anything about Dr. Raven."

"Okay," Annie said casually, ushering them back to the front, not at all concerned for a man who had been very involved in her business at one point.

CHAPTER FIFTY-ONE

Outer Limits Junkyard, Nicholson, Alabama, United States

"Hurry, hurry, hurry," Paris urged, feeling the tingling turning into a more intense sensation. She'd never been shrunk and then had to regrow back to normal size, but she knew enough about magic to infer this meant she was about to bound back to her regular form.

"I'm trying," Faraday said, choking on dirt, it sounded like. "I just have a little bit more until I poke through to the other side."

Paris pretended to hunt around in the pile of grass beside her, but her focus was mostly on the drone overhead. She willed for it to move on just in case she transformed right then. She didn't want to be shot with lasers then or any other day. Especially not after already having her brain melted. It had been a long day, she realized.

The drone hovered in place for a moment, going in one direction as if reevaluating a space and then going back the other way. Paris jerked her eyes to where Aunt Alicia was stationed and hoped she hadn't been spotted there.

"I'm through," Faraday said through a mouthful of dirt.

"Good," Paris said with relief, looking down at her squirrel body. "Let me get through before I'm huge again and can't fit through."

"I'm just crawling through to the other side to make sure it's wide enough for you," Faraday said, his voice sounding clearer. He must be on the ground on the other side of the junkyard.

"What do I do?" Paris asked, hopping up and running over to the hole he'd made. It was a tiny little tunnel. It was weird to think she'd fit through it, but she should, at least for another several seconds or hopefully a minute, in case they needed it. The last thing she needed was to get stuck.

"Just dive in and use your front feet to pull you through and your back feet to push you all the way," he instructed.

"You mean my hands," she laughed, sucking in a breath as if she was about to dive into a pool of water. Then she dipped her head into the hole, and just as he said, she wiggled and squirmed through the hole he'd made under the fence. The radiation protection Alicia had put on them was keeping them from getting poisoned. Her hands were helping to get her to the other side, but it was taking a lot of work.

"Use your feet," Faraday urged.

Paris was grateful for the reminder because, just then, she felt herself growing.

"No, no, no," she said in a rush, kicking so hard she felt like she was breaking up big bits of sand with her heels.

Paris erupted out the other side of the hole and jumped over the top just as she became her normal size.

"Pull sheet metal over us," Faraday urged as she rolled to her feet, indicating a piece of metal by the fence.

Not even thinking, just following orders, she did as she was told. Grabbing the piece of metal lying against the fence, Paris hauled it sideways and pulled it over her and Faraday like a blanket, shielding them just as a drone cruised overhead.

Paris couldn't see what it was doing, but she expected her kicking up the dirt around the fence to have gotten its attention.

"Hopefully, it just thinks it was a crazed groundhog and moves on," Faraday said, his eyes large under the darkness of the scrap metal.

Paris nodded, vibrating from the sudden change in size and taking back her human form. There was also the fear of getting blasted by a laser or bullets from the drones and the unknown of what resided in the magical junkyard all around them, which soon they'd be exploring once the drone was gone.

CHAPTER FIFTY-TWO

The University of Utah, Salt Lake City, Utah, United States

The college campus reminded Sherlock Holmes of his youth with the lush green rolling hills and tree-lined areas for studying or considering life's greater purposes. Sherlock had always loved college campuses where young minds were ripe with possibilities and primed to either think big thoughts or be homes for smaller things. Whatever the case might be, a college campus seemed like the right breeding ground for it.

He shook off the rare bit of nostalgia and reminded himself of what he was doing. "That's the building where Dr. Jessie Raven must have worked." He pointed to a red brick building surrounded by bright flowers and college students deep in conversation.

"Do you think that because it says it's the 'Center for Behavioral Sciences?'" Rudolf asked, leaning against a lush tree, across the courtyard from the building and many others in the open area.

"That's one reason," Sherlock said.

"Is it also because that's the information we had from his records?" King Rudolf asked.

"Yes."

"What about those goons stationed around the perimeter of the building?" Rudolf asked, quite seriously. "Was that also a clue?"

Sherlock nodded, grateful that his assistant wasn't as dimwitted as he appeared most of the time. "So you saw them, did you?"

"Saw them?" Rudolf asked, gawking in disgust. "The first to the east has a size ten shoe, wears a medium suit jacket, and has an unnaturally large head. The one to the north, right against the building we intend to enter, probably throws a mean punch based on the size of his knuckles and the angry glint in his eyes. The one to the west has a milk allergy based on the state of his face."

Sherlock blinked at the fae, unsure whether to be impressed or nervous about Rudolf's strange observation skills. "If they are here too, then they are definitely trying to find Dr. Jessie Raven. That means he probably hasn't turned up here yet, but like us, they think he might."

"Unlike them, we're going to go do some investigating," Rudolf said cheerfully. "So what disguises should we go for this time?"

"Oh, no," Sherlock groaned. "Not again."

"Hey, do you want to cruise into that building and ask questions that get us closer to the truth? Or do you want to meet Mr. Knuckles stationed by the door? I vote we breeze in there unnoticed, but that means we need to go incognito."

Based on the wide grin Rudolf was giving Sherlock, he was enjoying this too much. However, he was right. It was the best option.

The detective acquiesced with a sigh. "Fine, what did you have in mind?"

CHAPTER FIFTY-THREE

Outer Limits Junkyard, Nicholson, Alabama, United States

Only once they were certain the drone was gone did Paris slide the piece of sheet metal off them, leaning it against the fence. Looking up at the enclosure, she gulped. She had to get back out of this place in one piece and couldn't break her way out. She admittedly hadn't thought her way through the exit strategy, but now that seemed more than shortsighted.

Shoving down the concern that had to wait until later regardless, she turned her attention to Faraday and then to the mounds of junk all over the place.

"Oh my. Someone needs to clean their room."

"Isn't it wonderful?" Faraday exclaimed.

Paris shook her head, looking at the sea of metal and parts and trash that went on for as far as she could see. Most of the piles of debris were so high she couldn't see past them, even back in her human form.

A drone sounded overhead, and Paris made herself flush with the fence behind her. Faraday shook his head, casually looking up at the sky with a calculating look.

"I think its radar will be surveying the area on the other side of the fence," Faraday told her. "From what I can tell, there's often activity on this side of the fence, so the drones don't concern themselves with it."

"What type of activity?" Paris asked, looking around at the piles of electronics. There was everything from old pieces of equipment to newer-ish radios and speakers and televisions.

"You know, like I told you," he said, staring up at the hovering drone. "The magitech here has come to life."

"Yeah, you didn't explain what that means."

"Well, it's hard to explain," he reasoned, returning his focus to her with a smile. "See, there you go. It's gone. It's probably still inspecting the dirt pile you made coming through the hole."

Paris glanced at the much larger hole than the one that Faraday had made when she came through. Gulped. Nodded. "Yeah, that was a close one."

"We don't have to worry about security now that we're inside the borders," he assured her, sounding excited, almost giddy. "We just have to find the parts we need before the radiation protection spell wears off."

"We also have to figure out how to get me out of here," Paris added.

He nodded, still seeming to be on cloud nine and not his usual serious and nerdy self. "Right. I'm sure there will be a catapult or something I can engineer."

Paris halted. "Are you serious? That's your idea? You're going to—"

It wasn't the drones this time that caught her attention. It was the loud ding in her pocket.

Faraday glanced at the cause of the noise and pointed. "Your jacket doesn't usually make that noise."

She sighed, remembering what it was. "It's not just my jacket. It's my phone."

"Your phone doesn't either," he reasoned.

"Well, Subfar set it up to have special notifications," she said, retrieving her phone. "He wants to ensure that I'm notified when he needs me to make certain transactions."

"He's much savvier than his brother, isn't he?" Faraday observed.

"Much more," Paris agreed. "More pleasant, too. He doesn't have that whole thing where he wants me to die either, so that's nice. Overall, I really like Subfar."

"It doesn't hurt that he wants to make you rich," Faraday said.

Paris nodded, swiping on her phone, following the instructions the Protector of Wealth had sent her. They were pretty easy, surprisingly. "Buy, buy, buy. Now I wait."

"What are you buying?" Faraday asked.

"Stocks," she answered, not having had an opportunity to share the plan with him yet that Subfar had given her to get rich.

"Oh, stocks?" Faraday questioned. "Neat. What company?"

Paris decided right then wasn't the time to get into all that. She finished the transaction and put her phone back away. "So this part we're looking for. Where do we start?"

Faraday cut his eyes at her, sensing she was withholding something. They did have an important mission right then, so he allowed it. Pointing toward a pile of debris, he said, "Let's start there. It looks hopeful."

Paris laughed. "It looks like trash, but whatever."

CHAPTER FIFTY-FOUR

The University of Utah, Salt Lake City, Utah, United States

"Do you think that this scarf makes me look fat?" King Rudolf asked, frowning at the lavender paisley scarf he'd magicked on himself.

"It's a scarf," Sherlock replied dryly. "Not a pair of white pants."

Rudolf huffed. "I rock white pants. You don't even know."

"Are you sure this hat is necessary?" Sherlock asked, messing with the flat-brimmed hat the fae was making him wear.

"Of course," Rudolf said proudly, looking up at the detective. "You look like a west coast folk artist in that hat and not like you're about to go hunting in the moors with your dog named Murray."

"I'm not about to do either of those things."

"Don't you see that we have to look like hipsters if we're going to pass for college kids on this university campus?" Rudolf asked. "So you wear that hat instead of the one that makes you look like you're covering up male pattern baldness and…" He trailed away as he looked up curiously at the detective. "You know you have a fine head of hair. Why do you wear that dumb cap?"

"I happen to like that flat cap," Sherlock countered, not at all offended. Offenses were for people with fragile egos and a propensity toward anger. Neither characterized Sherlock Holmes.

"I'm just saying, you have a nice head of hair," Rudolf said. "I'm going to wear these thick scarves, and what else do I need?" He thought for a moment. "Oh, that's right." Rudolf twirled his finger and smiled when a frothy mug of coffee, complete with whipped cream and heart-shaped artwork made out of ground espresso beans on the top appeared in his hands. "There we go."

Sherlock Holmes glanced at the man. "That's what the young kids of America do? They wear scarves when they don't need them and carry around beverages that make art statements?"

"Isn't it cool and completely unnecessary?" Rudolf asked with a wide grin.

"Definitely," Sherlock agreed, pointing toward the building that was their destination. "Let's use these disguises now. We have work to do. This hat is messing with my blind spots."

"Oh, hipsters don't care about seeing," Rudolf remarked, striding out onto the college grounds with his coffee and flowing scarf. "They just care about looking cool even if it kills them."

"Seems like it might."

CHAPTER FIFTY-FIVE

Paris hadn't spent much time in junkyards. Actually, she'd spent no time at all, now that she thought about it. Still, she hadn't expected everything to be sorted so neatly. All the microwaves were piled together. The kitchen mixers and then the blenders. It was weird, as if someone had organized the junkyard.

Who would do that, she wondered just as the squirrel halted in front of her.

She paused too.

"What is it?" she asked, looking up and wondering if the drone was back. It wasn't.

"I'm trying to figure out which way to go," he said.

"I don't know, Dorothy," she joked. "Where's the junk man?"

"Ha-ha," he said, not meaning it. "Seriously. The parts are in specific places, but I'm not sure where that could be. It's not like someone handed us a map upon entering this place."

"No, just a mouthful of dirt," she related, coughing up some of the dirt still in her mouth.

"I bet it's that way." He pointed.

She narrowed her eyes at a mountain of familiar appliances. "Toward the mountain of toasters. Sounds about right."

He sighed. "You wouldn't understand. You just think this is all useless junk."

"I do think it's junk," she said. "You seem to think it's magical. Useful. What am I supposed to think?"

She glanced at the rusted-out appliances they passed, not understanding why this place was considered so protected and illegal. It seemed tame so far.

"You just have to understand how it can become something useful," he answered. "There are a lot of treasures here if you know where to look."

"I get it," Paris muttered, looking around at the piles of metal. "I cleared out the attic in Little Pleasures recently, and it was amazing."

"Oh, really?" he asked, turning to look at her with sincere surprise.

She nodded. "Yeah. Now I have one less thing hanging over my head."

He groaned. "Wow, that was just cruel. Just plain bad."

She laughed. "Yeah, but worth it."

"I don't think so," Faraday said slowly and then rushed forward.

Paris, catching sight of him getting away, ran after him. "What did you find?"

"I think the part is here." He paused in front of a huge pile of kitchen mixers, processors, toaster ovens, and electronic can openers.

"This is where you find a part to amplify a signal to broadcast thousands of miles to fix women from sleeping?" Paris asked, astonished. "In a pile of trash."

"Shhh," he said at once.

"Did you just shush me?"

"Yes."

"Why?"

"Because you're offending them, and I'm afraid of what will happen."

"Okay, we're getting you someone to talk to," Paris remarked, shaking her head and turning around to take in the other area of the junkyard. "Just tell me when you have what you need, Squirrel. We have work to do."

"Well, thanks to you, that work just got harder," Faraday said tensely.

Paris huffed. "What do you mean?"

She turned to find beaters and blades and hot coils from toasters all hovering in the air and pointed at the squirrel who was frozen in place.

Casually Paris stuck her hands on her hips. "This is what you meant about them being possessed?"

"Yes," Faraday answered tersely.

"I'm to blame for angering them, then?"

"Yes," he repeated.

"Fine," she said, drawing in a breath. "What do I do to fix things?"

"Make them stand down or fight them," he stated and then ducked as all the blades and mixers and heating elements rushed at her.

CHAPTER FIFTY-SIX

The University of Utah, Salt Lake City, Utah, United States

It had been too long since Sherlock Holmes had been out of the modern world. None of it made sense. The youth wore things that were uncomfortable and ill-suited for the seasonal climate even though it was "Cool." Not only that but the hat he was wearing obstructed his vision, even more than he thought. Rudolf couldn't keep up because he was afraid of messing up the frothy artwork on the top of the coffee. If this was a sign of the next generation, then things were going downhill.

The only good news Sherlock had to report out of the last ten minutes was they breezed past the goons without a second glance. If he'd been in his tweed suit with his cap, then they would have been watching his studious nature. Instead, he followed King Rudolf's lead and pretended to talk about the latest music beats and trends, debating whether Olivia Rodrigo was the next musical legend or not.

Sherlock Holmes didn't know what they were discussing, but it got them into the building without being noticed and up to the floor where Dr. Jessie Raven worked at the Sleep Study Institute for the University of Utah.

"Okay, let's have some fun with this one," Rudolf said, tossing the cup of coffee he hadn't drunk over his shoulder as they sidled up to the door. "You play good cop, and I'll play bad cop."

Sherlock glanced at the broken mug and coffee spilled everywhere on the floor. "I think you've already achieved bad cop status. What else is your plan?"

He slung off the scarf, abandoning it on the floor with the coffee. "I'm not taking any prisoners. Just me and my hardcore agenda."

Sherlock nodded, opening the door to the office and hoping to make progress on the investigation.

He realized that it should have involved questioning people who were awake, but they entered a room with three beds, all occupied by people deep in sleep.

"Oh, this just got totally meta," Rudolf stated. "We've got to enter their dream states to question them, I bet."

"Or we just find out who is in charge and talk to them," Sherlock countered, pushing through to the next room, hoping the fae was following.

Thankfully they came to another set of rooms where a woman was sitting at a desk with computer screens and seemingly off in thought. She appeared surprised at the sight of them. Then shocked. She jumped to her feet.

"Oh, I didn't expect any new subjects," she said in a rush, her brown hair piled on top of her head in a messy bun, much like Annie from the robotics academy. However, she was wearing headphones instead of goggles. Similar to Annie, she was wearing a plain white t-shirt, jeans, and Converse shoes. It was like they were weird twins.

"I'm sorry, did you come through the faculty hallway?" the woman said, pulling off the headphones. "That corridor is supposed to be off limits to students since we have subjects on that side. Anyway, how can I assist you?"

Rudolf stepped forward and shook his head. "From this point forward, we ask the questions, and you answer them, sweetheart."

CHAPTER FIFTY-SEVEN

Outer Limits Junkyard, Nicholson, Alabama, United States

Beaters and blades and other objects raced at Paris. She didn't have time to classify and catalog them all. Instead, she did the one thing she could think of and threw up a shield in front of her. All the metal deranged and possessed sharp objects rammed into it and then fell flat.

Feeling woozy, Paris backed up and looked down at the instruments on the ground. They all clambered to the dirt on the other side of her shield that would come down within seconds. She couldn't keep it up long. Not to mention that Faraday was hiding like a coward somewhere on the other side.

On cue, the squirrel poked his head up. "Did you survive?"

"Not thanks to you," she said, narrowing her eyes at him. "So that's what your magical junkyard does? The appliances are alive?"

"They are much more than that," he said, awe in his voice. "They have feelings and thoughts and memories from the lives of their owners. In doing so, they are very powerful. That's why the coils and springs and other parts I need will work so well. They have the emotional power of a lifetime of people."

"Well, the people who used those objects had anger management problems," Paris said, pointing to the objects lying on the ground that had hit her shield.

"They must have been relentless too," Faraday offered weakly.

"Why are you saying that?" Paris asked, but as the objects began to quake on the ground as if they were coming back to life, she felt she might already have her answer.

Running forward, she picked up her squirrel and continued to run as the sharp blades and mixers, and food processor attachments rose back into the air and came after Paris once more.

"How am I going to defeat them?" Paris asked.

"The same way you would anything else. Stop them," he stated. "A simple shield didn't work. Try something stronger."

Paris ran around a mountain of lawnmowers, hoping they didn't come alive. She really couldn't deal with serial killer lawnmowers right then. Not when she could hear the beating madness of blenders and more on her heels.

Sticking Faraday out of the way on her shoulder, she pulled out Amantis. The wand felt familiar in her hands, and she missed it since Uncle Clark had had it for a little while. She pulled out a potion she kept on her belt for these purposes. Pointing the wand at the potion, Paris muttered a defensive incantation, hoping it would work in such a short amount of time.

The potion turned from blue to purple suddenly. Paris didn't know if that was a good thing or not. However, it sounded like the kitchen tools had found her in the maze of the junkyard. Paris grabbed the potion in her throwing arm and waited until she caught sight of the metal objects.

When they rounded the corner, she threw the bottle at the instruments and then ducked, holding Faraday for support. The blast made many things around the junkyard jump. She was hoping she hadn't created more problems for herself in the process—waking murderous sleeping objects.

When the smoke and noise settled, Paris rose and looked

around to find the area around her was quiet once more. All the kitchen utensils that had been hunting her were dead on the ground once more. She was safe, for now...

CHAPTER FIFTY-EIGHT

The University of Utah, Salt Lake City, Utah, United States

"Are you with Zelle Corp?" the woman asked. "I told you guys everything I know. You stand outside my building every day, making me and the students uncomfortable, but I already told you that I don't know where Dr. Raven is. So just leave me alone."

"We're not with Zelle Corp," Sherlock began but was cut off.

"We're with a much worse organization," Rudolf said, trying and failing to appear menacing. He was like a puppy trying to attack.

"What do you want to know?" the woman asked.

"What's your name?" Sherlock asked, thinking de-escalation would be good.

"I'm Adina," she said at once.

"That means fragile," Rudolf stated, sounding angry but looking happy. "Does that mean you're going to break? Tell us everything you know."

Sherlock pulled in a breath, wondering if his assistant had lost his mind and then realizing that nothing could be truer. "Adina, we are trying to find Dr. Jessie Raven. We want to help him, but we can only do that if we know where to look. We're not with the guys from Zelle Corp. If you can offer us anything, that would be helpful."

She thought. Looked at Rudolf, who looked like a bulldog having a seizure, and then at Sherlock. Sighing, she said, "I don't know where he is. We couldn't pay him what he needed here, so he took the job at Zelle Corp. I didn't try to stop him, knowing he needed to make a change."

"Why would he need to do that?" Sherlock asked, picking up on a thread.

"Well…" She looked around the room, appearing uncomfortable.

"Answer the question," Rudolf barked.

She gulped. Nodded. "Well, you see, he was in love with me. He confessed his affections, but I turned him down. The next day he got a job offer at Zelle Corp. He might not have taken it, but things were tense between us. Anyway, I've felt bad about it ever since, like I'm the reason he's gone now."

"So you killed him!" Rudolf pronounced adamantly.

"No!" Adina yelled. "I turned him down. I think he took the job, but it wasn't what he wanted. He probably stole a bunch of confidential information from the corporation and went on that backpacking trip across Europe he was always talking about doing. That's my best guess. That's why those guys are after him. Who are you with?"

"The Feds," Rudolf answered at once, smacking his lips at her.

She shrugged. "Anyways, that's all I know. I haven't seen Dr. Raven since the day he confessed his love for me and left. I'd love it if those guys in suits left me alone."

Sherlock nodded, knowing she was telling the truth. "Thank you."

"Yeah, thanks for nothing," Rudolf said, storming out the door and down the hallway, staying with his role as a bad cop.

Sherlock wanted to laugh, but Adina reached out and grabbed his arm. "I hope what I told you helps. It's more than I told those guys in suits when they questioned me. There is just something about you and your partner that got to me. I don't know. Maybe it was because you seemed so nice and your partner, he's got a real attitude. I don't know how you put up with that."

"It's tough," Sherlock admitted, offering a nod to the woman before turning for the door.

He was astonished the king of the fae's attitude had haphazardly paid off for them. It got them answers they may not have gotten otherwise. Currently, they did him no good, but in time, he hoped they pieced together the puzzle and told him where Dr. Jessie Raven was located. Especially before Jackson Zelle's goons figured it out.

CHAPTER FIFTY-NINE

Outer Limits Junkyard, Nicholson, Alabama, United States

After being chased by kitchen appliances, Paris had a new and strange appreciation for the handy little devices. She didn't know what had possessed them to come after her, but she tried to remember going forward that the objects in the junkyard had feelings and not to offend anything else if she could manage it.

"Is everything in here possessed and alive?" Paris asked, following the squirrel who ran down one path and then back-tracked often, not seeming to know where he was going. In truth, the place was a maze, and it was hard to see anything but the current pile of junk in front of them.

"Yes, but most of it is asleep or not bothered by us," Faraday answered. "I'm guessing those kitchen appliances are a bit more energetic than something like that pile of old printers over there." He nodded in the direction of a large mound of printers of different ages and brands and in various states of disrepair.

"I never thought about the energy levels or personalities of appliances before," Paris related, thinking. "I bet the fittest appliance in the house is the refrigerator."

Faraday glanced down one narrow, cluttered path and then the next before setting off to the right. "Why would you say that?"

"Because it's always running," she replied with a laugh.

He paused. Shook his head. Grimaced. "You should stop. You're going to offend an appliance again."

"Hey, I fixed those deadly kitchen appliances back there."

"You killed them."

"Well, I could have fixed them. My mother's specialty is repairing electronics."

"Which I respect greatly." Faraday seemed to have picked up on a promising path and sped up. "I don't think you have her fixing skills. Leave that to me."

"If you think I can't repair electronics, then you're in for a shock."

He halted. Groaned. Turned back the way they'd come, changing directions.

"You're lost, aren't you?" Paris observed.

"I'm trying to figure out where the large appliances could be located," Faraday muttered, climbing up a pile of broken televisions to get a better view.

"How large?" Paris asked nervously. "Please don't tell me we need to find chainsaws and electric tools."

When at the top of the pile, the squirrel looked around. "Those are yard tools. They are that way." He pointed to the left. "No, I need large appliances for the coil and spring. Think washers and dryers and refrigerators and dishwashers."

Paris cringed at the idea of what those giant appliances could do if they had bad attitudes like the toasters and blenders.

"Oh! There they are!" Faraday exclaimed, running back down the mountain of old televisions. Many lit up when he stepped on them, but they didn't come to life or play anything on their cracked screens. Paris hoped that most of the electronics stayed asleep and ignored them while they finished this job. Time was running out, and she didn't want to be stuck in there when the radiation protection spell wore off.

"Will it take long to harvest these two parts from the large appliances?" Paris asked, trailing behind the squirrel, who was moving much faster now, knowing where he was going.

He skidded to a halt suddenly, appearing confused.

"What's wrong?"

"I'm lost again."

"Mmmm…" Paris mused, looking around, trying to logically decide which way to go based on the piles of junk around them. They were surrounded by old computers, furniture, and then cabinetry. Deciding to go with her gut feeling over logic, Paris chose the path beside the shelving and cabinets. "Let's try this way."

"Why?" Faraday asked, running after her.

"Because it feels right."

"Feelings aren't a practical way to make decisions."

"Feelings are one of the most important factors to consider when making decisions," Paris argued, just as a loud booming sound echoed from up ahead. Both of them stopped. Looked around. Listened.

Another loud noise sounded from just up the path, followed by creaking metal.

Paris tensed, looking sideways at Faraday. "What do you think that is?"

"The result of following feelings," he muttered, shaking his head. "Let's turn back and go the other way."

Paris was about to agree when from her higher vantage point, she caught sight of something large hopping in their direction. "Wait."

The loud noise sounded again, but this time it shook the ground under their feet. Faraday glanced at the dust that rose off the ground in front of him and then at Paris. "Wait? For what? Death?"

"For that."

Paris pointed forward as a washing machine bounded in their direction. Yes, it was huge and jumping in the air, its lid flapping up and down. It didn't inspire fear in Paris.

Unlike the murderous kitchen appliances, the washing machine bounding in their direction reminded Paris of a happy dog, just wanting to please its owner and do a good job.

CHAPTER SIXTY

Dr. Jessie Raven's Home, Salt Lake City, Utah, United States

"Okay, so what disguises are we using this time?" Sherlock Holmes asked as he and King Rudolf stood at the end of a tree-lined street in a quiet residential neighborhood. They were mostly hidden from view behind a delivery truck parked on the quiet road. Their investigation had brought them to the house that belonged to Dr. Jessie Raven and his mother, Brenda Raven.

The fae gave him a look of surprise. "Really? You want to dress up in disguises?"

Sherlock shook his head. "No, but I'm guessing that's what we're going to have to do." He nodded in the direction of the blue house that was Jessie and Brenda Raven's. "The goons are stationed around the house there."

Three men in black suits with sunglasses and earpieces were standing in various places around the residence. One was perched beside a large tree on the other side of the sidewalk. Another was on the other side of the house in a parked car. The third Sherlock had caught sight of when they walked by, hanging out in the alleyway at the back of the house.

"Okay, so what should we be this time?" Rudolf asked,

rubbing his hands together delightedly. "Oh, we can be vacuum salesmen. Or chimney sweeps! I've got it. Let's be Jehovah's Witnesses."

"How about we're with the local gas company and checking for potential leaks?" Sherlock supplied. "Brenda Raven will let us into the house, and from there, we can get our questions answered."

Rudolf deflated with a sigh. "That's practical but very boring. Can I at least talk with an accent and a lisp?"

"If you really want to."

The king of the fae held up his hand. "Okay, you're going to look ridiculous in a maintenance suit."

"Just get this over with."

Rudolf grinned wide. "If it makes you feel any better, I can pull off coveralls like a pro, although I've never done blue-collar labor a day in my life."

"Unsurprisingly, I have no feelings on the matter. Just don't make me wear a ridiculous hat or a scarf," Sherlock said, closing his eyes and waiting to be disguised.

CHAPTER SIXTY-ONE

Outer Limits Junkyard, Nicholson, Alabama, United States

Paris had always liked washers and dryers since they made her life much easier, and she relied on them often. This one definitely had a fun and inviting nature; she could tell from the start.

Feeling like she was greeting a friendly dog at the park, Paris smiled at the washer when it stopped in front of her. It was panting, its lid on top bobbing up and down. The machine's dials on the top resembled happy eyes. It was even wagging its back end, the connector hoses like its tail.

"Who's a good boy?" Paris asked, perching forward and grinning at the excited machine. "Are you a good boy?"

The washing machine hopped slightly.

"Or are you a girl?" Paris mused.

The machine's lid popped open, and a sound like a bark shot out of its basin twice.

Paris laughed. "You're a boy, then?"

Another bark, this time just once.

"What is happening?" Faraday said behind her, shock in his voice.

Paris turned, pursing her lips at him. "I'm making friends. This guy is much nicer than the killer appliances back there."

"Well, remember that you're talking to a washing machine," Faraday reminded her. "We're also lost and running out of time."

Remembering a quote from Snow White that seemed appropriate and well timed, Paris said, "It is when we are most lost that we sometimes find our truest friends."

"So now you and the washing machine are friends, are you?" Faraday questioned.

"Maybe," she chirped, turning back around to the large appliance that seemed to have animal characteristics and personality. "Hey, can you take us to where there are more of you and other big machines? Like clothes dryers, refrigerators, and dishwashers?"

The washer nodded somehow. Although it didn't have a head, the movement it made definitely resembled the gesture.

"Great! Will you?" Paris asked.

Another nod.

"Perfect, we'll follow you, Whirly."

The washing machine hopped, turning about, and then continued the way it had come, bouncing along loudly like before.

"Whirly?" Faraday asked, coming to stand beside Paris and watch the machine progress down the path. It wouldn't take much for them to catch up with it since they could walk rather than hop and didn't have to haul a couple hundred pounds of metal.

"He's a Whirlpool brand washing machine," she answered proudly. "He seems to like his name. I like him."

"You make weird friends," Faraday muttered, starting forward on the path.

She laughed. "That I do, Squirrel. That I do."

CHAPTER SIXTY-TWO

Dr. Jessie Raven's Home, Salt Lake City, Utah, United States

The coveralls fit Sherlock Holmes oddly, tugging at his legs when he moved his arms. The impractical nature of such a suit was strange to the detective. He reminded himself that many wouldn't want to spend their days in a three-piece tweed suit, and Sherlock couldn't imagine life any other way.

"Okay, so we tell Mrs. Raven her house is about to explode from a gas leak if she doesn't let us in to investigate," Rudolf said as they strode down the walkway that led to the porch and front door to the modest house.

"I think we can come up with a subtler reason to enter the house," Sherlock said, checking over his shoulder casually for the goons. They were watching but didn't appear suspicious. Why would they? Rudolf had done a good job making them look like they worked for the local gas company. The fae was even carrying a toolbox.

"Okay, we tell her that—"

Sherlock held up his hand, pausing the fae. "How about I take the lead on this one this time?"

The fae sighed. "Fine, but don't bore me. Come up with something fantastic that scares the woman into letting us in and quickly."

Sherlock agreed with a nod, rapping on the door and waiting for the woman to answer. Thankfully she didn't keep them waiting for long. The lady had a head of gray curls and a confused look as if she was alarmed someone would be calling on her.

"Mrs. Raven?" Sherlock asked when the woman looked them over.

"Yes? You're with the gas company? Is everything okay?"

"You have a gas leak, and we need to find it and fix it pronto," Rudolf said in a rush before Sherlock could continue. "Let us in before your house blows up."

Shaking his head, Sherlock grimaced at his assistant, giving him a look that said, "You just couldn't let me talk, could you?"

The woman clung to the open door even harder, blocking the entrance to her house. "That sounds like something that bad people trying to fool me would say. I want to see some identification."

Sherlock sighed internally, his instincts telling him the mother of a magitech scientist wouldn't be easily fooled by Rudolf's lies. "Mrs. Raven, we're not with the gas company." He angled his head to where the closest goon was located down the block. "We're working to find your son before those bad men. We want to help him and believe he's on the run, and for a good reason. If you wouldn't mind letting us in to answer some questions, I promise we will be fast, and you will be safe. More importantly, anything you tell us will help us to locate Dr. Jessie Raven faster."

The woman's eyes darted with hesitation between the two men. She considered what she'd been told but wasn't sure if she could trust them. Her eyes slid to the goon sitting in the car on the road, and this seemed to make the decision for her. Stepping back, Mrs. Brenda Raven ushered the two men into the house.

CHAPTER SIXTY-THREE

Outer Limits Junkyard, Nicholson, Alabama, United States

"Ohhhh!" Paris squealed at the sight of the crowd of clothes washers and dryers, dishwashers, and refrigerators and freezers all scrambling around in the junkyard, playing. "Can we keep them all? They are so cute!"

Faraday glanced up at her when they paused on the perimeter of the large appliance's play area. "You're talking about adopting electronics spelled with radiation to come alive."

"Look at how well behaved they are," Paris said, holding an arm out as a dishwasher threw cups from its "mouth" and a small refrigerator went to "fetch" it.

"They *are* like a bunch of puppies," he observed, stumped by the idea. "I guess it's because of the way owners treat washers and dryers and such versus the demands they put on other things."

"You're overthinking it," Paris said, waving him off. "They are loyal appliances. Not like those finicky toasters that sometimes burn the bread and the next day decide to hardly warm it."

"Do you think you can convince them to allow me to harvest parts from them?" Faraday asked. "I need a coil from a clothes dryer and a spring from a dishwasher."

Paris thought for a moment. Then she clapped her hands, getting all the puppy-like appliances' attention. "Who wants to play a game?"

They all bounced up and down, throwing dust into the air and making the ground shake under foot. Their doors opened and shut, making noises that sounded like "Yeah."

"Great," Paris cheered, pointing to the Samsung clothes dryer and then to the Maytag dishwasher. "Sammy and May, can I call you that?"

They both gestured in a way that seemed to say "Yes."

"Okay, you're going to be our judges, which is the most important job," Paris said, waving them over. "The rest of you are going to line up for a race. How does that sound?"

The large appliances all hopped around, their lids and doors clanging with excitement.

When Sammy and May arrived beside them, Paris turned to them as if they were dogs about to do a job. "You both just sit here, and my friend Faraday is going to check you over to ensure you're up to the challenge of judging. That means you can't have any defective parts. Does that make sense?"

The dishwasher opened its door and closed it several times to indicate it understood. The dryer did the same.

"Okay, well, he'll get to work, and if he removes anything, it's only to make you better," Paris said over her shoulder, heading for the crowd of large appliances. She clapped her hands. "The rest of you line up, and I'll go over the rules. When the judges have been checked over, we'll be ready to start the race, so you all need to be up to speed by then."

Paris glanced in Faraday's direction. He had already gone to work, checking for the parts on the back of the dishwasher. She just hoped he hurried because she couldn't keep the appliances distracted for too long before they caught on to her real mission. These might be machines, but they seemed intelligent. As long as they were happy, things were fine, but she didn't want to see the massive refrigerator angry.

CHAPTER SIXTY-FOUR

Dr. Jessie Raven's Home, Salt Lake City, Utah, United States

The inside of Brenda Raven's house told many different stories, but at first glance, none of them would tell Sherlock Holmes where the missing scientist was located. That information was locked in the minds of those who knew him best, and the detective believed his mother held the final piece of the puzzle. Once he had that information, he could construct an accurate picture.

"You're trying to find my son?" Brenda asked, shutting the door once they were in the hallway. Her face was full of worry. It appeared she hadn't been sleeping. "Why? Who are you?"

Sherlock saw that Rudolf was about to lie as he often did in these circumstances. This woman was smart. She was a magician. She'd see through things, and then she wouldn't trust them or help.

The detective held up his hand, pausing Rudolf from saying anything. "We work for the FGA. Are you familiar with the organization?"

"The Fairy Godmother Agency," the woman stated, eyeing

him. "You're not a fairy." She indicated Rudolf. "That one is a fae, though. Is he going to get bored if adults talk for too long?"

Sherlock almost smiled at this. The woman was clever and observant. Instead of grinning, he shook his head. "No, he'll be fine. We're here because your son got mixed up in something dangerous with Zelle Corp. Are you aware of that?"

She nodded, tying her hands together. "He took that job because of me. Because he felt he had to."

"Explain," Rudolf chirped, for once being brief.

"Well, I raised Jessie alone and have always had to work a lot to make ends meet," she began. "When I needed to put him through college, I hardly saw him; I worked so much. He promised that once he got through his doctoral program, he'd take care of me." She smiled affectionately as if seeing a distant memory. "I remember he used to tell me that one day I'd be able to put up my feet and that house elves would do all the work for me."

"Or dwarves," Rudolf imparted, his eyes lighting up.

Sherlock nodded, following the clues. "SnowWhiteRelaxes.com. It all makes sense now."

"I'm not following you," the woman said, confused. "My son has always loved that fairytale and named his robotic team after them, but I'm not sure what that has to do with me."

"Your son took the job at Zelle Corp to make more money," Rudolf said. "To help you out."

"Well, yes, because his other two part-time jobs couldn't pay enough," Brenda added. "The idea was always he'd get his Ph.D. and then move onto something bigger. However, I fear, based on what you've said and the fact that those men are always hanging around my house, he's gotten mixed up in something bad. Can you tell me what my son did? Where he might be?"

"He started a bad program," Sherlock answered, knowing the woman deserved answers. It appeared she needed rest and had probably worried herself to the point of sickness. "Realizing what he'd done, he fled, trying to get away from what he'd started and couldn't stop."

"Oh," Brenda said, looking at the floor, holding her chest as though this information hurt her.

"Do you know where your son might have gone?" Rudolf asked.

She shook her head. "I would have hoped he came home. He didn't, and then those men showed up and questioned me about him and haven't left since."

"Is it possible he is backpacking across Europe?" Sherlock asked as though he were crossing off an explanation he didn't think viable in the first place.

The woman laughed dryly, shaking her head. "No, that's just a lie he told that woman at the university to impress her. My son doesn't like to travel and has asthma. He likes his work and his friends and me."

"He loves you," Rudolf amended thoughtfully. "It's just he's in over his head and trying to stay away so he doesn't create more problems for you. We're going to find him and return him to you. Zelle Corp is going to pay for their evil agenda. That's no concern to you."

She smiled tenderly. "Yes, please help my son. You've got to help get these men off his back. They want him back to keep running the program. I just want Jessie safe and happy. I want him to have a real life."

"Of course you do," Sherlock said matter-of-factly. "One last thing Mrs. Raven, this career that took all your time. What is it?"

"Oh," she said, sounding surprised by such a casual question. "Commercial real estate. I own and operate a series of shopping centers around the area."

Sherlock nodded, having figured out exactly where Dr. Jessie Raven was located. He cut his eyes to King Rudolf, and by the twinkle in his eyes, he suspected he'd figured it out too. Or he was just excited about getting a drink and a snack after this.

If the fae had figured it out, Sherlock Holmes hoped it hadn't been too much earlier than he had.

CHAPTER SIXTY-FIVE

Outer Limits Junkyard, Nicholson, Alabama, United States

"I can't believe you just conducted a relay race between a group of magically alive washing machines, dryers, dishwashers, and refrigerators," Faraday said, sounding giddy and impressed. "It was by far one of the coolest things you ever did."

Paris rounded on the squirrel. "I defeated the oldest living demon on this planet. I went into a virtual reality that was real and stopped the game architect. I also stopped a deadly entity from escaping from another dimension and infecting our world, and you think that was the coolest thing I've ever done?" She pointed down the path they'd walked to where they'd happily left the large appliances playing track and field games.

He thought on this and then shrugged. "Okay, it's like the fourth coolest thing you've done."

Paris sighed, continuing on. After a moment, she laughed out loud. "It was really fun. Whirly was so cute when he pulled ahead at the last possible moment."

"Because he spit a bunch of old clothes at his opponents," Faraday added, also laughing. "Yeah, it was a very strange sight, but also interesting. The best part is that I got the magitech spring and coil that I needed."

"Our judges didn't even seem to notice either. They were so consumed with championing the races," Paris said, remembering how perfectly the whole thing worked out. She was relieved their treacherous journey through the magitech radiation-filled junkyard had turned into such a fun experience. "So, what else do you need?"

"A carburetor," Faraday answered.

"Like from a car?" Paris asked, not knowing much about electronics or machines, although she was her mother's child and should.

"Specifically from a 1978 Chrysler LeBaron Coupe," he answered.

It was Paris' turn to round on him. "That is very specific. How do you know there's one of those in this junkyard?"

"Why do you think I chose it?"

"Because you want me to turn you into a Davy Crockett hat," she guessed.

He shook his head. "I did my research, and there's at least a couple of those cars here."

"Why that specific make and model and year?" she questioned.

"There's a whole frequency contingency that we have to mimic in this..." Seeing the look on Paris' face, he shrugged. "Because of science."

"Fine, I'll take that answer because now I'm back to being annoyed, although the puppy party had put me in a good mood."

"Those were large appliances," he corrected.

She smiled. "Still, they were like large golden retriever puppies, so eager to please and lick you in the face."

"Just because Whirly kept spitting on your face, I wouldn't mistake that as licking you."

"Well, hopefully, getting the carburetor from your 1978

Chrysler LeBaron will be as easy and as fun. Which way do we go?"

"I know the answer to that," he said proudly, pointing straight ahead through the narrow path that snaked between the high piles of machines. "When I was up high, I saw the area of the junkyard with the cars. It's quite large. You can help me find what we're looking for."

"Then we'll be out of here before the spell wears off. I just have to figure out how to get over the fence without getting shot."

CHAPTER SIXTY-SIX

Dagny Bar and Grill, Salt Lake City, Utah, United States

Sherlock Holmes sat across the bar table, watching as the majestic and wealthy king of the fae polished off an entire party-sized platter of nachos. When the waitress informed him they usually served six to eight people, he told her to come back after twenty minutes to see if he wanted to order a second platter. To his credit, the fae didn't appear ready to stop, nor did he look like he was going to make the second order.

"Solving a mystery always gives me a big appetite," Rudolf said in between bites. "Doesn't it you?"

Sherlock glanced down at his cup of Earl Grey tea and shook his head. "I don't eat until the case is fully solved. We might have figured out where Dr. Jessie Raven is, but now we have to figure out the best way to get to him."

"We just go in there and wake him up," Rudolf said, licking his figures.

"What?" Sherlock asked, thinking the king had figured out the mystery, but maybe he hadn't.

"Well, Jessie was one of the sleeping subjects at the university, don't you think?" Rudolf asked, taking a sip of his beer and then shaking his head. "Oh, I can't drink this." He snapped his fingers to get the waitress's attention before glancing at Sherlock. "I thought I was a real man and could eat nachos and drink beer. Turns out I'm half a man in that regard. I need an appletini."

The waitress, having heard his order, nodded and headed back for the bar.

"You think he was one of the sleeping subjects at the university?" Sherlock asked.

"Of course. He and Adina are in love, and therefore she's hiding him and making up that backpacking business."

"Didn't you hear what his mother said?" Sherlock asked.

Rudolf nodded. "Yeah, he has asthma, but that doesn't mean he can't love a woman."

"No, it was the final clue that told me where he was," Sherlock stated. "I just can't figure out how we're getting to Dr. Raven and getting him out without the goons noticing. If they track us, then we might compromise his safety or Paris' attempts to stop Zelle Corp. We need the scientist unharmed, but I fear getting him out is impossible with the guards watching."

Rudolf smiled with gratitude when the waitress brought him his drink. "Okay. Tell me where you are guessing that Dr. Jessie Raven is, and I'll see what I can do to fix your worried thinking on solutions."

Sherlock huffed. "I'm not guessing. It all makes sense based on our investigations. There was one person who didn't act worried about Dr. Raven's whereabouts."

Rudolf thought. "Annie at the robotics academy."

Sherlock nodded. "Why would that be?"

"Because she knows where he is, and he's safe," Rudolf guessed.

"That's right," Sherlock agreed. "His mother gave away that she knew where her son was too, but that foretold me the challenge we faced getting him to safety."

Again Rudolf pondered on this. "She knew about the program, even though she pretended not to."

"Yes, which means she's been in contact with her son. She's tried to get him to a safer place."

"She did say all she wanted was for him to be safe and happy and live his life," Rudolf said.

"Which made me think back to where he could be trapped, having been trying to hide, but now is stuck."

Rudolf looked up in sudden astonishment. "Genius. So he's…."

Sherlock nodded, sensing what the fae was going to say.

"Can't we just portal him out of there?" Rudolf asked.

"The technology in that building probably prevents it," Sherlock answered. "Portal magic is so temperamental that it's usually ill-advised to do it in a place with that many electronics."

"So we have to at least get him outside the building."

"At least," Sherlock said.

"Why not use the students as a diversion?" Rudolf offered. "We can use their experiments against the goons, confusing them."

Sherlock's eyes widened suddenly. "That's it. You did it. Yes, I can see that working."

Rudolf flashed a toothy grin. "Great, so we go to the university and have the college kids all pretend to be sleep-walking like in a flash mob, and we use that as a diversion to get Dr. Jessie Raven free. I'm glad I figured it out."

Sherlock tilted his head to the side, giving the fae a look of uncertainty. "You get the scientist isn't at the university, right? You have figured out where he's hiding, right?"

"Yes," Rudolf chirped, leaning forward. "I want you to tell me and explain everything in detail so that I know that you know the truth."

CHAPTER SIXTY-SEVEN

Outer Limits Junkyard, Nicholson, Alabama, United States

Never in her life had Paris seen so many broken-down cars. She'd seen a huge number of them in traffic on the four-oh-five in Los Angeles, but those were all operational cars.

Standing in front of her were a sea of rusted, busted cars past their lives. Some had been wrecked. Some were sawed in half. Some were in pieces.

There were rows and rows of hundreds of cars, trucks, RVs, and vehicles of all types. Like the rest of the Outer Limits Junkyard, they were neatly arranged as if someone had taken pride in how the place was organized.

Each car was set end to end in even rows. She had the urge to jump up on top of the closest one and run across it and then leap onto the next and the next. Then she reminded herself these cars were part of the magical junkyard and would have feelings and thoughts, just like the owners during their time on the road.

Paris backed up suddenly, thinking that cars may not have as nice a disposition as the large appliances. Those electronics were all about helping. Cars were about driving and running over things and power and...road rage.

At first glance, she thought they might be classified by make and model. With her heart suddenly beating fast, Paris looked around. "Do you think there's a Chrysler LeBaron section?"

Sensing the tension in her voice, Faraday looked up at her. "What's wrong?"

"Just worried that if small kitchen appliances had bad attitudes, what kind these large vehicles might have," she said in a whisper, not wanting to wake the vehicles.

"I'm sure it's no big deal," Faraday said. "You have the spring and the coil, right?"

Paris nodded, pointing to her jacket. She was apparently mostly there to hold things.

"Okay. I think the LeBarons are over here," Faraday said, pointing to the right where some older vehicles looked to be stationed.

A horn blasted straight in front of Paris, making the squirrel halt. His ear flickered from the loud noise.

Paris froze, not wanting to trigger any problems.

"I'm sure it was nothing," he said, continuing forward.

The car directly in front of Paris blasted its horn again. It was a vintage Ford Mustang, but she didn't know years well enough to tell which one.

"Fare…" Paris whispered to him.

He glanced over his shoulder at her. "Just make friends the same way you did with Whirly."

Paris swallowed hard. Nodded. Forced a smile. "Hey, car."

The windshield wipers went off, making an awful noise. Paris backed up a few feet, but there wasn't much room to go anywhere with the fence to the perimeter behind her. She had somehow walked into a dead end.

Looking around, Paris spotted Faraday jumping onto a car's hood and then scurrying over one after another, moving across the junkyard. He halted, looking back at her. Seeing the Mustang with its windshield wipers going, he nodded. "That seems to be working. Just don't make it mad."

"How do I know what will make it mad?" Paris asked in a hiss.

He thought on this and then shrugged. "Beats me. Stall until I get the carburetor. I can't afford to have too much commotion."

"Stall," Paris laughed. "Like all these cars have."

The Mustang's lights shone on Paris, blinding her suddenly. Its engine somehow turned on, magically. She backed up, finding the fence.

Her gaze connected with Faraday, who had turned around again to see what had happened. He shook his head. "You just had to make a joke."

"They keep me calm," she admitted.

The Mustang revved its engine, and then its tires began to spin before it took off for her. Paris didn't have a chance to think about her next move. She darted to the side and leaped up on the closest car, on the row next to the Mustang. The car honked in protest immediately.

Crouching down, Paris looked over her shoulder to check to see if she was safe. The Mustang had turned around in the small space and was right in front of her. She didn't know what it would attempt next, apparently angered by her bad joke.

Then it revved its engine again, and she didn't have to guess. Like some awful Evil Knievel stunt, the car was going to try to crash straight into the one where she stood. This meant that Paris had no other choice than to indulge her earlier fantasy and take off running.

Jumping up, Paris ran over the hood of the car, its cab, and then the trunk before jumping to the next car. Then the next and the next.

"What are you doing?" Faraday yelled as the cacophony of horns and car engines and windshield wipers and more sounded off in the junkyard.

"Not having as good of a time as I figured," Paris admitted, watching as the cars all around her came to life in different ways. "Get to work! I fear we're overstaying our welcome."

"That's because you're the worst houseguest," he called back, diving into the open engine of a car on the far side of the junkyard.

"I made friends with the large appliances," Paris protested, realizing she was about to come to another dead end.

She paused, gauging the fence in front of her, wondering if she could jump over it from the car where she stood. It wasn't high enough, and she'd definitely fly into the barbed wire. That idea wouldn't work for getting out of the junkyard.

The car under her was starting to shake like it was going to turn into a bucking bull and throw her off. She jumped sideways to a different row, thinking of how to escape her current predicament and also how to escape the junkyard in general.

She looked from side to side, trying to find another path or exit. Unfortunately, her efforts to get away from the Mustang had put her in the center of the car lot.

A crash behind her nearly sent her off her feet, but she caught herself before she flew forward. Then she'd definitely be run over. No, she had to stay on top of the cars until she figured out how to get away from them for good.

Before another crash from the bumper cars could throw her off again, Paris jumped to another row. She wished Whirly was there to help her. Although she didn't know how, she liked her large appliance friends much better than these egotistical cars, who were all banging into each other and honking their horns.

"Paris…" Faraday's voice echoed across the junkyard that had come alive with screeching metal and other motorized noises.

She had to stay alert because, at any second, she could be thrown from the car where she stood and get hit. Keeping her center of gravity low, Paris looked around for a taller vehicle, hoping that might work for her purpose of clearing the nearby fence. There wasn't one, but maybe if she rearranged the vehicles by playing to their road rage, she wondered.

"Pare!" Faraday yelled again.

"What?" she called back, jumping back the way she'd come, looking for a different exit strategy. There had to be one.

"Paris Beaufont!" Faraday screamed. "Turn around!"

She huffed, her heart beating fast and sweat pouring down her face. Spinning around, she yelled, "What!"

Then she saw it and was immediately frozen with fear. The cars hadn't just come alive. They'd put themselves together to create a life-sized Transformer.

It was bearing down on her, looking like it was about to exact revenge for every traffic incident its many parts had experienced in their lifetime.

CHAPTER SIXTY-EIGHT

Annedroids Robotic Academy, Salt Lake City, Utah, United States

"How did you figure it out?" Dr. Jessie Raven asked from his place stationed beside the giant robot where he'd been hiding all along.

Once Sherlock Holmes had returned to Annie's academy and discreetly told her what he knew, she'd dropped the act. Then he'd explained how they were getting Dr. Raven to a safe place, and she'd been more than happy to help.

The truth of the matter was that after getting there, the scientist had been stuck. He couldn't leave because the goons would see him, so he'd been forced to stay. When anyone looked for him, he got inside the giant life-sized robot—the perfect hiding spot for a grown man.

"You weren't concerned about Dr. Raven's whereabouts," Sherlock said to Annie, who was stationed by her many students who were definitely in on things. They were the ones who nearly spoiled the secret when one of the kids went to get Raven the robot. She thought they meant the real Raven. "It was because you knew where he was. Also, you'd said it was because of Dr.

Raven that you got this retail spot. I didn't piece the importance of that together until I met you."

Sherlock directed his gaze to Mrs. Brenda Raven. "You were concerned about your son's whereabouts, but more about his safety and happiness, making me think it was a bad place. Then you said that your career was in commercial real estate, and you'd let slip you knew about the program Dr. Raven had been working on. I put it all together and realized that you owned this shopping center, which was how your son started working here. You knew he was here, but you couldn't get him out."

"That last part is where I come in," Rudolf said proudly. "Now, Mrs. Raven, as I instructed you, you've had the other exits to the shopping area blocked, right?"

The woman nodded tensely.

"That means that all traffic will be forced into the bottleneck here in front of the academy, making for absolute pandemonium," Rudolf said cheerfully.

He looked at the kids. "Do you have your robots? Are you ready to create some diversions?"

The kids all cheered, holding up remote controls.

"Great," Rudolf said, looking at the scientist they'd been searching for.

He wasn't a bad guy, Sherlock knew, just desperate to make money and help his family. When he knew what he was doing was wrong, he quit.

The detective centered his gaze on the scientist. "Are you prepared to make a break for it in the opposite direction as the diversion the kids create?"

Dr. Raven combed his hand over his thick beard, which made him look much older than his late twenties. He finally nodded. "My mother and Annie and the kids will be safe?"

"I'll see to it personally," Rudolf said proudly.

"You are?" he asked.

He scoffed, offended he had to introduce himself. "I'm King Rudolfus Sweetwater."

The kids all cheered again, excited to be in the same room as a king.

"You'll then go with me until we can get to a safe portaling area," Sherlock said to the scientist.

"You are?" Dr. Jessie Raven asked.

"Oh, he's just Sherlock Holmes," Rudolf said dismissively.

This got exclamations from the kids and grownups.

Sherlock ignored them. "I'll take you to the FGA Tower in New York City, where you'll be safe and under the protection of Agent Beaufont. She needs your help reversing the damage done to brides with the Snow White sleeping spell."

"You shouldn't have done that, son," Mrs. Brenda Raven admonished.

Her son hung his head. "I know. I tried to shut down the program, but all I could do was put an expiration date on it. That's why those meatheads are after me. They want me back, so can I turn the program back on in a few hours when it expires. Jackson Zelle also knows that I'm aware of a lot of his plans."

"Are you willing to share that and help the FGA?" Sherlock asked directly.

At once, Dr. Raven nodded. "Yes, of course. It would be my honor. The job I wanted originally, the one I applied for, which was how Jackson Zelle got my information was as an FGA IT director position."

"You're a magician, not a fairy," Rudolf pointed out.

"Yes, but I hear things are changing there," he said. "I was giving it a chance."

"Things are changing," Sherlock said. "Although that position has been filled, I'm guessing there might be a spot there for you. You'll have to take that up with Agent Beaufont."

"If you adults are done boring us, the kids would like to play with our robots," Rudolf cheered, exciting the kids. They yelled with anticipation.

Mrs. Raven rushed forward, hugging her son. "Take care of yourself and let us know when you're safe."

"I will, Mom," he promised.

"Once this all goes away, don't be a stranger," Annie said, smiling at the scientist.

"I won't," he agreed.

Sherlock Holmes nodded, ushering the kids and Rudolf to the front of the shop, where it would be busy with much more traffic than usual.

The kids all yelled and screamed as they put their robots to work on the ground outside the building and sent them at the goons. Sherlock watched from the back, waiting for Rudolf's signal.

When the goons had been chased from their stations, the king of the fae waved to Sherlock. He and Dr. Jessie Raven strode out of the Annedroid's Robotic Academy and past the dry cleaners, where they quickly portaled away to the safety of the FGA Tower.

They didn't even have to use disguises to get away in the end because King Rudolf's plan had been so smart, with the robots, kids, and traffic being a diversion. Strange enough, Sherlock Holmes missed having a disguise. He guessed that his adventures in the future with Rudolf would present more opportunities.

CHAPTER SIXTY-NINE

Outer Limits Junkyard, Nicholson, Alabama, United States

"Oh, holy smokes, Batman!" Paris yelled, nearly falling back on her butt from the fright of looking up at the mechanical monster towering above her.

The magitech vehicles apparently could work together when motivated. Two vans had been used as the legs for the monster. The body was the RV on its end. The arms were two cars, and the head with its headlights on and flashing at her was a Volkswagen Beetle.

Because the vehicles were very much alive and movable, they were transforming as Paris gawked up at the robotic creature. It shifted and moved, creating appendages from the parts of the cars that made up the arms and hands.

It was incredible, and Paris knew she should be making a move to get out, but the sight of the creature coming to life was fascinating. It appeared to be of such interest that even the car under her wasn't moving, trying to buck her off. Or, more accurately, the vehicle probably knew she was about to meet her end and wasn't bothering with her.

"That's a Transformer. Not Batman," Faraday corrected,

yelling at her from across the junkyard. That got the mechanical monster's attention, and it opened its hood of a mouth and yelled.

"Oh, hell!" Paris exclaimed, thinking the transformed cars might go after Faraday. "Get your part! I'll distract the thing… whatever it is."

"Okay!" he yelled, diving back into the engine, going to work.

Paris waved her arms, gaining the monster's attention, who appeared interested in what Faraday was doing to one of its brethren. The beast didn't even notice her. It lifted its van foot and took a step, thundering down on another car but not seeming to care.

It was going for Faraday. Paris had to do something!

"Hey!" she yelled, running over the cab of the car where she was and then sprinting over the trunk. She leaped, waving her arms. "Hey there! Bumblebee! Why don't you play with me!"

The transformed vehicle picked up its other foot and continued in Faraday's direction. Paris had to do more.

She pulled out her wand, and without thinking, she directed it at the monster and fired a firework. It hit the creature straight in the head, which meant the windshield of the Volkswagen Bug head.

The beast froze. Turned. Opened the hood of its face. Screamed.

She had its attention.

"Well, hey there, Sparky," Paris sang casually. "I have a friend named Whirly, and we get along just fine. Maybe you and I could—"

The blast of hot air and noise when Sparky screamed again cut her off and nearly blew her off the place where she stood, not far from the monster.

"Sparky!" Faraday yelled, materializing from the hood of the car where he'd been working. He was covered in oil and looked mostly black.

"I'm trying to stall. For you!" she fired back. "Did you find the part?"

"Not yet," he replied. "The one in this one won't work. It's burned out. I'll try the other Chrysler LeBaron."

"Hurry!" Paris called, but she'd taken her attention off Sparky too long, and he definitely didn't like that, apparently being an attention seeker. He reached forward, surprisingly fast, and hauled her off her feet in his makeshift hand made of car parts.

"Ouch!" Paris yelled, feeling like the girl in King Kong's grasp. All around her, she was encased in metal. Immediately, she was aware of how quickly the monster could crush her. It brought her up into the air, close to its face, looking her over with its head-light eyes. Paris glanced down, seeing she was well over forty feet off the ground. "I think that's a bit close for comfort. Why don't you put me down?"

"Actually!" Faraday interrupted because he was rude like that. "Paris, this is good."

"How's that?" she said, feeling the exhaust breath of the beast on her face.

"Make him angry, and maybe he'll throw you over the fence," Faraday offered. "I've almost got the part and can run. You, on the other hand, will be stuck here if you're not careful."

"Making him mad I can do," Paris said, watching the beast inspect her, sniffing her curiously. "He might crush me rather than throw me."

"True," Faraday said. "Try telling him jokes. Those always make me want to get as far from you as possible."

"Find your part, Squirrel! I'll deal with Sparky." She smiled sweetly at the strange robot. "So hey, did you hear about your brother? He's a Transformer made out of cardboard, and he shows up in two days."

"Oh, please don't," Faraday moaned as he worked.

"That's right. His name is Amazon Prime."

Sparky grunted, not getting the joke.

"Okay, well, you didn't like that one," Paris said, wiggling up and getting some space in the makeshift metal hand. She looked out and could see that Faraday was right. From this height and being this close to the fence, she could clear it if properly tossed. It had to be the right throw. Her magic could help. She just had to incentivize the monster.

The creature grunted at her. Shook her. Seemed to be looking for a reaction.

"How about this?" Paris began. "Your momma is so stupid she needed a computer password with eight characters, so she chose Snow White and the Seven Dwarves."

Sparky said, "Huh," like he didn't get it.

"Paris, he doesn't have a mother!" Faraday yelled. "He wouldn't get that joke."

Paris moaned. "I'm just trying to find his buttons, so he tosses me. Ha!" She laughed. "Tons!"

"That's just bad," Faraday called as he worked. "Try asking. Robots are people too. Not really, but…"

"Fine!" she replied and offered Sparky a smile. "Hey there. I'm just hoping you toss me that way, not too hard, but hard enough that I clear the fence. Soft enough that I can break my fall using magic. Not so soft I actually hit the fence. You get what I'm saying, Sparky?"

The robot yelled, his breath smelling like gas.

"So you don't," Paris muttered.

Just then, because the universe loved to mess with her, Paris' phone dinged in her pocket. It was the notification from Subfar she had to take when she got them.

She groaned. "Okay, let's press pause on this for a moment. I've just got to buy some stocks. You get it, right?"

Sparky yelled. Apparently, he didn't.

"You're not checking your phone right now!" Faraday yelled, shocked.

"Hey, I'm on duty right now," Paris told him. "I've got to."

She pulled out her phone and checked the alert. It told her just what to do. It was going to be hard to with Sparky shaking her like she was a can of soda he was trying to make explode. Her head bobbed back and forth.

"Hey, just give me a moment," she pleaded, trying to concentrate on what she needed to do on her phone. "This won't take long. I just have to…buy that stock…at that price. Yes, that many."

Sparky growled, obviously not happy with not being the center of her attention.

Paris finished the transaction and then looked up, giving him a pursed look. "Oh, my angels. You're a lot of work. I just needed one second to do that, and you couldn't give that to me."

He frowned, the grill of his mouth drooping.

"Yeah, you should feel bad," she continued, feeling strange cradled in his hand. "It was a really important thing I needed to do, and your tantrum nearly messed it up."

Sparky, out of the middle of nowhere, burst out crying. Water shot from his wipers, and then they went to work, going back and forth.

Faraday popped up from the hood where he'd been working, holding a greasy part. "Did you just make the magitech vehicle robot cry?"

"I did," Paris said with conviction. "He deserves it. Now, Sparky, you're going to toss me, and like I said, not too hard and not too soft. Aim for that patch of grass way over there."

She pointed to a section that was far enough away from the perimeter the drones wouldn't spot her. If they timed it right, she wouldn't be shot in midair.

Sparky grunted in protest, not a ball of putty in her hand like she'd thought. She reminded herself she was the one in his hand. Like with Whirly, she sensed the loneliness of these mechanical devices. They were partly human in a way and missed their owners. She could use that.

"Hey, Sparky, do you want me to come back and visit you?"

The creature nodded.

"Then you're going to have to help me get out of here. Otherwise, I'll die, and then I can't come back. Do you want that to happen?"

He shook his head.

"Good," Paris stated. "Then when I say, I need you to throw me."

Paris glanced in Faraday's direction. "Get out of here and meet me by the tree. I'll be there soon."

"Are you sure?" he asked.

Paris looked to the sky, waiting for when it was clear of the patrolling drones. "No, not at all, but I also don't want to die of radiation." She counted backward from three. Sucked in a breath and then said, "Now!"

Dutifully, Sparky lobbed her up and through the air, not hard but also at a force that ensured she flew straight over the fence, clearing it easily.

She pointed at the ground as she headed for it and muttered a spell that would help with her landing. It did, but she still landed on her head, rolling ungracefully onto her back where she looked up at the sky, blinking and wondering if the stars above her were real or in her head.

When she sat up, Paris realized she was alive, and all her parts were fine. Thankfully they had all the parts they needed to fix women from the Snow White spell too.

CHAPTER SEVENTY

Sleep Lab, Advanced Love Department, Level One, Basement, FGA Tower, New York City, New York, United States

Dr. Jessie Raven hadn't said a word since Paris and Faraday showed up and presented the magitech parts to him. She'd spoken fast, explaining what they needed and the urgency and everything else, but he stared at her like she was an alien.

Currently, he was standing in front of the device that Alicia and Faraday had made to fix the women falling further into comas all over the country. It still needed the magitech parts put into place to amplify the signal. More importantly, it needed Dr. Raven's coding reversed for it to work.

Sherlock Holmes had told them that getting to Dr. Raven had been an ordeal, and getting him there had been an adventure. King Rudolf hadn't returned yet and was busy playing with robots. After Paris' adventure in the Outer Limits Junkyard, she didn't really want to ask questions.

She recognized that this scientist had been through a lot, but she needed him to say something.

He looked at the strange device that sat in the middle of the sleep lab in the basement of the FGA and then up to Paris. Then to Faraday sitting next to Alicia, who was being patient but growing antsy.

"So, can you help us?" Paris finally asked. "I know that—"

"That's a squirrel," Dr. Raven said, interrupting her and pointing at Faraday.

Paris pulled in a breath. Of course, he was in shock. "Yes, that's Dr. Faraday. I call him Faraday or Fare or Squirrel or Jerky, depending on my mood."

He then glanced at Alicia and then away quickly. "You're Dr. DeLuca."

"I go by Alicia," the Italian said with a smile. "Faraday and I can get the reverse Snow White sleeping device ready, but we need your coding."

Paris was grateful for her aunt's no-nonsense approach. However, it appeared Dr. Raven was still coming to terms with things.

He pointed to the open department space where the others were. Uncle Clark was working on the fertility lab with Bermuda Laurens, and the rest were doing whatever they did. Paris had lost track.

"A-A-and Sherlock Holmes and King Rudolf of the fae," Dr. Raven stuttered. "They are the ones who came after me."

"I get where you're going with this. I have weird friends who work for me. I also have the very best. I want your help on this team."

"You're not going to punish me for what I did?" Dr. Raven asked, tugging nervously on his beard. "I mean, I came here because I didn't really have a choice, but I expected it was a trick."

Paris sighed. "You've obviously been working with Jackson Zelle. I get he's cruel. He had those goons following you. I hope they leave your family alone soon. We'll help how we can. To answer your question, I'm not into the business of punishing people, not unless I need to. You were desperate for a better job, from what I understand."

He nodded.

"So you took the job working for Zelle Corp," she continued. "You used your expertise to create SnowWhiteRelaxes.com and the magitech that puts brides to sleep."

"I'm sorry," he said urgently. "Jackson Zelle told me to take the experimental part of the project to completion, killing a woman, but I didn't do it. I just signed my reports saying that I did."

"Which is exactly why you're here," Paris said, "and why I have no interest in punishing you. You made a mistake, and this is your opportunity to make it right." She pointed to the table with the magitech parts. "Will you help these scientists complete this device and then reverse-code it so it fixes all affected by the Snow White sleep spell?"

"Of course," Dr. Raven said at once. "I was just so surprised that you trusted me to help and that you weren't going to do something to me before or after I helped."

"No. Instead, I'm going to offer you a job," Paris told him.

"You are?" he asked.

"First, we have a time-sensitive project. As a woman who suffered from this spell, I want your undivided attention on getting the device up and the amplifier working. Do nothing else until it's completed. Then when you're done, come to my office. We'll discuss your future, how to help you and your family, and how you can be a part of something good."

Paris glanced at Alicia and then Faraday. They both gave her looks of determination, followed by curt nods. She smiled and turned for the door.

"Thanks, Agent Beaufont," Dr. Jessie Raven said behind her.

Paris turned and gave him a sturdy look. "You're welcome. Now get to work so that I can thank you. Here in the Advanced Love branch of the FGA, we work together so we can exchange gratitude. It's better when we spread it around."

Faraday grinned at her. "About like love."

She returned the grin. "Exactly."

CHAPTER SEVENTY-ONE

Paris' Office, Advanced Love Department, Level One, Basement, FGA Tower, New York City, New York, United States

Paris couldn't believe it.

She had her own office. It didn't have a broken chair and makeshift desk. It also didn't have a view, but she absolutely didn't care.

She'd had a corner office on the third floor, but the walls weren't even real, and nothing about the space felt like a real office. The one Uncle Clark made for her was perfect.

"Do you like it?" Clark asked, appearing in the doorway.

She opened her mouth to answer and then found herself speechless. Looking around the large desk, Paris shook her head.

"I can make the desk more modern or less, or I can make it smaller or larger," Clark said, looking around. "I can put more shelves on the wall or less or add more artwork or less."

Paris stood up, looking at the space, which was already perfect. There was a place to pace when she needed to. There was a perfectly sized desk with a computer, like a real one. There were bookshelves with all her favorite books and then ones perfect for referencing. There was a large armchair for thinking and a place to welcome visitors.

"Uncle Clark, it's absolutely perfect. I can't believe you made this, and for me."

"Of course," he said. "You're the director of the Advanced Love branch for the FGA. You need an office."

She pointed to the open area that still didn't have workstations. "My employees need places to work too. We need a conference room and break area and so many other things before a place for me."

He smiled at her. Shook his head. Laughed. "The reason you're the perfect boss is that you think of what your employees need before you. That's why there are people like me who get to decide. I decided that you needed a place to think and make the hard decisions and have meetings. You're a director and deserve to have a proper place to manage."

Paris looked around at everything, so elegant and new and perfect. She didn't know what to say, so she smiled and said, "Thank you."

"You're more than welcome," he replied. "Now I have to get back to work in the fertility lab. Bermuda is very demanding."

Paris laughed. "Funny how she's not even a part of the department or the FGA, but she's moved in."

"I know, but it's an important mission, helping mortals and magicians and other races to cross breed," Clark said. "I like it, although I think I've been hit by quite a few doses of whatever rays she's experimenting with."

Paris laughed, although she wondered what effect that could have on her uncle.

"Well, good luck," she replied. "You're right. It's important work."

What she didn't say was that creating halflings would have its drawbacks, as she knew firsthand. None of them would ever be able to breed.

The thought reminded her of the promise she'd made to the Protector of Wealth to help the FGA. She pulled out her phone, checking for any new messages from Subfar. So far, there weren't any, but her stock portfolio was already showing promise.

She just wished she understood why Subfar wanted her to buy up shares in that particular company. It didn't make any sense. She thought it could be the strangest long game in the world.

CHAPTER SEVENTY-TWO

Paris' Office, Advanced Love Department, Level One, Basement, FGA Tower, New York City, New York, United States

A timid knock broke Paris' concentration. She had been deep in thought, working on several projects at once. She was shocked at how efficiently she could work when given such a wonderful space devoted to her purposes.

She looked up, surprised to find Dr. Jessie Raven in her doorway. "Oh, hi."

He sighed in reply. The scientist wasn't tall or short, and he wasn't attractive or unattractive. He was a plain guy with a beard and funny laugh and kind eyes. Strangely enough, he reminded Paris of a dwarf from Snow White, but she decided to keep that to herself.

He motioned to the chairs stationed in front of her desk. "Can I come in?"

Paris smiled brightly, remembering she had a place to welcome people to sit. "Of course. Take a seat."

"Thanks," he said, striding into the office and seeming to try to decide which chair to take. Finally, he took the one closest to the exit, which was probably wise. After perching on the edge of the seat, he smiled at her. "It's done."

"Can you elaborate?" she asked. "Do you mean you choked my squirrel because he was condescending for the last time? Or you tripped the giantess because she insulted you? Or that you helped with fixing Snow Whites?"

He chuckled, playing with the hem of his cargo shorts. "I meant the last one. We put together the device, which was incredibly crafted. I was surprised by the level of expertise your magitech scientists have. I mean, they put a P1 with an F15 and—"

Paris held up a hand, pausing him. "I do know the smartest people. Believe me; I know that. They are smart enough to know not to tell me the details of their nerd projects. You should learn that too."

"That makes sense. If you're not into that type of thing, you wouldn't want to hear about it." Dr. Raven caught himself in mid-sentence from elaborating, and to Paris, that meant he was trainable. This was already looking promising.

"So the device worked?" Paris asked. "You helped them with the coding or the reverse coding, as it were?"

"Yes," he answered. "Really, they made my job easy. They already knew everything, except how I had specifically coded it, which was my own unique brand."

"Did you all send out the signal?" Paris asked.

"We did, and it will be breaking the spell for anyone who was affected." A look of shame covered his face. "Again, I'm so sorry that I did this. I didn't realize what I was signing onto. Then it was too late. Then I was afraid of what would happen to my mother if I didn't go through with it. Then I didn't care what happened because it was all too much and only getting worse. I wanted to protect my friends and family, so I ran."

"I get it," Paris said. "The important thing is that brides aren't being affected anymore."

"They aren't," he agreed. "I'd already put the expiration on the program at Zelle Corp, so they can't spell new people. Even if they did, then we can send out the signal and fix them."

"Good," Paris said. "Now we have three other items to discuss, all of great importance."

Dr. Raven tensed.

"The first is Terrance, the wedding planner," Paris began. "Were you aware that Zelle Corp and those goons abducted him?"

"I was planning my escape then, so I didn't hear much. I just know they brought someone in who was snooping."

"Where would he be kept?" she asked.

"At Zelle Corp," he answered.

"Do you know why?"

He shook his head. "They won't hurt him, I don't think. It's just that Jackson Zelle will want to have anyone in his back pocket who can offer him expertise on love and the industries surrounding it. He was snooping around. Really, it was just a matter of time before the wedding planner was taken by Zelle Corp. Jackson has a way of 'acquiring' talent."

"I'm sure he does," Paris muttered, drumming her pen on a pad of paper. "So that brings me to the third thing. Can you offer any insights on what other projects Jackson Zelle is working on? We need to know what we're dealing with, and I have to believe he's launching something else after this. Or, more likely, this was a diversion while he got his missiles into place."

"You're right. He has another project that was considered much more important than Snow White. I don't know much about it by design. He called it Project X. I do know it had to do with robots."

Paris groaned. After her time in the Outer Limits Junkyard, robots would haunt her. "Anything else you can tell me about Zelle Corp? You realize they are up to no good by now. We can fight them together, but not unless your heart is in it."

"Not only do I want to fight Zelle Corp," Dr. Raven began, "but I want to break them down from the inside. One of the reasons I applied for the IT position was because I want to use magitech and science to help love. There have to be so many ways, but I think I'll only understand them with the right direction. Science is full of facts. Love is emotions. Together, they must complement each other."

"You're very good at what you do, aren't you?" Paris asked.

"I like to think so," he said.

"Originally, you applied to be the director of IT and operations here at the FGA?"

"I did, but I'm not really a leader. I realize now."

"You're still good at what you do," Paris observed. "What would you think about working on special projects here at the FGA in the Advanced Love branch? We need someone with your expertise. As it happens, I'm hiring for all positions."

His beard and mustache hid his smile, but it surfaced in his eyes. "I'd like that very much. After working with your team, I'm excited to see what else we could do together."

Paris leaned to the side, looking out the door at the department area. "Well, if you hang out with the squirrel, you'll get into trouble because he's always doing edgy things. If you hang out with my aunt, you'll learn something, because she's brilliant. My other employees are insufferable, rebellious, and childish in that order."

Paris stood from behind her desk and offered the man her hand. "Stay and make your own observations. We're all friends here at the FGA, and I'd like to have you on my team."

"Even if I'm a magician and not a fairy?" he asked nervously. "You won't get in trouble for that?"

Paris smiled. "Probably. Can I be honest with you?"

He nodded, not having taken her hand, so she lowered it.

"The FGA is a sinking ship and we're on the bottom deck, meaning we're going down first," Paris explained. "However, no one has more to lose than us. When we do save this place, then we're going to the very top."

Once more, Paris held out her hand and gave him a sturdy look. "What do you say? Want to join the team?"

The smile Dr. Jessie Raven brandished was unmistakable, even under his beard. "Yes, of course. I'll go down on this ship. I think under your leadership and with this team, we'll weather this storm and sail to new places."

CHAPTER SEVENTY-THREE

Saint Valentine's Office, Matters of the Heart, Fiftieth Floor, FGA Tower, New York City, New York, United States

"The board isn't going to like this," Saint Valentine said, his voice coming through between wheezing breaths.

"I know," Paris said, sitting back after informing the leader of the FGA of everything that had happened and what she was planning going forward, including the financial strategy she was working on with Subfar.

A smile flickered on Saint Valentine's face. "I absolutely don't care."

"Really, sir?"

He nodded, although it seemed to cost him a great effort. He sat behind his large desk, looking smaller than ever, the New York City skyline behind him. Paris had hoped helping brides to wake up from the Snow White sleeping spell would have recovered the love meter, but it didn't swing back the other way quite as fast.

There were other unseen problems hurting the FGA. There was the turmoil with the board and money. Everything in the institution was about faith, and currently, some powerful people in high positions were doubting the importance of love and their purpose there as fairy godmothers.

"Of course," he answered after a long pause. "The right thing to do is to hire Dr. Jessie Raven. He's a brilliant scientist who can help the FGA to achieve new goals."

"He's a magician," she argued, knowing that would be one of the board of directors' many complaints.

"So are you," he countered. "We are fairies and should be in charge of protecting love. That doesn't mean we shouldn't allow other races into our ranks. I've been saying that for a long time. I was finally allowed to hire faculty who were magicians and a giantess' and other races at Happily Ever After College, and that's made a world of difference."

Paris smiled, knowing he was referring to her mother, her aunt, and Bermuda Laurens, who worked part-time at the college, teaching the fairy godmothers.

"It is overdue that we hire outside our race here," Saint Valentine said. "The board has blocked me every time, with the exception of you. You have fairy blood, so they couldn't really. Now… well, what are they going to do? Fire me?"

He laughed at this. Paris did too.

"Yes, but Dr. Jessie Raven isn't just a magician," Paris said when their laughter dissipated.

"He's a previous enemy to the FGA who attacked love with the Snow White sleep spell. He's also the one who fixed it."

"I think he's good at his core," Paris said.

A unique wisdom shone in the eyes of the man across the desk from her. "You know, the ability to turn our previous enemies is a skill that few have. Usually, those names are engraved on people's souls, and they die hating those who have wronged them."

"I don't have the energy or inclination for such things," Paris said, shaking her head.

"Which is why you're the perfect director for the Advanced

Love branch," he stated. "You could have forced Dr. Raven to fix what he'd done and then turned him over to the authorities. He would have done time for this. No one lost their life, thanks to you and your team's quick work, but many women were in comas for a startling amount of time. Love was hit. Now it's recovering and very well, I would say." He smiled with delight. "Sometimes it takes losing someone for a short amount of time to remind others how much they love them. I think fiancés are more in love with their brides than they were before."

"That is a nice perk to all of this," Paris related. "Dr. Raven is a good man, and he wants to do good things here. I trust him. As a benefit, he has inside information on Jackson Zelle and what he's planning next at Zelle Corp. Although we don't know what it is, we are poised and ready for the potential attack on love. Dr. Raven thinks it has to do with robotics, and he's in a great position to help us."

"Knowing Jackson, it will be a mighty blow, I believe," Saint Valentine said. "He's been gearing up for this, it seems. When I sit back and look at everything he's been doing, it feels as though all the rest have been diversions. Robotics seems like something big."

Paris thought, her brain not working as fast after the long mission. She needed rest. Thankfully she would be allowed it soon, without worries of not waking. "Yeah, I don't know what it could involve. There are so many possibilities."

"Trying to figure them out might limit us," Saint Valentine said. "Sometimes when we home in on finding a problem, we don't see the real one rearing its head before us. All we can do is keep our eyes open and protect our hearts."

Paris smiled thoughtfully at the man across from her. "Good advice for all times."

"I think so," he said, pushing back from his desk. "This financial plan you and Subfar have. Are you comfortable with it?"

"Are you, sir?" she countered, knowing how risky and bizarre it was.

"I don't have to do anything. You're the one who is borrowing the investments, making all the transactions in your name, and inevitably putting everything on the line." Saint Valentine tilted his head, giving her a meaningful look. "You're risking more than just money for this."

Paris didn't know how, but she sensed he knew she'd promised her firstborn child to Subfar in exchange for the funds. She gulped, shaking her head. "It's worth it. I'll figure it all out in the end. Right now, everything is unclear, and we're at the stage of shorting the stocks. I don't know much about it, so I just do what I'm told."

Saint Valentine chuckled. It was a nice sound, and it made him look not as old and sick. "Yes, Faraday told me a story of how you conducted a stock transaction while being held by a giant robot. It was quite the adventure you had."

Paris laughed too, remembering that Faraday had briefed Saint Valentine while she had spoken with Dr. Jessie Raven. The squirrel had explained how the Snow White sleeping spell had been shut down in technical terms. Apparently, he'd also told of their more humorous adventures. It had been a whacky set of activities over the last several days. That reminded her of her next concern.

"Sir, at some point, I've got to get into Zelle Corp," Paris said seriously. "Maybe I can get evidence and have the House of Fourteen issue a warrant, or I break in, but one way or another, I have to get in there and rescue Terrance, the wedding planner. It's my fault that Jackson Zelle's goons took him. I can only hope he's okay."

Saint Valentine regarded her for a long moment and sighed. "You see everyone's personal safety and well-being as your responsibility. This must be a deep-seated trait of the Beaufonts.

I see it in all of you, and in ways I've never noticed in others. It's a beautiful thing."

"Thank you, sir—"

He held up his hand, pausing her. "I caution you, though. If you feel responsible for everyone, then you will inevitably suffer heartbreak because it's impossible to save all people."

Paris swallowed the knot in her throat. "I know, sir. Terrance was there because of me. I have the capability to save him. I just have to do it the right way. We know how dangerous Jackson Zelle is. Hopefully, all this will work together, and we can storm into Zelle Corp, shut down this new Project X, and save Terrance. That's how it would go in a perfect world."

He closed his eyes for a long moment, and when he opened them, they were sober. "I've lived a long time, and I've given up hope for a perfect world. With you working alongside me, I'm starting to think that we might find perfection in small ways in this world. That would be enough."

Paris forced her face to remain neutral, although looking at the man before her was breaking her heart. He was right. She couldn't save all people. She didn't even know if she could save him, and that was her main goal right then. Saving Saint Valentine meant rescuing the FGA and saving love.

"Sir, I know we're running out of time," Paris began. "I know the board of directors is looking for buyers for the FGA, and the company is dying and taking you with it. I just need you to hold on a little longer. I believe we can persevere. I believe we can weather this storm. That we'll sail onto better days. We need you as our leader to do that."

He pressed his lips together, rubbed them, and then sighed deeply. "I appreciate your optimism. I believe if anyone can save us, it will be you. Although I have complete faith in you, I also know that every hero suffers a defeat. We might not make it. I might not. That's a cold hard fact that I need you to come to terms with.

Because if that happens, you'll have to start over without me. You'll have to champion love without the FGA. Paris, whatever happens, you must continue to protect love—it is quite simply your destiny."

"I promise. I will always fight for love. Don't count yourself out yet, sir. I'm not going to start thinking of starting over. You don't start thinking of giving up."

CHAPTER SEVENTY-FOUR

Little Pleasures Farmhouse, Outskirts of Boulder, Colorado, United States

"So wedding colors," Hemingway mused, sitting on the porch and rocking in the swing. "What do you think? My favorite and your favorite?"

Paris snuggled into him, enjoying the sunset over the mountains in the distance. "You know, I've fretted over that silly simple decision for hours, and you boiled it down so easily. Of course. Yes, blue and green. That's perfect."

"Do I have to wear a blue or a green cummerbund?" Faraday asked, sitting on the deck of the porch beside them, tinkering with a strange electronic device in the waning sunlight.

"No one will be wearing a cummerbund," Paris stated.

"The flowers?" Hemingway asked.

"Mama Jamba is doing them," she answered.

"The cake?"

"Lee from the Crying Cat Bakery," she replied.

"Clark is doing the catering with Chef Ash's help," Hemingway added proudly.

"Christine and Penny are in charge of decorations," Paris

continued. "Jeremy Bearimy at the Silk Armor is doing my dress and the suits. Punch Line is the band. Faraday is in charge of lighting, photography, and all technical things."

"So we just need a venue," Hemingway said. "Here? Right?"

"That seems like the logical option," Paris muttered, chewing on her lip. "It doesn't feel right, though."

"Well, what feels right?" he asked.

"You should get married where you met," Faraday interjected, half paying attention as he concentrated on his current project.

Paris brightened with a smile. "That's it. Yes. That feels right. We met at Happily Ever After College. That's where we fell in love. It's because of the fairy godmothers that we found each other. We should be celebrating that."

"I like that idea, and the grounds of the college are magical."

"Thanks to you and your hard work," Paris offered.

"Talk about remote," Faraday said. "I still haven't figured out where that place is since you can only portal there. It's like it is in a bubble."

"Which makes it even more magical," Paris said.

"Okay, it appears that we've figured out all the main details," Hemingway said, pulling Paris in closer.

"Just one minor decision left," Faraday mumbled, concentrating.

"What's that?" Paris asked.

"The date," he chirped, flicking his tail. "You haven't picked a wedding date."

"Oh," Paris coughed. "Yeah, I guess I was thinking it would be when things settled down, which will be—"

"Never," Faraday interrupted. "There will always be a challenge. A job. A world to save. Love to protect. More. That's just the life you signed on for."

"I don't remember signing anything," Paris joked.

"You love it, and you're incredible at your job. We will just get married in between the drama and cases. Whenever works best for you, my bride."

Paris thought. "I guess I've got to think about when would be best."

Faraday glanced up from his work. "You don't have to worry about weather since it's always spring at Happily Ever After College."

"True," Paris imparted. "I say the sooner, the better."

"You do?" Hemingway asked, surprised.

"Well, of course, I do," Paris said. "I can't wait to be married to my best friend. Although I've never been a girl dreaming of the fairytale wedding, how could I not want that now that I've found my prince?"

"Aww," he said, leaning down and pressing his head to hers. "You're definitely my princess. Soon to be my queen."

"You all are going to make me throw up," Faraday teased, but he was regarding them fondly.

"Hey, Fare, will you be my maid of honor?" Paris asked.

He thought about this. "Do I have to throw you a trashy bachelorette party?"

"Not unless you want to be served as the appetizer at the reception," she teased.

"Great, then yes," he said.

"You know I once went to a cannibal's wedding," Paris said casually.

"You did?" Hemingway asked, surprised.

"Yeah," she replied. "Everything was going well until they decided to toast the bride and groom."

Faraday groaned. "Oh, wow. That was painfully bad."

"Oh, sorry. I guess cannibals are in bad taste."

Faraday just shook his head. "She doesn't know when to stop."

"Yeah," Paris went on casually. "You, Fare, probably would have preferred the wedding I went to where two satellites got married."

He shook his head urgently. "Don't. Just don't say it."

Paris laughed. "The ceremony wasn't great, but the reception was amazing."

He pressed both his paws to his ears, continuing to shake his head. "Make her stop, Hemingway. Please."

Hemingway laughed, kissing Paris' forehead. "I refuse. I happen to love her jokes. They show her wit and playfulness."

"Or how my patience can be tested continuously," Faraday muttered, returning to work.

"You know you adore my jokes, Squirrel," Paris said.

He glanced up at her with an affectionate look. "I adore you. I stand your jokes. I'd be honored to be your maid of honor."

"Thank you," Paris said, snuggling into Hemingway's arms and lying her head more on his chest. He pressed her in close, enjoying the glow of the sun behind the ridge of the mountain. Paris was so grateful for the man beside her and that one day soon, he'd be her husband. She was also thoroughly grateful for the squirrel beside her and that forever, he'd be her partner in helping love to thrive.

Another day had ended, and love had persevered thanks to the efforts of the halfling and her squirrel. Tomorrow they'd discover new mysteries, solve bigger problems and work to bring more love into the world.

For now, Paris Beaufont was going to fall asleep in the arms of the man she loved, with her best friend tinkering on the deck, knowing she'd awaken to another day full of possibilities.

Familia Est Sempiternum. There were no truer words for Paris Beaufont as she fell off to sleep. Family was definitely forever, and she was about to prove that.

Thank you so much for taking a chance on this new series. Thanks for buying and reviewing the books. Thanks for supporting LMBPN and for being awesome! If you're reading this, you are definitely awesome!

Have I told you all lately how much I love writing? It is seriously the coolest profession. Not only am I always wowed by it and all the weird and wonderful ways my books come together, usually against my planning and attempts. Something amazing like that happened in this book and blew me away. This is book 95, so if you think if gets old, it doesn't...ever.

But also, I love writing because it gives me a legit reason to be crazy. Right now, I'm on a plane to London, en route to Scotland, as I do, and I finished this book yesterday. A week early. In two weeks. A day after book 7 was finished. Which also happened in rapid time.

So I get on the plane, with my daughter, which is another story in itself. I'm full of them, haven't you heard... Anyway, all I was doing was working to get done so I could get on this plane. So I get Lydia and I on the plane and I just pass out. Literally. The next morning I wake up and apologize to the flight attendant, who says, "You are the easiest passenger ever." But literally I just passed out. And I tell them, "I finished a book in three days and got on this plane."

And there you go. Writing makes me cool. And gives me excuses. Enough said.

So I am on this plane to Edinburgh with Lydia and I'm a bit of an emotional mess when I'm not sleeping. You see, in 3 years, I've gone to Scotland 10 times. This is my 11th. And my first time with another person. Ten times I've crossed the Atlantic by myself. The first was to find Sophia's Gullington. The next 9 times were because of love. And there was a pandemic. But today, well today, I go with my best friend, to show her where I pictured dragons live.

The Scotsman always says they are in Wales, but I tell him, that's what they want you to think, so you don't look in the right places.

And so, I'll take a piece of my heart to Scotland in a few hours and reunite the pieces.

Don't cry, Sarah. Don't cry.

Okay, so I'll tell you about the other, other cool part of this book. It was inspired by Lydia's summer camp. While all the so called cool kids were off at outdoor camps and canoeing and horseback riding and getting fleas, my daughter was at robotic camp. Oh yeah!

And she loved it. Like so much. At the end of every day they had their robots compete. Well, day one I come to pick my daughter up and I'm worried when I see that she's one of six kids and they are all boys and being taught by this bearded geek (hence our inspiration for Dr. Raven). Then they compete and she comes in last.

I take her home and she says, "I like that it was all boys. No drama."

I can relate, girlfriend.

Then day two and she comes in 4th. I'm proud.

Then day 5 and she's 1ˢᵗ. And my daughter wins the 1ˢᵗ spot every day for the rest of the summer camp. The geeky instructor then comes up to me and says, "I run a professional robotics competitive team and I'd really like it if Lydia joined us."

Yes, please!

So that will be our spring. Robotics tournaments. Can't wait.

And until then, the robots inspired this book in so many ways. I love how life sets us up for success, if we let it.

We're about to land. Yes, I'm taking my 11 year old to Edinburgh. There was this one time I took her Bali. I'd like you all to ask Mike about how he looked across the dinner table at me in Bali and pointed at Lydia and said, "I thought you were mad to bring a 7 year old here."

Ask him…Ask him how wrong he was… It's a great story.

Much love and Peace,

Tiny Ninja

MICHAEL'S AUTHOR NOTES

SEPTEMBER 2, 2022

Thank you for not only reading this story, but these author notes as well. I'm presently at the house in Cabo San Lucas, and it is the first time I am writing anything here while it is dropping BUCKETS of rain on our heads.

I feel like I'm going to float away. Not that we should since the house is made of concrete and heavy shit, not wood and shingles, but the sound as the water plummets from the roof ten feet into the walled brick courtyard—three of the four walls are hard and sound-amplifying—gives you the impression of a raging waterfall.

When I look, it's not nearly so bad. I sit back down, and the sound belies my memory from seconds ago...

I could believe waves of water are lapping against the walls.

Which is a possibility since this house isn't too far from the beach, but it's only the sound making me feel this.

Ok, I'll get back to the author notes now.

I ADMIT I WAS WRONG

Let's just get it out of the way that I was wrong ;-).

I am tempted to leave the fall-on-my-sword to the heading

above and let Sarah stew in her expectations a little longer, but I can't do that.

Well, I could absolutely do that to Sarah, but not to Lydia!

With Lydia's robotic (read: future sci-fi author in training) effort going fast and furious, any smart publisher (like myself) will make sure to stay on her good side until we get a chance to lock in our working relationship.

If I have to play nice with her mother for a few decades…so be it. ;-)

I'll get my digs in with Ms. Noffke until then. I suppose she's a pretty good sport about it all.

Just wait until I divulge my evil-short-Sarah video…

Talk to you in the next story!

Ad Aeternitatem,

Michael

If you want, I have a couple of short stories you can read that I am sharing from my STORIES with Michael Anderle newsletter here: (No requirement to sign up.)

https://michael.beehiiv.com/

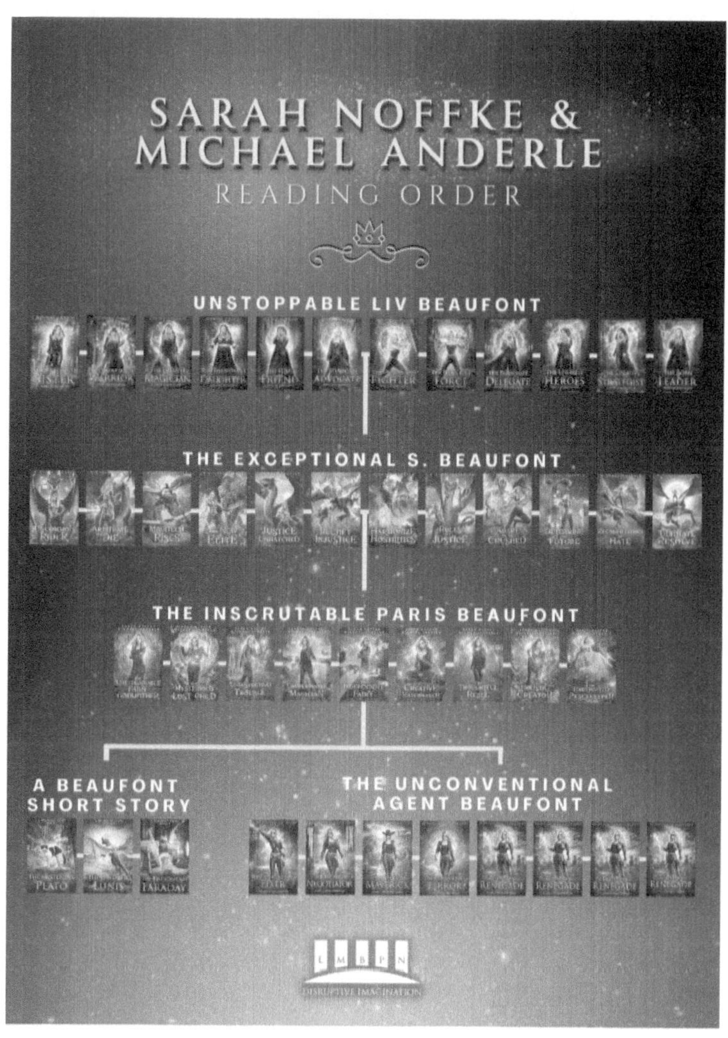

For the most up to date list please visit
https://lmbpn.com/reading-orders/sarah-noffke-and-michael-anderle-reading-order/

BOOKS BY SARAH NOFFKE

For a complete list of books by Sarah and a suggested reading order, please visit:

www.sarahnoffke.com/reading-guide/

ABOUT SARAH

Sarah Noffke is a prolific USA Today Best-Selling Author, who writes YA and NA science fiction, fantasy, paranormal and urban fantasy. Most of her stories draw on her experiences living on the West Coast, growing up in Texas or traveling the world.

Her passion for art, culture and literature drives her to create stories that are full of whimsey, humor and philosophy. Her books appeal to readers who enjoy an escape, a bit of magic mixed with science and the unexpected--like a dragon who tells bad jokes and has a video game addiction, but fights for justice.

Noffke's books are top rated and best-sellers on Amazon. Her books are available in paperback, audio and in Spanish, Portuguese, German, Dutch and Italian.

To stay up to date with Sarah, please visit her website and subscribe to her newsletter: www.sarahnoffke.com

For a complete list of books by Sarah and a suggested reading order, please see: www.sarahnoffke.com/reading-guide/

BOOKS BY MICHAEL ANDERLE

Sign up for the LMBPN email list to be notified of new releases and special deals!

https://lmbpn.com/email/

For a complete list of books by Michael Anderle, please visit:

www.lmbpn.com/ma-books/

CONNECT WITH THE AUTHORS

Connect with Sarah and sign up for her email list here:

http://www.sarahnoffke.com/connect/

Michael Anderle Social

Website: http://lmbpn.com

Email List: http://lmbpn.com/email/

https://www.facebook.com/LMBPNPublishing

https://twitter.com/MichaelAnderle

https://www.instagram.com/lmbpn_publishing/

https://www.bookbub.com/authors/michael-anderle

www.ingramcontent.com/pod-product-compliance
Lightning Source LLC
Chambersburg PA
CBHW032351310726
48973CB00007B/1959